JOHN ELLSWORTH

THE GIRL WHO WROTE THE NEW YORK TIMES BESTSELLER

VINCI BOOKS

JOHN
ELLSWORTH

THE GIRL
WHO WROTE
THE NEW
YORK TIMES
BESTSELLER

VINCI
BOOKS

By John Ellsworth

THE THADDEUS MURFEE LEGAL THRILLERS

THE MICHAEL GRESHAM THRILLERS

The Lawyer

The Defendant's Father

The Law Partners

Carlos the Ant

Sakharov the Bear

Annie's Verdict

Dead Lawyer on Aisle 11

30 Days of Justis

The Fifth Justice

Lies She Never Told Me

Girl, Under Oath

Lawyers in Gray

SISTERS IN LAW

Court Order

Hellfire

The District Attorney

Justice in Time

Vinci Books

vinci-books.com

Published by Vinci Books Ltd in 2025

1

T hey were head hunters.

Twenty-first century head hunters.

They wanted the jihadist's head, severed from the body, lifted to the lens on *Al Jazeera* network.

So they summoned her, Christine Susmann. She appeared as ordered. They deposited her in the waiting room while they conferred.

The sudden, overwhelming threat posed by MESA was the topic late that afternoon in Langley, Virginia. Outside, the maples and oaks—leafless—looked stunted, birds flitted among the branches, securing shelter in the deep winter, and men and women in peacoats and watch caps scurried around in CIA spy school, hopeful of making the grade and grabbing choice field assignments. But inside the conference room, long-ago graduates huddled around the broad curve of cherry conference table at one end of the Assistant Director's office. Coffee was poured, pastries were plucked from silver trays and cigarettes set to burning. Notes were exchanged, viewpoints aired, and then came time to vote. Or almost. Two more files to be passed around the huge table. One file was yellow, addressing civilian matters. One file was olive-colored, addressing military matters.

The Assistant Director was a man of rigid bearing, ex-Army, a West Pointer with the required ruby class ring, crewcut, and proud of the thirty-two inch waist he had maintained since college thanks to daily workouts and weekend hundred-mile-bike rides. He plucked the first artifact from the olive file and passed it to his left.

"News clipping, *Chicago Tribune*, 2005," he said into the system that recorded all conversations in the room. The four intelligence officers did quick reads and handed it around the table. The ten-year-old military news clipping reported:

Sgt. Christine Susmann, a military police officer in the Illinois National Guard, was awarded the Silver Star for her role in thwarting a Taliban insurgent ambush, the military said Thursday.

In a two-hour firefight, Sergeant Susmann and two other soldiers fought off more than 35 insurgents armed with AK-47s, machine guns and rocket-propelled grenades after the force attacked a supply convoy southeast of Kabul, Afghanistan. The Americans killed 30 and wounded or captured 3 others. Sergeant Susmann, 23, received her medal on Thursday in Kabul."

Heads nodded and looks were exchanged. She was an American patriot, which elevated the conversation. They could work with her.

The Associate Director next passed around a single

sheet from the olive file—bullet points from her military jacket.

Papers were flipped, read, and re-read. Assent was by silence: so far, she was their choice for the assignment.

A second set of papers came from the yellow file. Her FE—family/education sheet. The father was Afghan and the mother was French, both medical doctors, both naturalized U.S. citizens. The genetic admixture produced a dark-skinned woman who could pass for Middle Eastern. She would require no makeup, no disguises for the role. Her father had raised her proud of her heritage, and daily conversations with him in Arabic were required. As a young soldier serving in Afghanistan, she interpreted for the MPs. She spoke perfect Arabic to Arabs who didn't know she wasn't a local. So the language skills were in place.

Against her parents' wishes, she had enlisted in the Army straight out of high school, so she was headstrong and independent, two traits required of spies.

The Assistant Director prepared to close the deal. He strode to his desk, unlocked a drawer, and carried four final files to the table. They were identical in content and pinned inside red covers. He passed the files around the table and waited, contemplating while the officers read.

The AD drummed his fingers on the table while the red files were finished off and evaluations made.

Then the last file was closed. All eyes turned to him.

"Vote?" he asked.

Four heads nodded.

"Afghanistan?"

"Yes."

"Syria?"

"Yes."

"Terrorism?"

"Yes."

"Military?"

"Yes."

"And I'm a 'Yes' too. It's settled, Christine Susmann is selected. Now to find out if she'll serve."

They had voted she would be the operator sent to Syria to behead the leader of MESA. His name: Abu Nidal al-Zaqari.

"Have you contacted her?" Syria wanted to know.

"We have. She's in the outer office as we speak."

"You were very sure about her," said Terrorism.

The AD smiled wryly. "She was my choice all along. I've actually met her. It was ten years ago, but she impresses, as you'll see."

"Family?" asked Afghanistan.

"Husband, two kids. The husband is a problem."

"He objects?"

"He doesn't know the specifics, of course. But when we sent for her he fiercely objected."

"She told you this?"

"Of course. Availability interviews were completed and it surfaced at that time."

"What was her feeling about him?"

The AD spread his large, thick hands.

"You can ask her that yourself. Let me bring her in."

He buzzed and a receptionist opened the door to admit a young woman in her early thirties. All eyes were watching her. Christine was five-five and average weight, but that's where "average" ended for her. For one thing, she was beautiful. She had won a county beauty pageant in the summer of her senior year, right before enlisting. For another thing she was built like an NFL safety: broad, heavily muscled shoulders and upper arms, muscular thighs and calves.

Physical Eval reported she could bench press 275 yet she only weighed 145.

The AD smiled at her. He waved her to a chair halfway down the table.

"You are Christine Susmann; we've met before."

She wasn't smiling. She wasn't frowning, either. She had slipped into military-ambiguous-affect.

She pulled a wave of hair from her forehead. "Have we?"

"At the military academy, 2004. You had just completed basic and were partway through your advanced MP training in leadership."

"All right."

"Following Basic Training, you served in Afghanistan, correct?"

Christine's dark eyes narrowed. "Am I confirming what that red file says? Or do you really not know?"

The AD looked at his assistants. One gave an approving smile. That was Syria.

"Touché. So let me get right to it."

"Yes, please. I'm on the seven-thirty back to Springfield."

"Sure. The people you see seated around this table all hold commands inside the Agency."

"CIA. That's what the big gold seal said out in the lobby."

He smiled. "We brought you here to ask for your help."

"I did my tour. I will help with anything I can. Just don't ask me to serve in Kabul again."

"Why's that?"

She all but spat it out.

"Shit hole."

"Your opinion seems to be a majority one."

"Whatever. So how I can help my country other than going back to Afghanistan?"

"What we're going to ask you to do is allow us to put your military training and experience to one more use."

"You want me to arrest someone?"

"We want you to kill someone."

"Okay, well, thanks for the trip back here, the luxury hotel, the great steak last night, and the chauffeured tour of the city. But I'll be on my way now."

She stood and began to turn away.

"Please. Sit down and at least hear me out. You will be able to catch your flight in plenty of time, I promise."

"That's a must. I have a very upset husband at the other end."

"We appreciate that. Please try also to appreciate our quandary. Your government has underestimated the consequences of allowing the Middle Eastern State Army to fester and spread."

"MESA."

"MESA. All over the news, in everyone's mind, people are nervous about getting on subways or flying—it's much more of a perceived threat than we expected."

"Which is worse, the perceived threat or the actual?"

"Both, I would say. Both are equally unacceptable. So your President has decided to declare war. Starting with the top down. Cut off the head and the body will wither and die. That's the administration's best thinking."

She shook her head. "Which we all know is nonsense. Cut off the head and the organism will instantly grow another. That's the reality of terrorism."

The AD raised an eyebrow. "Maybe, maybe not. Cut off the head and immediately address the body and you just might prevent that prediction from coming true. There can be no head without a body."

"There can be no efficacious head without a body, you mean."

"I stand corrected. Yes, that's true. Which is where you come in. We want you to take off the head. Give them some of their own medicine: a public beheading."

"You mean literally? You want me to take off his head?"

"On TV."

"TV. This is your best plan?"

"It's a world stage."

"And how do you see me pulling off this act where the head of MESA disappears?"

"You will gain admission to his inner circle."

"And I would do that how? You still haven't answered my question."

"We would smuggle you in-country. You would use your military skills and great beauty to get close to him. You would prove yourself worthy of his utmost trust."

"And after I have terminated his command, how do I get home to my family? I'm sure my husband will want to know."

"We haven't got that far. We thought we'd ask your help there."

She slowly shook her head. She blinked hard. "Got it. I was afraid it would be something like that. Long story short, I probably don't get to come home."

"We'll have a plan for that. We'll have helicopters, S.E.A.L. teams—whatever is needed, you'll get. We can promise that. No one has to die there. Except their leader."

"But the chances are good that I will die. In that event, what does my family get?"

"The usual assassin's package, ten million cash, full ride

for the kids to any university, college, or other post-high school training desired, paid mortgage."

"Sounds like they're better off financially if I don't make it back."

"Then you'll do it?"

"I didn't say that. No, I won't do it. I'm leaving now. Your Middle East strategy needs to change. It's wrong. Wrong approach."

"I'm sure you have recommendations in that regard."

"No, actually, I don't. I'm a paralegal, not a political scientist. And I'm no longer a soldier. I was a soldier once and I killed my share of bad guys. But I was young and hung then. Now I'm a mother and lots wiser. Gotta go."

She stood to leave.

"Wait. Ten million cash if you come back, as well. Plus the paid mortgage and education perqs. Now what do you say?"

Christine settled back into her chair.

"That's my family's economic future you just guaranteed, either way."

"True. One million today, balance on your return or confirmation of your death. Either way."

She squirmed in her chair. It was getting very difficult to keep saying, "No."

"You people are real assholes, you know that, don't you?"

The Assistant Director allowed a small smile. He wasn't totally against acting human. Just mostly. "Your opinion is noted. Now, suppose you give us some account numbers. You will find the money in your account before you even leave here."

"What about training?"

"Don't have time for that. Besides, you're ready for this. You always were."

"Leaving when?"

"Sunday night."

"What? This is Friday. I get one day with my family and then I'm gone?"

"This can't wait, Christine. It will take you probably six months to make your way inside the castle walls. Time is of the essence."

"You people amaze me."

The AD smiled. "Then it's mutual. We're glad to have you on-board."

She unzipped her bag.

"Here's a check. Routing number and account number."

"And here are plane tickets out of Chicago. In your name."

She accepted the packet. "Pretty sure of yourselves to buy these in advance, weren't you?"

"Sergeant Susmann, you have an asthmatic daughter who visits the ER at least once a month. Your son has been treated for cerebral palsy since birth. He's going to need a lifetime of medical care. Your husband drives a dump truck and you earn sixty-five-thousand as a paralegal working for Thaddeus Murfee. Meaning you make more than your husband, but even if your salaries were doubled you still wouldn't be able to guarantee the health care your son will need after you're gone. So the airline tickets sounded to us like a solid investment."

She opened the packet and studied the tickets.

"My name is Ama Gloq? I'm flying Chicago to Zurich? Then what?"

The AD touched the side of his head. "Need-to-know."

She shrugged. "I find out when I get there. But I'm certain it's Turkey then Syria. Correct?"

He smiled.

He extended his hand. She stared at it. Then shook her head.

"I'll shake it when you cough up the other nine million. Or won't."

"Fair enough."

"And Gloq? What kind of name is that?"

The AD crossed his arms on his chest. Slowly, right before her eyes, he made a pistol of the fingers on his right hand. He pointed it at Christine.

"Glock. You code-named me after the most popular gun in history."

He lowered the thumb hammer and said, "Bang."

"Is that it?"

The AD sighed. "Not quite. We need cover for you in case you're recognized. So we've made arrangements for Thaddeus Murfee to fly on the same flight. But he'll be turning around and coming home once you land in Zurich. You will part ways."

"Does he know about this? He hasn't said anything about it to me."

"He was called this afternoon. Thaddeus Murfee is a patriot. He didn't hesitate to commit to riding along to provide cover for you. Good man."

"Yes, he is a good man. He won't be in any danger, will he?"

"Of course not. Milk run. Chicago-Zurich-Chicago. One and done."

"I'll talk to my husband. I'll let you know."

"Uh-uh. Too late for that. In or out?"

Her chest heaved in a heavy sigh. "We need the dollars. I'm in. Stupid, but in."

"Excellent. Then, away we go!"

"One last thing. What is my nationality?"

"See the passport. It says you're Afghan. Do you have a problem with that?"

She grimly shook her head.

"Would it matter if I did?"

"Not in the slightest."

"There you are, then."

"Yes, here we are."

2

They operated out of a converted lube shop in Grozny, Chechnya. There were three of them, plus two PC's that still accepted floppy disks, a blue-eyed Bassett hound and four feral cats living in the windows.

But they were well-funded. They spent a stack of cash and received an untraceable email that listed all Swissair pilots age sixty-three or older. They filtered that list to those who flew to Zurich and of those they chose the one who was sixty-four. His name was Royal Evans and his was the perfect profile: mandatory retirement in six weeks, happily married, no criminal record, retirement fully funded. The seats were confirmed and Zurich was confirmed. They knew they had their man.

The Chechens entered the United States and made their way to Chicago. They set up housekeeping in a down-town Hilton suite and went to work.

The pilot, Royal Evans, had to be taken down. Only then would he be useful.

First order of business: they made sure Evans caught his wife with another man. The other man was one of them, name of Maritan. He was a physician and handsome. Mrs. Royal Evans was swept off her feet in just three days after a chance meeting at the Starbucks she visited every weekday morning. He was wearing scrubs and he wore the requisite stethoscope around his neck like a Hollywood producer sporting gold chains. He reeked of status and riches like lounge lizards reek of Musk.

Maritan was several years Mrs. Evans junior, a surgeon trained at America's oldest hospital, Bellevue. He told Mrs. Evans he'd never known love before. It took her all of seventy-two hours to fall madly in love and phone her sister in Poughkeepsie to tell her so. The man wanted her to come away, she told the sister, but he insisted she first confront Royal Evans and tell him she wanted half of everything. Including his Swissair retirement.

Her sister asked, would she do it? Would she demand half of everything?

Mrs. Evans didn't equivocate. Maritan was the nicest man she'd ever known. He was considerate, caring, and soft-spoken. He wanted to know everything about her, hung on every word she uttered. Two blissful nights with a youthful, virile, intelligent doctor—what woman in her fifties could resist? Especially when Royal Evans was distant and growing angry in his advancing years. He hated the kids crossing the lawn, he hated dark skins, he hated Europe, and he hated her family. When he was home he refused to shave and their time together consisted of white whiskers and regret. The thought of it: that she had thrown away thirty years. It came down to an easy choice for Mrs. Evans.

"Go for it," her sister encouraged. "You only go around once."

Mrs. Evans told Royal Evans there was no way she could ever turn away from Maritan the surgeon. She demanded half of everything. Including his Swissair retirement. He imagined himself living in a studio with a foldout bed above a butcher shop, the victim of a sack and pillage.

He decided to dig in and let it blow over. But she was having none of that.

Mrs. Evans demanded he leave the house that night. He tossed down two scotches and refused to leave. She dialed the police while he watched and listened to her report a domestic disturbance. Taking the scotch bottle, he grabbed his flight bag and left. Now the Chechens had them separated. They followed him and checked into the room next door in the Palmer House in Chicago.

The following morning, the Chechens noisily settled around the next table as Royal Evans ate breakfast in the hotel cafe. Evans couldn't help but overhear. The topic was an upcoming flight to Zurich. The Chechens erupted into a violent argument about flying times and time zones. Evans was astonished, because it was his flight and he would be flying their plane, so he interrupted their argument and offered his thoughts.

Ayub, the younger of the two, eyed him with bristling suspicion as he spoke.

"And you know this how?" Ayub said sharply.

Evans smiled his friendly, Welcome Aboard smile, hiding from them the fact he actually loathed them because they were dark and spoke with accents. "I know it because I have been the pilot on this trip probably two hundred times. To make a long story short, your friend is right and you are wrong."

Ayub relaxed and let the pilot see he was warming to

him. "Well, this is unexpected help. How can we thank you?"

"Not necessary. Call it serendipity. Just let me finish eating in peace."

"I shall call it that. And I shall buy your breakfast as well, if you will allow it. Then you won't hear us again. Not one single peep."

"No need for that."

"We insist. Please—join us for coffee."

"I'm fine over here."

"Are you on a layover?"

"No, I live here as of last night. Problems at home."

Ayub winced. "Aniji, he knows all about that. He had an American wife once."

The older man, Aniji, shook his head sadly. "Never again. No American women."

Evans nodded and found himself oddly sympathetic. "I hear that," he said.

"And what is your name, captain?"

"Royal Evans. And you can forget about the captain stuff. I'm off-duty."

They traded stories. They were petroleum engineers visiting Russaco's home office two miles away. They explained they were from Russia and they found America inspiring and wonderful. Which pleased Royal Evans. Everyone likes to hear visitors admire their home. They asked if he had ever toured a petroleum refinery and he laughed and said no, he actually had not thought about visiting a refinery. One thing led to another and he agreed to accompany them on a tour of the local plant. It just might help take his mind off the problems at home. And for Russians, they weren't so bad after all, thought Royal Evans. And who knows, the Chechens said, maybe Mrs. Evans will have come to her senses in a day or two. Evans said he doubted that, that she hadn't strayed even once in thirty years. No, this was serious and he dreaded the worst.

They toured the refinery. They gave him a Russaco hard hat to keep. Little stuff, including buying his dinner. That night they drank together and they spiked his scotch. When Evans woke for a bladder call at five a.m., he was horrified to find with him in a bed a female who couldn't have been more than fifteen. His two new friends were at the foot of the bed, video recorder in hand, stony-faced as he regained consciousness. It swam into view for him and he realized.

He had been had.

They played the video, showing him the hard drive version of the *Kama Sutra*. Evans ran to the bathroom and threw up. By the time he came back he was shaken and ashen. A quick look around. The girl had disappeared. But his new friends were still there. In fact, they had just ordered up a carafe of coffee and six Danish. They wanted to talk. Man to men. For they had a proposition.

They held tickets on his next flight. A thousand miles out over the Atlantic he would turn over control of the plane to his co-pilot and go to the restroom. When the cabin door came open, they would rush the cockpit and take control. The 777 would be diverted to Moscow and he would fly it there. His reward: $1 million. He did the math: his 401k was at $1.3 million after thirty years of toil. Mrs. Evans was in for one-half, her community property share. The Chechen's deal looked better to Evans. Plus they would destroy the recording of the sex-with-a-minor incident and he would not have to spend his retirement behind bars. The math worked top-down and bottom-up, so Evans agreed.

Two days later his flight came up.

They took one cab to the airport. One big happy outing,

at that point. Royal Evans rode in back, sandwiched between them. It turned out they had British passports, good as gold in the U.S.

Captain Evans moved from back seat in the cab to first chair in the 777. In the cabin of Swissair Flight 3309, Chicago to Zurich nonstop.

In a cockpit lockbox, Captain Evans kept a small pistol. He always swore he would use it to prevent a skyjacking. But this time, when they breached the cabin doors, he was busy in the restroom. When he emerged, he played the victim role and immediately assented to re-program the autopilot and head for Moscow. After all, there were 324 civilians onboard his flight and his first thought was for their safety. The co-pilot and First Class stews all heard the threats to kill the two pilots and crash the plane in the Atlantic. Captain Evans couldn't—wouldn't—allow that.

So Moscow was dialed in to the autopilot. No announcement was made to the passengers.

The first skyjacking since 9/11 had just been committed. Not a shot fired, not a throat cut. Just a sickening video recording on a cheap camera starring Royal Evans and a street teen. Jail bait wasn't even the right term. *Prison* bait was more like it.

Captain Evans looked into the dark night at stars above and pitch black below, diamonds tossed at velvet. At 450 knots and slipping into the northern hemisphere polar jet stream, there was no stopping the Moscow-bound aircraft.

Captain Royal Evans was out of good ideas.

At that point, he was just driving.

3

S ergei Barishnakov's passport and papers said he was Steven Barry, when he arrived in America. He obtained a student visa under that pseudonym, using the falsified identification papers provided to him by Russia's GRU—the Russian counterpart of the CIA.

He attended Dartmouth, where he was a member of the ski team. During winter months he skied every weekend. He became a ski bum and in doing so looked very upper-middle-class American.

After six semesters and six summer schools, he earned a degree in Cyrillic languages. Next up: UCLA and Ph.D. studies in linguistics. With practice, all Russian accent was erased and a wholly new personal history penned in the books. Following graduation, he was hired by the CIA and posted stateside, working out of Langley as a ciphers expert. The CIA knew nothing of his Russian bloodline and history. The Agency's own records confessed that out of every 10,000 hires a foreign agent from an unfriendly state would make it through. Steven Barry proved the statistic.

He married another Russian Agent, one Mary Anne Junpay of Philadelphia and they had two children. Mary Anne stayed home with the kids and encrypted Sergei's stolen CIA data and then broadcast it to Russia via a trawler operating off Kodiak, Alaska, and in later years by encrypted tweets.

When Christine Susmann went deep-cover using the credentials of Ama Gloq and the full extent of the CIA ruse had become known by Steven Barry, the false identity was superimposed on the actual identity and relayed to Moscow GRU. Russian intelligence added one more face and one more phony name to its list of CIA intelligence assets.

"We might as well be trading agent identities right out in the open," said GRU agent Karli Guryshenko, the Muscovite in charge of CIA spying. "We know their agents and they know our agents. Maybe we should put them on baseball cards." This last part was never said aloud except one time: knee-walking drunk on Evanota Vodka, Karli had made this statement to Irina, his wife, at a mandatory state dinner. The next day she told him about his comments and his face turned white. Had anyone heard him? No one, she assured him. "But you and your baseball card spies better pray President Irunyaev never gets wind. It's very cold in Siberia and the woods there are full of fools who didn't know when to shut the hell up!"

It was Karli who reviewed the Christine Susmann— Ama Gloq— pedigree. He saw to it that her fake identity was keyed into Russian computers and made available to GRU agents worldwide, all 22,500 of them.

Christine's secret had remained unknown to the Russians all of 4.5 hours.

Back in Langley, Steven Barry was impressed. Christine's outing was the fastest since the Bush Administration threw Valerie Plame under the bus. Luckily for her, Plame at the time was in the United States. Christine—Ama Gloq —was headed toward Moscow on a skyjacked 777 when it came to be her turn.

A new record, which would likely result in a vacation award for the skier Steven Barry.

Aspen Mountain just moved that much closer to his skis.

4

The passenger in 14D blinked awake. He called the steward. The steward hurried back to him.

"Yes? What can I get you?"

He carefully studied the steward's face.

"I feel a slight turn in the flight path. Why would we be turning over the Atlantic?"

"My goodness, Mr. Murfee, aren't you the astute one?"

Thaddeus Murfee shook his head.

"Not at all. It's just that I own a Gulfstream and I know a turn when I feel it. And I've been feeling it the past five minutes. Slow, almost like they're hiding it. But we turned and I know it. What's up?"

"We had a slight cross-wind. The autopilot adjusted. Happens all the time."

"No, it doesn't happen like that. Crosswind corrections are long arcs. There's no sensation of turning with those."

The steward stood upright.

"Well, I've told you all I know. Would you care for a nice glass of wine to help you relax?"

"No. I won't be sleeping. Nor will I relax."

"Good night, Mr. Murfee."

Thaddeus stared out the black window. He saw only the reflected blink of navigation lights skipping along the clouds far below. Beside him, to his right, sat Christine. Although her eyes were shut as if sleeping, he was certain she had heard every word of his exchange with the steward. Lawyer and paralegal had boarded the plane together, joking and talking like employer and employee off to accomplish a law task in Europe. Nothing unusual, just another day at the office for the very busy young lawyer and his assistant. They had found their seats in business class and gotten comfortable.

To Thaddeus' left, a young, Hispanic woman was sleeping as the plane added 150 knots in the jet stream. She had a laptop perched precariously on her lap. Thaddeus' inclination was to reach across and take it out of her hands before it dropped to the floor. But he knew his move could be misinterpreted, so he let it go. He found the button on the arm of his seat and reclined the back. He closed his eyes.

———

THE YOUNG HISPANIC woman blinked awake. Something had changed. She closed up her laptop and wiped a drop of sleep spittle from her mouth. A tinge of excitement ran down her spine. At last, she was on her way. A story on Nazi banking in Zurich had been used by her as the reason for her trip. But she had other ideas. She shivered and draped the airplane blanket across her knees. She placed the laptop on the floor and sat back. Now what had changed?

Her question was answered when the man beside her called the steward back. He was told the plane had made a course correction; that was all. The passenger seemed satisfied so she relaxed back into her chair.

Eyes closed, she dreamed of the *Pulitzer Prize* awaiting her. She would follow that up with the required book. A *New York Times* bestseller.

Her name was Angelina Sosa and she was a 2012 Honors grad from the University of Chicago School of Journalism. In college, her heroes were Bob Woodward and Carl Bernstein of Watergate fame. Her latter-day hero was Edward Snowden. A millennial herself, she saw in Snowden a servant of the people, by the people, and for the people. Her parents violently disagreed with her, calling him a traitor and someone who should be locked away forever, but that's how it was with parents, she decided. There would always be this gulf or that.

At UC she had a minor in Russian and a second minor in Russian Literature of the Czars. The motto "autocracy, orthodoxy, and nationality," expressing the principles applied to a new system of education, was used by her first anti-hero, Czar Nicholas I. He was dedicated to suppressing liberal thought, controlling the universities, increasing censorship, persecuting religious and national minorities, and strengthening the secret police. With Pushkin, Lermontov, and Gogol, a golden age in literature began. For her, this was literature to be adored. Better yet, it should be read in the original Russian, and so she did, even training herself to think in Russian at will.

At first her visions of winning worldwide acclaim for her reporting had been hazy. She knew she needed the inside track on some sort of problem, some sort of mess, or some measure of governmental intrigue that would catch the public's fickle fancy. Maybe something about some politician, or office holder; even a governor. Chicago was rife with ne'er-do-wells who were too often gracing the front pages of local papers. Ferreting out their unsavory political schemes and under-the-table/behind-closed-doors dealings. *That's* what Angelina had in mind. Exactly that. In fact, two previous—living—Illinois governors were incarcerated, doing time for crimes committed while they were in service to the people who had elected them. But how to get that inside track? How, exactly, does one go about digging up the dirt on wickedness? Where to begin?

She stiffened as the man beside her took a deep breath and slowly exhaled. Evidently he was asleep. She eyed his profile from the deep shadows of the nighttime Business Class. He wasn't too shabby-looking, she thought, maybe a little too preppy. He hadn't changed all that much since the last time they sat together. She was sure he wouldn't remember. As for her own taste in men, Angelina gravitated toward someone a little more edgy, a little more unshaven, than the guy in the next seat. Then she felt flustered at her naiveté about the world. Here she was, leaping to conclusions about someone based only on what he looked like. She knew better; she knew how successful this attorney was. She mentally kicked herself for being so childish. She wouldn't find any great story if she kept allowing her prejudices and illogic to lead her blindly through the world. *Grow up, Girl!* She corrected herself. *Grow the hell up!*

At that point she lapsed into a four hour fuzzy state of being, situated somewhere between coma and twilight sleep. Business class didn't lend itself to sleeping any more than any other part of these international flights, she guessed, never having flown internationally before. But she was abruptly jolted back to a state of wide-awake when she heard a passenger complain loudly to a stewardess, "Miss, we've just flown over Zurich and we're not descending! What is going on?"

5

K aty Murfee was young—only twenty-eight—and her stomach was as flat as a girl's. Which she hated, because she wanted another baby. She wanted to see her stomach swell and protrude and grow a baby. Thaddeus Murfee's baby.

They'd been successful once before, with Sarai. But Sarai was now six and needed a brother or sister before the age difference became too great. In fact, Katy wondered whether they had already passed that magic age when siblings that follow siblings are considered by the older ones to be too young to play with. She prayed that time hadn't come, but she knew the time was now or the playmate link would be lost. Katy had come off the pill six months ago and had expected to immediately conceive. But it hadn't worked that way.

And now she was genuinely concerned.

She was working long days at *Lodzi Ashstein Miracle of Life Community Center*. She would generally be onsite by seven a.m. to oversee the breakfast feeding and she would generally stay until ten at night. She always wanted to make sure everyone got a bed or at least a bedroll if the beds were all filled. It was a labor of love; no work had ever been more rewarding to her than working with the homeless, the sick, and the hungry. Plus, Turquoise had co-opted what now amounted to four good-size rooms for the chemical dependency groups that met there and, oftentimes, played cards there and held dances and raffles. That was a whole other organization and Katy felt blessed by it and blessed by the fact that Turquoise usually had it under control with Katy's help. As an added bonus, Lodzi Ashstein himself spent his mornings in the building, helping meet the needs of veterans and their families. His specialty, he called it.

It was six a.m. when Katy stood before her dresser mirror and rubbed her flat hand up and down on her flat stomach. Last week with Thaddeus had been good; she hoped she had hit the ovulation cycle on the money when she had seduced him after he got home late. She smiled. Whatever else could be said about it, he hadn't complained. He was obviously devoted to her and only had eyes for her, for which she was grateful—but not *too* grateful, she didn't want to spoil him.

As a physician, Katy knew there were five steps for women to consider when trying to get pregnant, before making an appointment with an IVF specialist.

First up was a complete physical. Check, she had been to see Evelyn Meier, her OB-GYN.

Second step was genetic testing. Why? Because she and Thaddeus were different genetically, she being Native American and he being Irish-English. Or at least she thought the difference might be significant enough to justify testing, so they had opted for it, each one giving up a sample of saliva to the lab. Her doctor had convinced her—and

Thaddeus—the genetic screening might be the single most important thing they could do to help ensure a healthy baby. And all it required was a saliva sample from each of them. Better yet, their insurance had covered it.

The remaining steps required Thaddeus. He would soon be home from Zurich and she would guide him from there.

Not that he actually needed guiding, she thought, smiling.

6

J acques Lemoneux was a minor talent in the French Embassy in New York.

He was mid-fifties, balding with a dyed black fringe of hair, a graduate of the École d'économie de Paris, and an expert on American wheat exports to France. He had been in Chicago visiting the Board of Trade when he purchased a one-way ticket to Paris, with a stopover in Zurich. Lemoneux flew between Paris and New York every weekend, leaving late Friday and returning late Sunday. His airborne pastime was dialing in his GPS to follow the plane's speed and flight path. His phone's GPS had proven infallible: one time, at 38,000 feet, several hundred miles south of the Aleutian Islands, he had been able to lock onto eleven GPS satellites within six seconds, a personal best. He always knew where he was, a small eccentricity he allowed himself when traveling.

At two a.m. he opened his eyes for a quick look at his phone. He noted the plane was four hundred miles short of the European continent traveling 553 miles an hour. On time, he saw, but definitely north of its usual flight path by at least two hundred miles. Lemoneux attributed the odd geolocation to a thunderstorm bypass and immediately went back to listening on his ear buds. The audiobook was entitled, *A Western Survey of Eastern Terrorism*, a study Lemoneux was perhaps one-third really interested in, but, the economist in him demanded he finish listening to the book, since the price had been paid.

The audiobook's narrator droned on:

The Chechen–Russian conflict is the centuries-long conflict, often armed, between the Russian government and various Chechen nationalist and Islamist forces. Formal hostilities date back to 1785, though elements of the conflict can be traced back considerably further.

Since the end of the Second Chechen War in May 2000, low-level insurgency has continued, particularly in Chechnya, Ingushetia and Dagestan. Russian security forces have succeeded in capturing some of their leaders, such as Shamil Basayev, who was killed on July 10, 2006. Since Basayev's death, Dokka Umarov has taken the leadership of the rebel forces in North Caucasus.

Radical Islamists from Chechnya and other North Caucasian republics have been held responsible for a number of terrorist attacks throughout Russia, most notably the Russian apartment bombings in 1999, the Moscow theater hostage crisis in 2002, the Beslan school hostage crisis in 2004, the 2010 Moscow Metro bombings and the Domodedovo International Airport bombing in 2011.

At that point Jacques Lemoneux angrily jerked his seatback to the upright position, yanked the ear buds from his ears, and summoned the steward. "Coffee," he said, exasperated with the increasingly dull audiobook, "two sugars on the side. And hurry, please." He was wide-awake; the audiobook had failed its key use, which was to transfer useful knowledge to Lemoneux which might possibly increase his chances for a promotion at the Embassy.

Chechen-Russian relations bore no foreseeable possibility of giving his career any kind of boost, so Lemoneux kicked himself for buying the audiobook. $11.95 shot to hell. Amazon and its five-star rating system had been skewed with this particular offering, Lemoneux was certain of it. But the returns period had lapsed and so he was stuck with the book. Hopefully a strong swill of coffee would remove some of the bad taste left from reading it.

Lemoneux tugged the phone from his breast pocket. He jabbed the GPS icon.

He was shocked to see the plane was even further north of its usual path. Plus, it hadn't begun descending for the stopover in Zurich.

"Now what?" he wondered.

The plane was closing on Moscow at 577 miles an hour.

7

"**M**iss, we've just flown over Zurich and we're not descending! What is going on?"

Four passengers complained to the flight attendants. Three men and one woman. The foursome was following their flight on GPS phones and, according to the GPS geolocation, they had overflown Zurich and were turning northeast. What, they demanded of the attendants, was going on?

At which point, Christine Susmann opened her eyes.

Paralegal Christine Susmann had received her professional training in the U.S. Army. Following Basic Training, she had begun her career working as an M.P. and had served two years at a Black Ops detention center in Baghdad. She was under lifetime orders to never discuss what she had seen or done on that post, which was fine; she never wanted to discuss it anyway. Following two successful years working hand-in-glove with the CIA field officers, she had her choice of Army schools and selected paralegal school. She had seen all she ever wanted to see of detention centers, prisons, jails, or any other institution where people were held against their will. Paralegal training had dragged on for almost a year, but when she finished she was assigned to a JAG unit of busy lawyers in Germany.

Now she was traveling as Ama Gloq on the Swissair flight to Zurich, and she overheard one of the complaints about overflying Zurich. She looked to her left at Thaddeus, who was asleep and oblivious to the minor upset of their fellow passengers. An idea occurred to her and she dug through her carryon and located the phone the CIA had issued her under the Gloq identity. She paged across the icons until she found the GPS button. She jabbed it and waited.

Sure enough. Off-course by several hundred miles. Her pulse quickened. Something was up, wasn't it? She couldn't be sure. She nudged Thaddeus with her elbow. He moaned and moved away. She did it again, this time poking him hard in the ribs. His eyes opened—just barely, but opened.

"What?" he said.

Christine looked around. No one listening from behind.

"We're off-course." She lifted the GPS screen to him. He studied it and raised his eyes.

"I asked that steward if we had turned. He tried to tell me it was only a weather correction."

"Huh-uh. We're several hundred miles northeast of where we should be."

"Damn," said Thaddeus, coming fully awake.

It was then that he noticed the young woman to his left. Her eyes were wide open and she had clearly been eaves-dropping on his exchange with Christine.

Her pupils were fully open in the dark cabin and the whites flashed.

"What's going on?" she asked Thaddeus at a conversational level.

He shrugged. "What do you mean?"

Angelina eyed him closely. "I heard what you and your friend were saying. We're off-course. How come?"

"Don't have the answer to that," he said. "Wish I did. Probably weather."

"We wouldn't be east of Zurich if it was just weather, would we?"

She'd stumped him. She had him there.

"I don't think it's anything to worry about. You can probably go back to sleep," he reassured her.

"You think? You think I should sleep through a skyjacking? What are you, nuts?"

Thaddeus looked away. She was speaking much too loudly for the confined space. Others were surely hearing every word and he wanted no part of her.

"Sorry. I guess I meant that I should go back to sleep," he said, and leaned back against his chair. He closed his eyes and lapsed into a sequence of shallow, even breaths, meaning to indicate to the young woman that he was no longer available for dialogue.

But she was anxious. "You're a surgeon, am I right? Going to Zurich to give a paper?"

Thaddeus cracked one eye open. "Me? No, you have me mistaken for someone else. I'm going to sleep now, if you'll let me."

"So what do you do? *Talk* to me! Can't you see I'm dying over here?"

"Dying? Why are you dying?"

"Fear, man. This shit scares me to death, flying across the Atlantic in the middle of the night and now going past our destination. Why aren't you scared too?"

At which point, Christine brought her seat-back upright.

Christine said, "Miss, this man is trying to get some sleep. And you're keeping me awake. Do you think you could just back off a little and let us both get a few winks?"

The young woman's jaw tightened. Her dark eyes flashed.

"Who appointed you Mother Superior? What, you're the queen of the flight? Why aren't you both getting a little nut-so like me?"

Christine did the best thing she could think of. She gave the younger woman a wide smile. "We're seasoned travelers and we're probably both thinking there's a weather detour here. That's all."

"Show me on your GPS, please. Show me where we are."

Christine sighed and activated the screen on her cell-phone. She punched the GPS icon and waited while the software accessed a geo-satellite. Then she held the screen up for the young woman to see.

"OMG," the young woman said. "OMG. We're way past Zurich!"

Christine turned the phone to her face. In the dim light her profile was clear. Anyone watching would have had a good look at her, but at that moment she was ignoring that possibility.

"OMG is right," said Christine. "Thaddeus, we're four hundred miles past Zurich. What the hell?"

Thaddeus took the phone and studied it. He turned it horizontal and obtained a wider view of the area. Then he handed it back to Christine.

"I'm clueless," he said. He reached overhead and summoned a steward. Looking up the aisle, he could see they were all busy, to a man and to a woman, speaking in whispers with other passengers. Evidently the odd news was traveling fast.

8

I nside the cockpit, the Chechen national, Ayub, stood behind Royal Evans as he piloted the plane. Ayub held the pilot's Walther PPK jammed against the pilot's head. Captain Evans thought the gun's placement was meant to impress the crew, but he wasn't entirely sure of that. It could have been that the original hijack plan had been abandoned and now the Chechens really meant to kill them all if the Russians didn't meet demands.

Both Captain Evans and Ayub were staring intently out the windshield. The wipers were flipping aside a mixture of ice and rain pelting the Plexiglas at 600 miles per hour. The co-pilot was flicking through switches on his console, monitoring flight metrics as they reported on his screens. So far, he had announced minutes ago, all values were within normal ranges.

The stewardess named Leona Lacey stuck her head inside the door.

"Captain Evans, someone needs to say something to the passengers."

Royal Evans gave her a look over his shoulder. "GPS'ers got the word on the street?"

"They do. Everyone knows something's up. We're going to have a revolution back there if someone doesn't say something."

Ayub laid a hand on Evans' shoulder. "Make no announcement," he said. "I'll go back and talk to them when we've crossed into Russian airspace."

"About that," said Evans. "You don't just fly into Russian airspace unannounced. They're going to scramble Sukhoi Su-24 attack aircraft to intercept and turn us around. Or worse. A missile up our ass doesn't sit well with me, how about you?"

Ayub smiled. "Couldn't care less. We're prepared to die, Captain. The only question is, when does it happen? However, we have a trade to make with the Russians first. So what do you recommend?"

"We need to call up Moscow Center and announce our intention and route. We need to get on their screens as a known aircraft in their airspace."

"So call them up."

"Now? You're saying I should call them now?"

"Why not? We don't want to anger them. Not yet, anyway."

Captain Evans looked across at his co-pilot, an ex-Air Force airman with 2500 hours in 777's.

"First Officer Manfred, please contact Moscow Center. We need to advise."

First Officer Manfred was a small, crew-cut co-pilot who couldn't leave the coffee alone. He swore by it on long flights and always had his favorite mug in his hands.

"Roger that," said Manfred. He began punching

numbers into the dash and soon was receiving data from the Swissair mainframe.

"Okay," said Manfred, "Here we go. Evidently after the fall of the Soviet Union, the Federal Air Transport Agency assumed responsibility as the authority in charge of civil aviation in Russia. It's under the control of the Ministry of Transport of the Russian Federation. The agency is responsible for the all aspects of civilian air operations including the operation of the nation's navigation and traffic management system. Rosaviatsia is similar to the Federal Aviation Administration in the United States. All transmissions are in English."

"Fair enough. Dial them up, please, Manny."

"Roger that."

Manfred punched numbers into the radio and immediately began speaking in a monotone into his mike.

"Moscow Center, this is Swissair Flight 3309. We are declaring an emergency and are thirty minutes from entering Russian airspace. We have been hijacked."

Manfred repeated the same call several times.

Then Moscow Center came back. It was English, as advertised, but dripping with Russian inflection.

"Swissair 3309, this is Moscow Center. You are not authorized to enter Russian airspace. Will say again, do not enter Russian airspace. You are prohibited, your emergency is denied."

"Oh, hell no!" moaned Captain Evans. "How the hell does he deny an emergency?"

"Negative, Moscow," said Manfred. "The situation is out of our hands. We have been hijacked by three men who are demanding we fly into Sheremetyevo."

"Permission to enter Russian airspace is denied. Repeat,

permission denied. Please divert elsewhere or you will be intercepted by fighter aircraft."

"Notice he didn't say what that would mean," Evans said to the Chechen. "My guess is they play very rough. Just ask the Koreans, if I recall correctly."

"Captain, yes," said First Officer Manfred, "here's a data update." He began reading from his dinner-plate-sized green screen. "In 1983, 1551 Zulu, Korean Air Lines Flight 007 deviated from its intended course and entered prohibited Soviet airspace over Kamchatka. Soviet ATC dispatched Sukhoi S-15 fighter aircraft to intercept. Non-incendiary rounds from cannons went unnoticed and, long story short, the fighters shot down the flight. 269 aboard killed."

"Of course," said Captain Evans. "Textbook intercept and shoot-down for the Soviets. We're about to find out if the new and improved Russian ATC is so short-sighted, I guess."

Captain Evans thumbed his mike.

"Moscow Center, this is Swissair 3309 Captain Royal Evans. We are hijacked and declaring an emergency. We have no choice but to enter Russian airspace. We will cross-over in sixteen minutes. Please advise."

Dead air followed. The tension in the cabin was mounting. A bead of sweat broke out on the captain's forehead. Having his aircraft brought down by a Russian missile hadn't been part of the deal. No, the deal was cash money and every passenger delivered safe and sound. He drew a finger across his forehead and wiped the moisture on his trousers. He couldn't let the situation degrade further.

"Repeat, Moscow Center, this is Swissair 3309 Captain Royal Evans. Permission requested to enter Russian airspace for declared emergency. Please advise."

Now he was making a transmitted record of the intrigue between a Swiss aircraft and the Russian Federation. Whatever followed would be the topic of the next week in the press. CNN and the BBC would be all over it. *Al Jazeera* would feature it. *Time* and *Newsweek* would do analyses. The world would judge the Russians on the next hour. They would compare any antagonism to the shoot-down of the Malaysian airliner over the Ukraine several months earlier. It was well known a Russian SAM missile had been responsible. Public opinion would warrant severe U.S. and Euro economic penalties, not to mention furor in the U.N.

Captain Evans predicted, correctly, the Russian controllers were in touch with the Kremlin, maybe President Piotor Irunyaev himself. Another public whipping was the last thing the Russians needed, what with the Ukrainian sanctions already underway, not to mention the horrendous financial impact of the collapse of oil prices. Russia was in dire straits and another international incident was the last thing the mother country needed.

Just then, the Russian ATC came back over the dashboard speakers. The aircraft was advised to set a course for Moscow, Sheremetyevo Airport.

Ayub pounded the captain on the back.

"Well done, captain!" the Chechen cried. "Well done!"

Four minutes later they flew across the imaginary line in the air. Two attack aircraft had been scrambled and were waiting. They assembled at both wingtips and began the escort.

Russia now spread out below their wings.

9

P assengers who had a view of the wings were astonished to see fighter aircraft take up positions twenty feet beyond the wingtips. Russian red stars adorned the aircrafts' rudders. Word passed quickly among the passengers. Russians were out there; you could all but reach out and touch them.

Pandemonium erupted.

Thaddeus and Christine quietly conferred.

"My guess? That's Russia down there," he told her.

"My GPS is confirming that."

Too close not to hear, the journalism graduate chimed in.

"OMG! My first real story!"

Thaddeus ignored her. Until she punched him in the ribs with her elbow.

"We're in Russia!" she cried. "Let me do a one-on-one with you," she said excitedly to Thaddeus.

He turned to look at her.

"What?"

"You know," she said. "I want to do a piece describing what the hijacking means to one passenger. A biopic."

"Can't help you there. Find someone else. And sit back and try to relax, please. You're going to hyperventilate."

Christine looked across Thaddeus at Angelina.

"Seriously, slow your breathing, girl. Put your head back, close your mouth, and breathe through your nose. There you go."

Angelina did as instructed. The pretty young woman turned her head to the side and watched the flight of the Russian fighter out her window.

"OMG, we're in Russia. We've been hijacked."

Ayub then entered the passenger cabin and picked up the yellow phone used by the attendants for in-flight announcements. He punched the button on the hand piece and blew into the mouthpiece. "Testing," he said softly, then heard his voice reverberate through the passenger compartment. His dark eyes narrowed.

"Ladies and gentlemen," he began, "may I have your attention? First, let me reassure you. My friends and I have borrowed your aircraft for a few hours. Our country needs us in Moscow and you're along for the ride. No harm will come to you, as long as you do exactly as you're told. We will be landing in Moscow and we will remain on the aircraft until the Russian President meets certain demands. My friends and I are Chechen. The Russians are holding captive certain comrades. They must be released and in turn you will be released. You will then continue your journey. Thank you."

He abruptly slammed the phone into its wall mount and disappeared back inside the cockpit.

All was quiet for several seconds, and then everyone tried talking at once.

"What is your name, sir?" Angelina asked Thaddeus. She held her phone as one would hold a mike, waiting to record his words.

"No names, no interview. Please. Sit back and try to relax, miss."

"Angelina."

"Angelina. You're excited and not thinking clearly. You won't be doing a story about me. Try to think bigger, in terms of the overall skyjacking. There's your story."

"No can do. I need to personalize the experience. Now, what's your occupation?"

Thaddeus turned away. He looked into Christine's eyes and rolled his own.

"Miss," said Christine in her command voice, "Put that thing away. And leave this man alone."

Ignoring the order, Angelina passed the phone/recorder nearer to Christine.

"What is this man's occupation? Names, please."

Thaddeus relented. "Look, miss. My name is Thaddeus Murfee. I'm an American lawyer out of Chicago. I'm as upset as anyone on this plane. Now remove your phone and do something constructive for yourself."

"Mr. Murfee, are you married? How will your wife react to the news? Any kids—children? Ages?"

Thaddeus pushed the phone away. He twisted in his seat until he was facing the ambitious reporter.

"Now look. You know everything about me you're going to know. You're going to have to back off now and find someone else to interview."

"You're beside me. I can't very easily find someone else. Besides, everyone's trying to talk at once. You and your friend are the only ones not exploding. You would be doing me a huge favor if you would help me with a story. Didn't anyone ever give you a hand up when you were young and starving? Didn't you get help along the line? Please think about how that happened and how it changed your life. That's all I'm asking."

Thaddeus turned forward. She had struck a chord. He had received help not five years ago. A young woman had come into his office with a terrible disfigurement. Christine and the District Attorney had really helped him make the case. The young reporter had him there. Maybe he owed. Maybe it was his turn to lighten up and give back a little bit. Whatever.

He said softly. "My name is Thaddeus Murfee. I live and practice in Chicago. I'm trying to get to Zurich, where I have business. The young woman seated next to me is my paralegal. Her name is—"

He broke off. Christine was traveling as Ama Gloq. He couldn't very well give out her true identity. He was immediately sorry he had mentioned her.

"Yes? Her name is what?"

"She'll have to self-identify if she wants. I'll leave that up to her. She doesn't owe anyone."

"How are you feeling about now? What's your reaction to being hijacked?"

"Like everyone else onboard, I'm greatly concerned."

"No, everyone else onboard is terrified. You seem to be somewhat cool about the situation."

"Look. People react differently to different things. Right now I'm trying to keep my head and see if I can help the situation somehow. Help get us out of this mess."

"And how do you see yourself helping?"

He sighed. "Who knows? But if I fly off and start running around like a chicken with its head chopped off,

I'm useless to anyone. Call it my training. Keep your head while others are losing theirs. That's all. No biggie."

"What kind of business were you going to transact in Zurich?"

"Law business. Like I said, I'm a lawyer. That's all I can say. Attorney-client confidentiality."

"Why have we been hijacked? Did you understand the man who talked?"

"He said he wants to trade passengers on this plane for inmates in Russian jails. Same old story, Angelina."

"How does he plan to do that? Speak slowly, please."

"He is going to threaten our lives—let the Russians know he'll kill some of us if the trades aren't made. Same old story, again."

"Do you think he will kill anyone?"

"These situations are never good. Most often, hijackers take over planes with the mindset they're not going to escape alive. Like the 9/11 attacks. Those hijackers knew they were going to die. But it was okay with them because they believed in their cause. It's that simple."

"Do you have any plans for taking back the plane?"

He blinked hard. "Me? Are you talking to me? Did you see the gun the guy was holding? Very hard to imagine me going up against that."

"So you're just going to wait and see?"

"Like everyone else, yes. I mean they could crash the plane right now if that was their plan, pure terrorism. But these guys have an agenda. We'll see if the Russians do business with them."

"And if they don't?"

"I hate to think of that."

"What are you feeling right about now?"

"Scared to death. Don't make me out to be a hero. I'm not. I'm just like everyone else. Scared and bewildered."

"Is there anything you'd like to say to your wife? What's her name?"

"Her name is Katy. No, I don't want to say anything right now. This has gone on long enough. I'm done answering questions. Turn that damn thing off, please."

Angelina moved the phone away from his face and touched the screen.

"Good," she said. "That's in the can, as they say. Hey, you know what? I think this story fits a novel format better than a news story. It's going to go on longer than a pure news story. I'm going to write a *New York Times* best seller."

"Rock on," said Christine, her voice angry. "You go, girl."

"Yes I do. One best seller, coming up."

10

Three Chechen radicals were aboard the plane. They were Ayub, Maritan, and Aniji.

Ayub was the youngest, at twenty-six the leader and formulator of the plot to disrupt Russian imprisonment of key Chechen dissidents and freedom fighters. Ayub was six-two, swarthy, blue-eyed, and was always at least three days away from a razor blade. His chin was strong and his carriage was erect and proud. He was a graduate of Chechen State University with a degree in philosophy and a minor in government, odd areas of study in what was known predominantly as a technical university. He smoked French cigarettes and drank thick Turkish coffee and spoke four languages, English being his second. He prided himself on his dedication to his religious beliefs and intellectually considered himself a socialist and fully supported Chechen separatism. A natural leader, Ayub had carefully selected the two men who would accompany him on the death mission the hijacking represented, for none of the three expected to get out of Russia alive.

Maritan was the surgeon, a graduate of Donetsk National Medical University when it was still located in Donetsk, before being moved in 2014 due to the war in Donbass. He was light complected, a youthful thirty-eight, and had been radicalized by what he had seen in the Russian-Chechen War in 1995. The war had left over 100,000 Chechens dead and another 200,000 seriously wounded. Maritan, then eighteen, had served as a private in the Chechen army and was witness to thousands of civilians and soldiers who had been tortured and brutally murdered by Russian Federation troops. While financially independent and a green card holder in the United States, the physician's bank account was directly linked to Chechen radical groups, which he only too gladly supported in their continuing war with Russia. He personally was acquainted with three of the Chechens then imprisoned by Russia whom the hijacking meant to set free. Mrs. Evans—wife of Royal Evans, the pilot—had immediately fallen in love with Maritan when he made overtures to her in the hospital where she worked as a scrub nurse. She had been flattered and hungered for the body and services of a younger man. Quickly arriving at the point in the relationship where she was willing to tell the pilot she wanted a divorce and fifty percent of his assets, she had surprised even herself with her willingness to fall madly in love even in her fifties. Truth be told, unbeknownst to her, she had been waiting for just such a love and Maritan had agreeably provided the opportunity in her otherwise dull life. Being married to an airline pilot who was always away had left her miserably lonely. Maritan, with his love of opera and French cuisine had simply swept her away. His desire was obsessive and hers immediately became its equal.

The third hijacker was a brutalizer of men. His name was Aniji and he was a martial arts specialist in three fighting regimens. He was expert in all makes and calibers of small arms, automatic weapons, and even heavier military weapons both U.S. and Russian. Aniji taught bomb making to other radicals and was relentlessly pursued by the Russian GRU for terrorist crimes against the motherland. Aniji was medium height and heavily muscled, moving catlike on the balls of his feet and capable of cold, unforgiving stalking of Russian agents unlucky enough to be targeted by him. Aniji could always be found wearing black leather jackets, even in the mild summers of Chechnya, sometimes even going without a shirt while preferring the jackets that just did hide the guns always carried inside the waistband of his black denim trousers. "The Man in Black," his comrades called him, and he made every effort not to disappoint. "I am warrior," he once told a newcomer to the cell controlled by Ayub. "My job is to ensure you never leave."

The newcomer stayed.

The threesome entered the passenger cabin full of bluster and threat.

Aniji—as one might expect—was the keeper of the pistol and he waved it around, pointing it at this passenger and that. He finally settled on an Iowa grain farmer and pointed the muzzle of the gun at the man's aisle-side ear. He held it against the man's head while he addressed the passengers.

"This man has been selected to die. His death will show the Russian authorities that we are here to free our Chechen brothers and nothing less will do!"

The grain farmer winced and shrugged his head away from the gun. At which point the terrorist Aniji squeezed the trigger and the gun blasted away the quiet of the cabin. The man's distal skull broke into pieces and spattered against the neck and face of the elderly woman sitting beside him, who all guessed was the dead man's wife. She cried, "Uh-uh-uh-uh-uh!" as she plucked bits and pieces of skull and brain matter and tried to put them back into place on her dead husband, pressing bone into the gaping wound. "Uh-uh-uh-uh-uh!" the old woman moaned and cried, her bloody fingers flying up and back like a potter's hand at the clay, trying to create reason from chaos.

Not a sound, not a movement, among all the passengers. Then it broke loose, and some began quietly sobbing, heads down, crying into their hands and pillows. Others simply sat and stared, ashen-faced, disbelieving. The first man had promised, hadn't he—the first man who made the announcement—hadn't he said all would be well and they would all continue on their journey? Slowly, shock at the ease with which the Chechen had snuffed out another's life began to loosen its hold on some of the witnesses. Moans were heard and there were whispering and terrified looks directed at the Chechens.

"That being said," said Ayub, the hijacker who had first spoken to them, "we sincerely hope it won't be necessary to take more lives. But know this: we won't hesitate to do so. The Russians must accede to our demands or more of you will die here. Now put your heads back, close your eyes, and think good thoughts."

11

Karli Guryshenko hated three a.m. postings. The landline had rung, something about an inbound hijacking, report immediately to Sheremetyevo Airport. He dressed in the same gray flannel suit he'd already worn two days in a row, and slipped his pistol into its shoulder harness. He leaned to his left and checked his image in the small bathroom mirror as he stood urinating in the cramped bathroom. Crewcut, gray hair, long face, boxer's flattened nose, physique of an Olympic weightlifter, and tired, very tired facial muscles. He sighed and returned to the bedroom, where he tucked his GRU identification into a side pocket.

He locked up and then rode the elevator down to the lobby of the apartment house where he and 650 other souls made their nests. The apartments were tiny, cramped, dimly lit, and always reeked of the neighbors' dinner smells, which seeped around walls that were unfinished with quarter-round and seam woods meant to beautify and reduce intra-apartment transmissions of smells and sounds.

Moscow was like that: heavy on the price, light on the amenities.

"What amenities?" he thought, as he started up the Volga and pulled into traffic on Dimitri Street. As usual, he was amazed at the heavy traffic flow in the middle of the night. Didn't these fools ever sleep?

Waiting at a red light, Karli drummed his fingers on the freezing steering wheel. His fleece-lined gloves muted the sound, of course, as winter wear in Moscow muted everything. Everything, that is, except traffic sounds and those horrendous rap music machines on wheels with the ear-bursting speaker systems that rocked your car when they pulled alongside. How he wanted to take out his pistol and blow those speakers into the driver's lap, just one time. Karli's life wouldn't be complete without a quadrophonic speaker slaying.

Coming up to Wavinchi Street, he absently slapped his shirt pocket for a cigarette. Then he remembered for the ten-thousandth time that Dr. Andreza had finally won out: Karli had been tobacco-free all of six weeks now, and seemed to miss the little papery cylinders and their smoke more than ever. The urge was increasing when it should have been going the other way. Or so Karli had thought. He continued motoring another two miles on secondary roads.

At last he jumped on the expressway and began the ten-minute commute to Sheremetyevo Airport. Cars passed him at high speeds on both sides as he tried to maintain a consistent 90 KPH in the center lane. Government transportation sported speed governors now in an attempt to keep speeds down and impose fuel economies. This was totally foreign to most Russians, given their country's enormous business in oil exports. Karli was fond of telling the other agents, when they broke for coffee and were arguing this or that government action—the Russians had petroleum to burn. Literally. The entire sub-strata of Russia was awash in easily-mined oil. Oil fields ten thousand kilometers long. Enough to supply Eastern Europe for a hundred years at peak usage. So why the governors on the government cars, especially the GRU-issue vehicles, where speed just might be a deciding factor if pursuit were undertaken? Why that? He slapped the steering wheel with his gloved hand and noticed it was so cold he felt nothing. He slapped it again. What, his flesh had frozen? He looked at the dashboard temperature: -30 C. Not bad, for Moscow in January.

Just then his cell phone erupted into the *William Tell Overture*. He flicked its face and pressed the appliance to his left ear.

"Karli."

"Yuri. What's your ETA?"

Yuri was second-in-command at GRU, Russia's Main Intelligence Directorate. He was also Karli's best friend and a go-to asset whenever Karli found himself frozen atop some bureaucratic land mine. He wanted to know how soon Karli would arrive at GRU Sheremetyevo Airport.

"Ten minutes. Maybe less, everyone's passing, no one holding me up this time of day."

"Everyone's here."

"The Intercept Team?"

"Yes. Malinda is wondering where the hell you are. I hate that woman," this last part being said in a low tone, almost a whisper. Obviously Yuri was somewhere in the supervisor's general area at Sheremetyevo Security.

"What are we looking at?" Karli asked. He pulled the phone briefly from his ear, making sure it wasn't frozen to the side of his face. It had been known to happen.

"Flight from Chicago. Hijack, perps being Chechen. That's about all we know."

"Body for body."

"Right, you give us one, we give you one kind-of-thing."

"Has Malinda said anything?"

"Only to remind us the GRU doesn't make deals with terrorists."

"So it's a terrorism posting."

"Exactly."

"Which means a high body count."

"Probably. We won't know until they actually start shooting passengers and tossing them onto the tarmac. But knowing the Chechens, I have no doubt there will be blood. Lots of blood."

"Is our assault group assembled?"

"All but one or two stragglers."

"God."

"I know. Try to explain this mess to the American president."

"Bad press all around."

"See you in ten."

"I'm at kilometer post 345.2. See you in five."

"There's night construction at the off-ramp. Take care there."

"Roger that. And out."

Karli slipped the phone into his suit coat. He felt the warmth from his phone briefly warm the skin on his chest. Madness. It was all madness. You kill one, we refuse to negotiate, so you kill another. Lives would be snuffed out tonight, Karli had no doubt.

He watched the construction lights flare up ahead and the intermittent red arrow pointing at the off-ramp to the airport. How he would love to bypass the ramp and just keep driving. Would that day ever come for him? The day when he would turn in his gun and badge and resume life under his birth name? He seriously doubted it. Men like him grew old and chair-bound and suffered a series of heart problems until the big one put them under. He should be so lucky as to be the exception.

He guided the Volga along the off-ramp and took his foot from the accelerator. The little car reduced speed and rolled up to the first red light. Green and white signage offered four choices for airport action: long-term parking, departures and arrivals, curbside, and pass-through. He chose curbside. He would select a security spot and head inside. Airport police would run his plates and immediately protect his VIP status. The car would remain un-towed and untouched. Perqs, he thought, and wheeled in curbside, thirty meters south of the Aeroflot entrance.

One and done.

12

J
acques Lemoneux felt his bladder demanding deflation. But he was afraid to stand up and ask to use the restroom. *Now what?* he wondered. *Just piss in my pants?* As he had these thoughts, his eyes never left the form of Aniji, up at the front of the plane, still waving the gun about and glaring back at eyes that dared meet his own. The man moved like a cat: deliberately, on the balls of his feet, always with considerable grace and well-defined goals. No wasted motion there, thought Lemoneux, and he decided he definitely would not ask the murderer if he might use the restroom. He had been the recipient of certain training in the United States and knew better than to draw attention. But then he had let his guard down and now his bladder was pounding. Rather than draw any attention, he chose wet pants and relieved himself where he sat. The urine flowed into his underwear and forward along his thigh to his knee, where it abruptly fell away, heading south and wetting even his socks. He regretted all the coffee he'd ingested and promised himself he would avoid all liquids

until this present horror resolved itself. One way or the other.

The woman to his left smelled the urine. She flounced uncomfortably in her seat and then stood up and shrieked, "This man has wet himself! Come quickly!"

"Sit down and be still!" Jacques hissed at her. He tugged at her wrist. "These animals won't care about that. Sit and be glad they haven't heard you!"

But she ignored him. She was wearing a red wool suit with a black and white scarf around her throat, dangly bracelets of gold that weighed down her wrist, and a ladies' Rolex of gold and silver. Her hair was cut to a perfectly even length and her gray eyes were full of horror at the notion that the man sitting beside her had relieved himself where he sat. *Clearly*, thought Jacques, *this is the worst thing that has ever happened to her, being forced to sit beside a urinating stranger on a 777.*

At that moment, the man up front noticed her. He widened his eyes in response. She saw that she had his attention and spoke up again.

"This fool has wet himself! I must move!"

The man's expression didn't change and he didn't respond to her statement. Instead, he slowly began moving along the aisle, closing the distance between the woman and himself. As he moved, he surveyed the passengers on both sides of the aisle, probably half of whom were hanging their heads in order to avoid making eye contact. He had made his point when he had shot the elderly gentleman. *So why*, Jacques wondered, *had this fool woman missed the point? What on earth?*

The man with the gun strode up alongside Jacques' row and stopped. Without a word he stuck the gun in the woman's face. Using his free hand, he roughly shoved her back down in her seat. He then put a finger to his mouth in the universal shush sign. Whether he spoke English was unknown. Jacques was relieved that he came back only to quiet the woman. The fact no one was shot after her outburst was a huge relief. While his heart thumped in his chest, he hadn't made eye contact with the killer. He dumbly stared at the seat back facing him.

"Did you piss your pants?" the killer suddenly asked.

Jacques couldn't ignore him. Better to answer the question.

"I did. I was afraid to ask about the restroom."

"Smart man. We won't be needing the restrooms tonight."

The killer then raised his voice and shouted to all passengers. "No restroom for anyone! You must relieve your bladders and bowels where you sit. This is no longer a friendly Swissair flight. You are now flying Chechen Air and we don't intend to please anyone!"

No one dared respond.

"You," the killer said to Jacques. "What is your name?"

"Jacques Lemoneux."

"Passport, please."

Jacques two-fingered the passport from an inside pocket in his jacket.

The killer flipped it open and read.

"French?"

"Yes, sir."

"Why in Chicago?"

"I'm attached to the French Embassy. I was attending an official function in Chicago."

The man scratched his head with the corner of the passport.

"I hate the French. I hate you. Your countrymen dishonor Islam."

"That isn't me, however. I believe in live and let live."

"What does that mean, live and let live?"

Jacques shrugged. "Well, it means you should get to live your life and in return I should get to live mine. Any way we choose."

"That is unacceptable. Our way is the only righteous way. You will die first tonight. I hate the French."

Jacque suddenly needed to urinate again, though his bladder was empty.

"I don't want to die. I will do whatever you say."

"You will be our first offering, Monsieur Lemoneux. Our burnt offering."

"Meaning?"

"Meaning we will trade your life for the life of a Chechen brother imprisoned by the Russians. If they refuse to trade, you will be the first passenger shot and pushed out onto the tarmac. Live and let live that, please."

With that, the man motioned Jacques to his feet. Jacques complied and the man guided him from his seat into the aisle.

"To the front of the plane. Now!"

Jacques led the way to the front of the plane, where he was ordered to sit down and place his back against the bulkhead. He did as he was told and found himself sitting in his urine-soaked pants, on the floor. He thought briefly of telling his captor about a heart condition—contrived—but then decided against it. No sense creating another reason to make his sacrifice that much more reasonable, since he might be about to die from fright anyway. He dropped his chin to his chest and spread the palms of his hands against the hard carpet. The very floor trembled beneath his hands as if the aircraft were frightened for its safety. He fought back tears and closed his eyes. He made it appear he didn't dare allow them to see him crying. As it would turn out, Jacques was an accomplished actor and his fear and near-tears were part of his drama.

Seated four rows back were Thaddeus Murfee, Christine Susmann—traveling as Ama Gloq—and Angelina Sosa, the wannabe *Pulitzer-Prize-New-York-Times-Bestseller*. They witnessed the man's plight who had been selected from among the passengers and made to come forward. Why he was there, they didn't know, but Thaddeus guessed the man had said the wrong thing or done the wrong thing or maybe he was the man the woman back behind them had cried out complaining had wet himself. Probably that, thought Thaddeus, and he felt a deep sense of concern for the man's well-being. He had come up on the killers' radar and that was never a good thing.

"What are you feeling just now?" Angelina asked Thaddeus.

"Knock it the hell off," Thaddeus abruptly whispered back. "This isn't the time or place for that silliness."

"Silly? I want my story, that's all."

"Thad, you have my permission to crack her across the mouth," Christine whispered loud enough for Angelina to hear. "If you want to trade places with me, I'll do it myself."

Angelina leaned across Thaddeus.

"Then give me your best shot, sister," said Angelina. "My older brothers trained me to knock the shit out of nosy old women. Now sit back and shut the hell up or I'm coming over there!"

"Hey, hey!" said Thaddeus. "You're going to get numb-nuts back here if you don't knock this crap off. Both of you sit back and quiet down. Angelina, I'm feeling concerned right now, very concerned, that's how I'm feeling. Write it down."

As he said the words he turned in his seat to get her attention with his eyes. As he did so, he looked straight into one of the most wholesome, attractive faces he'd ever run into. She returned the deep look and a small muscle twitched in her lips. Then he remembered Katy and how much he loved her and how such feelings as he was experiencing right then, were saved exclusively for her. So he turned away. "Write it down. The old guy feels very concerned."

She huffed beside him. "I will. I'll write it in my tablet, no thanks to Miss Come-Kick-My-Ass next to you."

Of course Christine heard. She suddenly reached across Thaddeus and jerked the tablet from Angelina's hands.

"I'll settle this," Christine proclaimed to Angelina. "You can have this back once this mess is cleared up. Until then, shut the hell up before you get him back here."

She was referring to the hijacker Aniji, whose focus had shifted to the arguing threesome. He seemed to be weighing whether he would confront them. Then he looked away as a woman a dozen rows back, opposite side of the plane, fainted. Her seat-mate cried out for help and Aniji's attention was diverted away from Thaddeus and the women flanking him.

Which relieved Thaddeus and Christine. Angelina, on the other hand, was half out of her seat, leaning across Thaddeus, trying to grab back her tablet. But Christina had it wedged between her right leg and the side of her seat. "Not until I say so," she hissed at Angelina. Whereupon Christine seized one of the younger woman's flailing hands and bent her fingers back. Christine half-rose out of her seat and used her leverage to force the young woman to sit back down. It all happened in seconds, without a word being said, but Thaddeus could sense that Angelina realized she had met her match. Even her better.

The young reporter sat back and crossed her arms over her chest, flexing her fingers as if feeling for damage. She looked out her window and Thaddeus could see her reflection in the plastic window, glowering and, he hated to admit, probably planning a counter-attack. It would take everything he had to keep these two apart. At the worst of all possible moments, he had found himself refereeing a catfight—for want of a better term for the melee.

He had words for them both but he dared not speak up.

He sat back and closed his eyes. He heard the killer talking to someone several rows back, assessing the unconscious woman. Clearly, the killer didn't give a damn and was only there to quell any uproar caused from her faint.

Thaddeus settled into his seat.

He was at once glad and regretful he was seated between the two warring factions. One was a proven warrior with a phony passport and ID, the other a starry-eyed reporter in search of a big future.

How he wished he were alone just then.

Alone and looking for an opening, instead of wedged between this twosome that seemed intent on calling attention to themselves. He swiveled his head and peeked past his seat-back.

The killer was standing in the aisle, arms-crossed, tapping the gun against his forearm. Thaddeus was certain the guy had no use for anyone else on the plane except his comrades. Everyone else was just expendable inventory to be used however he wished.

Even if that meant killing another of them just because....

He came back up the aisle and paused beside Christine, seated in the aisle seat. Evidently the man had noticed the commotion involving Christine and Angelina.

"Passport?" the killer said.

Without glancing up, Christine took her passport from her pack. The man studied it, his lips moving slowly as he read. He held the passport up for Ayub to see from where he stood at the front of the compartment. He motioned Ayub to join him. The smaller man hurried back and without a word took the passport and scanned it. He reached down and took Christine's face in his hand and turned it up to meet his gaze.

"Ama Gloq? Is that supposed to be a joke? Come with me."

13

A nother group had no less interest in Ama Gloq than did the skyjackers.

Karli Guryshenko and his GRU supervisor Yuri Andrelisov were poring over the flight manifest. It had been forwarded from Swissair in Geneva, and nothing had especially jumped off the screen at them until they came to that one name: Ama Gloq. She was trying to pass herself off as a Middle Easterner, always a person of interest on a transatlantic flight. But the agents knew better; she had been outed; she was CIA.

Yuri said, "Afghanistan? She's from Kabul. Capital city, it says."

"She might have fought with the resistance, for all we know," said Karli.

"You are referring to the war between the Soviet Union and Afghanistan."

"Yes, the one where we got our ass handed to us."

"Don't think so. Not old enough. Maybe her father or her uncle, but not her."

"What else do we know about her?"

"Her employer is listed as Shell Oil. She's listed as a geologist, Ph.D. from MIT."

Karli nodded. "So the CIA is trying to sneak her here, trying to make this look like a true hijacking. This makes no sense, why would they go to such trouble?

"You're thinking what I'm thinking?"

"She's CIA and she's coming here so America can make some kind of political success."

"My thinking exactly. My guess is, she's never set foot in Afghanistan. Unless she was there as a U.S. combat soldier." Yuri smiled and sadly shook his head. "This entire hijacking might only be meant as a way to get her inside Russia."

"You are a devious man, Comrade Andrelisov."

"It pays to be. What if I'm right?"

"Could be. Let's run her through Central ID. See what else we turn up."

"I've already got that started. We should know something in the next thirty minutes."

"Naturally we will put a hold on her. She's of great interest to the State."

Yuri stood and stretched. It was the middle of the night and he missed being at home in his own bed, soundly sleeping. "She is of interest to the State."

"Either way Central ID reports back, we'll hold her then. A nice comfortable jail cell."

"Maybe not so comfortable. We want her cooperation."

"Agreed. Not so comfortable, then. I promise you, I will have her spilling her guts ten minutes after I have my hands on her."

Yuri gave his underling a blank look. "I'll pretend I didn't hear that."

Karli smiled. "You didn't hear it from me. Just make sure I'm the arresting officer."

"Done."

———

SWISSAIR FLIGHT 3309 landed thirty minutes later and taxied to the Swissair pod. Airport security swept the exit doors with blinding spotlights. A coterie of security personnel gathered at the Jetway where it connected with the airport terminal. Whatever happened, they would be ready.

Karli arrived behind the others and immediately passed the word. GRU would be running things. Nothing would get done except upon the direct orders of Karli himself. He placed himself at the gangway phone and waited for the pilot to call. Within minutes the red light flashed. Karli waited while the light blinked insistently. Finally he picked up.

"Airport security. Who is speaking, please?"

"Call me Ayub," the voice crackled over the house phone. "I am in charge of this aircraft."

"All right, Ayub. My name is Karli. Please tell me your plans."

"Prisoner trade. We trade a passenger for an imprisoned Chechen. It's as simple as that."

"You know we don't negotiate with terrorists. No First World country negotiates with terrorists. So a trade, passengers for prisoners, is definitely out. Why don't we talk instead about you leaving Russia alive? Would you like to leave here alive?"

Karli knew the conversation was being recorded. He

had come across tough and was taking charge from the start. Exactly on-script.

Except the phone went dead. Karli held the phone away from his ear and studied it for several seconds. Then he put it up to his ear again. "Ayub?" he said. "You still there?"

No answer.

For the benefit of the GRU tacticians listening in, Karli said, "What now?"

Dead air. No instructions came back. And Ayub was gone. For the first time, Karli felt both angry and helpless. He wasn't accustomed to being ignored. His hands clenched and unclenched. For a brief moment he considered sending an armed force into the plane and taking down the hijack-ers. But reason and training overcame that egotistical thought and he slowed his thinking. The next move would be up to the hijackers. It had to be: he was left out of the equation at this point.

His earpiece suddenly came to life.

"Karli!" it was Yuri's voice. "Our eyes-on are reporting the aircraft's rear door has been opened and something—or someone—pushed out onto the tarmac. Our ground crew is checking it out."

Karli replied through his throat mike. "I will re-establish communication when you're ready."

"All right, here it is. Comrade Portovia is reporting a dead body has been unceremoniously pushed out the door. An elderly gentleman. We're going through his papers as we speak."

"He is dead, of course."

"Cold and dead, I am told. There is lividity. He has been dead for some time."

"I don't like this. Who are these people? I am wondering."

"Chechens. We are in touch with the president's office as we speak. He was advised thirty minutes ago and he wants to run things, I am told."

"Fair enough. Please advise when you hear."

"Roger that."

Karli surveyed the crowd of armed security personnel waiting behind him. They were very quiet, very professional, very determined. Most of them were older, what the Service called Pskov Storm Troops Division. Men whose happiness was in direct proportion to the body count from any operation. They were hooded and carrying the latest in automatic weapons, with a shotgun or two thrown in for what could only amount to wholesale slaughter, given the tight quarters of an aircraft compartment. Karli shook his head and determined it was up to him to keep them under control. Surely the Russian president would want that.

Just then, the lights in the aircraft blinked out. Agents switched to night scopes but there was nothing to report. No movement, just an aircraft at rest, looking tranquil in the Russian night, belying what all knew was likely happening on board: the selection of the next victim would be underway. That was how it always went in these scenarios.

———

AYUB DUCKED from the cockpit into the passenger compartment. He kept a low profile, aware that night scopes would be following any movement aboard the darkened aircraft. He found Jacques Lemoneux sitting with his back against the bulkhead, where he had been earlier deposited. "You," he said. "Come with me. Do not stand upright. Crouch, as you see me doing."

Jacques climbed to his feet, keeping a bent-double

profile. He didn't need to be told twice. Ayub pushed him roughly into the stewardess staging area of the aircraft. A red gangway phone hung from the cockpit bulkhead. Ayub lifted the phone.

"Who am I speaking with?" Ayub asked.

"Call me Karli. We are preparing to assault the aircraft."

"I wouldn't do that. We have several guns on board and will kill everyone on the plane before you can break through the doors."

"Have it your way. But know this: prisoners will not be released. The Russian president himself has given his orders."

"Orders?"

"No negotiations. If you surrender and the remaining passengers are released unharmed, you will be allowed safe passage out of Russia."

"Not interested. My comrades are willing to die here tonight. As am I. Our efforts will be repeated by those who will follow us. Hijackings will continue and innocent American blood will be spilled on Russian soil until our demands are met. You have been warned."

"So be it. No negotiations."

"Then prepare to collect the next dead body," Ayub said, and slammed the phone against its cradle. He calmed himself and replaced the hand piece. He turned to Jacques.

"Are you prepared to die?"

"I'm a Frenchman. What good does it do to kill a Frenchman? I just heard you tell them you would be killing Americans. Killing me will only make you look foolish."

Ayub paused. The man was correct, said his puzzled expression. He smiled wryly. "Well played, Monsieur Lemoneux. Well played. Take a seat back where you were."

With a feigned sigh of relief, Jacques turned and crept back into the passenger area and all but collapsed into his earlier position against the bulkhead. Tears came to his eyes and he gasped for air. That had been close, his behavior said. So close.

Ayub re-engaged with the passengers. "Show your passports!" he commanded them. "I will be coming through the plane and ask all Americans to hold up their passports. I am also looking for the next volunteer."

"Volunteer for what?" cried a muffled voice from the rear of the plane. Ayub couldn't make out the speaker in the dark.

"Volunteer to die. We are here to secure the release of Chechen prisoners. Every time our demands are turned aside, one of you must die."

Silence ensued. The man with the question didn't follow up. There would be no volunteers, the silence told the hijacker. Just then, Aniji appeared beside Ayub.

"Who do you want next?" he asked Ayub.

"We will be democratic. Start with the first row, window seat. Work across the row."

Without another word, Aniji stepped across the bulkhead row to the young black woman seated at the window. His hand swept forward and he had no sooner placed the muzzle of the gun to her forehead than the gun erupted. A bright red flash followed, coupled with the roar of the gun. In one motion Aniji unbuckled the woman's seat belt and lifted her dead body away from the seat. He carried her to the rear door of the aircraft, passing boldly through the piercing white glare of the spotlights where they entered the plane's pod-side windows.

The third hijacker, Maritan, was waiting there, and he twisted the handle, pushing the door open.

Aniji pushed the dead body out the door and it fell in a clump to the ground.

Up front, Ayub again placed the telephone handset to his ear.

"Well?" Ayub said.

"You are a dead man. You have committed murder on Russian soil. You will die for it."

"The first prisoner we demand be released is Kebiriam Vachagayev."

"Ah, the presidential aide."

"Exactly. We will trade the next American in line to be assassinated for Comrade Vachagayev."

"Only because I have to, we will speak with our people and call you back."

"Ten minutes. Then we throw out the next American."

———

THADDEUS MURFEE HEARD bits and pieces of Ayub's instructions to the Russians. He was considering options—which were virtually non-existent—when a foot kicked the back of his seat. He waited. The foot kicked again.

Without turning around, Thaddeus said, "What is it?"

"I'm an air marshal. You American?"

"I am."

"Will you help me put an end to this?"

"Whatever I can do to help," said Thaddeus. "What is your plan?"

"Trade places with the woman on your right. Lift the armrest to do it, have her slide onto your lap, then you slide into her seat."

"I can do that," said Thaddeus. "Christine?"

She immediately slid over onto his lap and he moved to his right. Her seat was warm and it was on the aisle.

"Now what?"

"When they come back up the aisle, I am going to shoot the one with the gun. The killer."

"And you want me to rush the cabin?"

"Exactly. Your job is to make certain they don't force the plane to takeoff again. Can you do that?"

"I can," said Thaddeus. "I will move when you shoot."

"Yes. And I will be right behind you, with my gun."

"Good. I am ready, then."

"Wait for the killer to come back up the aisle."

"What if they have guns in the cockpit?"

"They won't. I checked the manifest. The only gun on the flight is the pilot's. That's what they're using to kill Americans."

"Got it."

"I'm going with you," said Christine. "You need backup."

"You stay put," Thaddeus said. "I've got this."

"In fact, I should be on the aisle, not you, Thad."

He gave her a dull look. "I guess not. I've got this, Christine."

At which point, the killer came striding back up the aisle, headed for the front of the plane. Evidently it was time to shoot another passenger. Just as he passed and his back became visible, there was a commotion behind Thaddeus and he instinctively lowered himself in his seat as the pistol barked out behind. Then he was up and leaping over the fallen killer, whose blood was draining from a cork-size hole in the back of his head. The cockpit door banged open just as Thaddeus reached it and he grabbed the first man through by the arm. Ayub was smaller than Thaddeus, and wasn't expecting to be jumped, so when Thaddeus pulled sharply on his arm the Chechen flew forward and sprawled in the aisle. Thaddeus dropped down and jammed his knee against the back of the man's neck, facedown as he was, and bore his entire weight downward. Christine leapt around him and disappeared inside the cabin. The air marshal then rushed forward and followed Christine into the cockpit.

A struggle was underway in the cockpit between Christine and Maritan, the surgeon. The connoisseur of French cuisine/opera fan was outmatched. Christine instantly had him in a headlock and dragged him back through the cockpit entrance, now being assisted by the air marshal, who had one of the man's arms and had jammed the gun to his head.

"Come out and drop to the floor," the air marshal ordered, and Maritan complied.

At this point the two remaining hijackers, Maritan and Ayub, were facedown in the aisle, Thaddeus astride Ayub and pinning him with a knee and full body weight; Maritan also face-down with the air marshal's boot on his neck. Christine was straightening her suit jacket, torn up the side in the tussle, and pulling down her cuffs. She was none the worse for wear and saw that Thaddeus and the air marshal had things fully in control, so she returned to her seat.

"What's your name?" Angelina Sosa immediately asked Christine. "Spell it, please."

The reporter had her tablet open in her lap, fingers on the keyboard.

"My damn," Christine moaned, and looked off to the side. "Would you please put that stupid thing away? This is neither the time nor the place."

"Please. I'm just asking for your name."

"Ama Gloq."

"I thought I heard someone call you Chris or Christine."

"I don't think so. My name is Ama Gloq."

"No, I'm sure Thaddeus called you Christine when you traded seats. He said it again when you blew by him and hit the cockpit door with your shoulder."

"Ama Gloq. G-L-O-Q. That's my name. First name Ama. Now shut the hell up and let me catch my breath."

"That was very heroic, what you did. I'm impressed, girl. You rock!"

"Please."

14

T wo weeks before the hijacking, Jacques Lemoneux stood outside Christine Susmann's Schaumburg condo. It was 7:25 a.m. and the couple's two children left the house first, on bicycle and on foot, followed by Christine's husband. Which left Christine alone in the house. Parked down a half-block in a nondescript white van, Lemoneux waited until Christine left home driving a ten-year-old SUV. Lemoneux followed behind, hanging back 100 yards, until Christine turned into day parking at the Palatine Metra station. He pulled up to the adjacent stop sign and waited, watching her out of his rearview mirror. There was no follow-on traffic behind him, so he dawdled at the stop sign. She parked and walked the fifty yards up to the station, where she disappeared inside.

Lemoneux went on around the station and circled back to Christine's house.

He boldly pulled into her driveway and got out. His locksmith's picks opened the front door lock in less than thirty seconds and he went inside, carrying his bag of tricks.

In the kitchen, living room, family room, and bedroom he quickly hid miniature wide-angle cameras with built-in mikes. The devices were tiny and easily hidden inside sound system speakers. As he worked, he wore latex gloves, always sure to leave no prints on the off chance a device was discovered.

Which they were not.

For the next week, Lemoneux monitored all conversations in the household. He wore an earpiece that made him privy to all exchanges. While he listened he also followed Christine everywhere she went. Albertson's Foods, L.A. Fitness, Salads n' Such, pediatrician (ear infection, youngest child), Roser Toyota (lube and checkup), and cleaners, delis, McDonald's and all the rest of the dozens of stops she made while Lemoneux tailed her. Other workers monitored family cell phones, courtesy of the NSA.

They hit pay dirt on the ninth day, as Christine was talking with the Chicago PD Records and Reports officer. Evidently her employer, Thaddeus Murfee, was defending the owner of a tri-state office furniture wholesaler on tax evasion charges, and a prior arrest for embezzlement twenty years earlier was on the books at CPD. Christine wanted a copy of that report and was having difficulty with the records custodian, who apparently didn't want to be bothered with a twenty-year-old record. Lemoneux listened half-heartedly while the conversation droned on, but suddenly pricked up his ears when the topic of calendaring the expected delivery date came up.

Lemoneux heard Christine say, "Look, we need these records within seven days or we'll have to come after you with a *subpoena duces tecum*. Please don't make me do that. You don't want to appear at our offices and I don't want to go through the headache of having a subpoena issued by the clerk and served by the sheriff. How about just overnighting the records to me, certified?"

"Can't do," said the records clerk. "We can't send certified records by mail or FedEx or anything else. And we can't email them. You'll need to come here and sign in, show proper ID, and have the pickup recorded on our documents diary."

"I have to do this personally, or can I send someone by?"

"You're the requesting agent. It will have to be you."

"Damn, man," said Christine, "you must have a heavy flow of traffic through there every day."

"You have no idea. The idea behind this is that these aren't public records, but we've streamlined the Freedom of Information Act rules for our own purposes and made that much simpler. Trust me, this is the best way. Now, when can we expect you?"

"I have to be overseas tomorrow and for the next week. So it can't be right away. Can I swing by today?"

"No can do. These are paper records. They have to be retrieved from storage. That takes two days, turnaround. Where are you going?"

"Pakistan."

"Pakistan? As in the country Pakistan?"

"That's right."

"Isn't it dangerous for Americans to go there?"

"Not necessarily."

"Does your boss make you do this?"

"I have family there. It's a personal trip. But enough about me. Can I calendar my visit when I return?"

Which was all Lemoneux needed to hear. He immediately reported the upcoming visit to his secret employer, the CIA. The CIA wanted to know more. But nothing more was said about the trip that could be intercepted by eavesdropping. Travel visas were checked at all embassies, airline reservations searched, and thirty days of telephone conversations between U.S. citizens and Pakistani country encodes were traced and sifted by NSA. Nothing turned up that explained the travel plans. In the end, it was decided that Lemoneux would continue his tail of Christine, even out of the country.

Her plans made the CIA all the more anxious to follow through on its original plans for Christine as well. The Assistant Director sent for her and she traveled to Langley for the recruitment that would take her to Afghanistan, but which ended up hijacked to Moscow, as she traveled under the CIA cover of Ama Gloq.

Lemoneux missed none of it. It was a simple case of the CIA watching the CIA. There were even cases where the overseers were two deep, watchers watching watchers watching CIA agents. But that was deemed overkill in this case because Christine had an impeccable record as a soldier and a patriot. It was believed by the Directorate that she would exclusively represent CIA interests overseas. The possibility of double-agency was remote, less than a two percent chance, it was concluded.

But when her plane was sidetracked to Moscow, all records of any CIA involvement with Christine were destroyed. It was as if her name had never appeared on Agency computer screens or been accessed on Agency data farms.

She had vanished and was left entirely on her own. She was no longer numbered among agency assets.

Her value to her country was at an all-time low.

15

G RU Central ID reported in a one-liner to Karli:

"RE: Ama Gloq/AKA/Christine Susmann. Known CIA
operative—Arrest and interrogate."

AT 12:02 a.m. the night/early-morning of the hijacking, the
GRU and Russian Security Police stormed the Swissair
flight. The cockpit crew had notified Sheremetyevo Ground
Control the crew had reestablished control of the aircraft
and the hijackers were in custody. Immediate assistance was
requested and Karli was among those who boarded the
aircraft. Unlike the others he was not wearing a face mask
and was not brandishing an automatic weapon. But it
immediately became clear he was in control of the
operation.

"Who are you?" he demanded of the air marshal, whose service weapon was in plain sight.

"U.S. Air Marshal's Service, Tennyson Durant. These are my prisoners." He indicated Ayub and Maritan, handcuffed together face-down in the aisle, the air marshal hovering over them, service weapon drawn and daring the duo to resist.

"Who is Ama Gloq?"

The air marshal answered Karli's question with a blank look. Karli went to the front of the plane, to the phone, and picked up the handset. Pandemonium had set in; the aircraft was noisy, like a busy movie theater after the lights go up. Karli keyed the mike.

"Attention, please. Russian security seeks a woman named Ama Gloq. Will you please self-identify?"

It wasn't until he announced a second time Christine—Ama—heard and responded.

"That would be me," she said and raised her hand. "I'm Ama Gloq."

Karli lifted his hand and motioned her up front. She gathered her carry-on and stepped into the aisle, carefully stepped around the hijackers, and picked her way to Karli.

"What do you want with me?" she asked. She had just struggled in the cockpit with one of the hijackers and was still trying to calm down, to return her breathing to normal. Dealing with Russian bureaucracy hacks was not at the top of her priority list. "What?"

"We need to speak with you."

"Who is 'we'?"

"Please, come with me."

Karli took Christine by the elbow and worked her out the front door of the plane. The Jetway had been attached to allow the boarding and now he took Christine from the plane, the first two to leave.

Thaddeus watched them disappear out the door and attempted to follow, but a hijacker had reached up and wrapped his arm around the young lawyer's leg.

Thaddeus turned to the noisy police and lifted his hands. "What? You're just gonna let this guy take me down?" They were jostling and pushing, try to move him away, and he was trying to disengage—he wanted nothing more to do with any of it—but the cramped space was making it very difficult to indicate with his body language and movement he wanted the same thing they wanted.

At last he kicked his leg free and made it through their cordon. He shrugged through a tight knot of passengers to his seat and twisted in next to Angelina. She was standing, snapping stills with her smart phone and narrating furiously into its mike exactly what she was witnessing. She had no time for him just then, for which he was thankful, but there was a major problem, he realized. Christine hadn't stepped back in. She had evidently been escorted into the terminal, something Thaddeus had intended to prevent. Still, she was nowhere to be seen.

He stood up and looked over the top of the crowd, now crowding into the aisle and pushing each other, three hundred anxious passengers clamoring to de-plane.

Thaddeus pushed through the nearest bunch and began moving forward, stepping around the two hijackers who were standing and submissive, free arms outstretched, allowing their pockets and bodies to be searched.

"Tennyson," Thaddeus shouted through the uproar, "what happened to Ama?"

The air marshal looked between the nearest passengers and located Thaddeus as the speaker. "Unknown. The big

Russian took her off the plane. I've been a little bit distracted here."

"What happens if I leave the plane and try to find her inside?"

"Without a visa? You won't make it past the first cluster of ugly Russkies. I'd wait here until the civil authorities come aboard."

Either he didn't hear or didn't care, but Thaddeus seemed oblivious to this last admonition as he pushed through to the Jetway and turned right, headed for Russian soil. Nor did he notice that Angelina Sosa, intrepid reporter for the *Chicago Tribune* and wannabe *New York Times* best-selling author, was in hot pursuit.

"Thaddeus!" she called to him.

She was ignored. He was of one purpose: the status of Christine Susmann. His pace quickened as he imagined her in the grip of the Russians under an assumed name.

That couldn't be good.

16

A ngelina Sosa was twenty-three, a modest five-feet-six-inches, brown-skinned (Hispanic father and Italian mother) and possessed a thrice-tested IQ of 152. Her interests belied her off-the-charts IQ: she was a raging Pink fan, a constant checker and poster of and on Instagram, a Saturday-Sunday fitting clerk at the downtown Victoria's Secret, and a rookie reporter on the courthouse beat for the *Chicago Tribune*.

She knew very little about law and criminal court processes. To say she was struggling with her profession would have been an understatement. Why, she found herself worrying over and over, were some criminal cases with indictments and why were others filed only with what was called an "information" and why were some filed only on a police officer's ticket?

And then there was the matter of search warrants. She witnessed search warrants forever getting quashed and evidence banned from use in court on the oddest of technicalities—which always astonished her. The willingness of criminal court judges to turn loose obvious criminals guilty of obvious crimes itself seemed criminal. Cases where, for example, the police hadn't knocked before kicking down a door, or where crossing traffic lanes without a blinker wasn't serious enough to predicate a drug bust based on a traffic stop—how could the black robes live with themselves? So, she was learning, and her boss wasn't making it any easier.

Her editor was a fiery mid-forties single woman named Carson McCutcheon. She was an iron-fisted martinet who demanded at least two unimpeachable sources on all stories before she would publish. In today's news environment where CNN anchors interview CNN reporters and call it news, the gluey, plodding news team, slowed by McCutcheon's bi-source requirement, was no competition for the "Breaking News" environment of cable. Which meant the *Chicago Tribune*, where Angelina labored, had become more an in-depth purveyor of news, suited more for the serious news consumer than was the drive-by flash reporting of cable.

While this was the difference between *Tribune* reportage and cable news slash-and-burn reportage, there luckily remained a place in Chicago's environs for newsprint: thousands of trains trundled into and out of Chicago every twenty-four hours. More often than not, their passengers passed the miles with a newspaper in hand, buried nose-deep in the *Pulitzer Prize* stylings of *Tribune* reporters.

Angelina's beat was the criminal court. Criminal court reporting under the *Tribune* umbrella was a tremulous tightrope for Angelina to mount each day as she looked for the truth of important cases, the truth that always seemed to lay just out of her grasp because she had no law degree. Sometimes, however, she won the trip across the wire because she was the perennial student who just never gave up. In her spare time, she read books on criminal and civil procedure and studied law cases from the same hornbooks used in law schools. Her skill on the wire was gaining momentum and balance.

Her editor Carson McCutcheon had early-on challenged Angelina:

"Win a *Pulitzer*. Then I'll have you over and we'll swill Chateau-Rothschild and I'll cook scrumptious soufflés for you. Plus, I'll tell you all my secrets, even my shoe size."

Always one for a challenge, Angelina had replied, "I'll win a *Pulitzer*, sure enough. I'll see that and raise you a *New York Times* Bestseller."

"Why not? The one you can frame and hang, the other you can spend on Italian cars and Tommy Choos. Simultaneous would be an impossible coup for a cub, and I would actually be impressed."

"Then get ready to be impressed. I'm like a jaguar, just waiting for my chance to spring and drag my prey to the ground and suffuse my soul with the most important story of the season. Lady, I'm on it."

"I can hardly wait."

"Any chance of getting me out of the criminal courts?"

"Why? Aren't there *Pulitzers* enough for you there?"

Angelina scoffed. "Truth be told, I wouldn't know a legal *Pulitzer* if it walked up and bit me on the ass."

"Hang in there. You will."

"Really, I would prefer the political beat."

"Stick with it. One of these days the scales will fall away and you'll get it. Now you see but through a glass darkly, but then, etcetera, etcetera."

"I'm trying."

"There is one other way, Ms. Sosa."

"Which is?"

"Sometimes the *Pulitzer* stories fall out of the sky. They happen right before the reporters' eyes without behest or prayer."

"Like Woodward and Bernstein. Watergate just fell into their laps."

"Precisely. So keep your eyes open. You never know."

Which was exactly what Angelina was doing the night her plane was hijacked.

She decided Thaddeus Murfee would be the main character of her story—that she would see the event through his eyes—especially after he tackled one of the hijackers and brought him to the floor of the aircraft, pinning him there with a knee. With that development, she was sure she had her man.

Now he had returned to his seat and was obviously searching the crowd for his friend, Ama Gloq. The woman with whom she had gotten off to a rocky start. She kicked herself for that childishness on her part and determined that it would not interfere with the story developing around her.

She climbed to her feet in the confined space and joined Thaddeus in looking for his friend.

"See her? I don't," she said just as Thaddeus stepped into the aisle.

He ignored her. Then he was pushing forward and was gone.

Angelina returned to videoing the scene and narrating into her smart phone. Like her, the phone was capable of multi-tasking and she was giving it all she had.

A *New York Times* bestseller had erupted all around her and damned if she was going to miss a second of it.

Surely a *Pulitzer* wouldn't be far behind. But wait! Her quarry was getting away.

She clambered into the aisle and began making her way in the direction Thaddeus had gone. He was her story. She would run him to the ground.

She made her way out of the aircraft, into the Jetway, and found herself calling to Thaddeus as he increased the distance between them. He was in a terrible hurry and she stopped to remove her heels and stuff them inside her carryon before running after him.

The story was underway and she had been promised a front row seat. Except Thaddeus Murfee didn't know it. He also didn't know she spoke Russian fluently thanks to her college minors.

He needed her.

Just like she needed him.

17

Jacques Lemoneux knew his duty and he knew his own limitations. While he was a CIA agent placed in the French Embassy under French cover, he, as he liked to say to his lover, was "more desky, less fieldy." Meaning he didn't carry guns and ordinarily wouldn't be called on to terminate a target; with the exception of hand-to-hand, where he was a top-rated knife and razor man.

His key expertise and usefulness to the CIA was micro-electronics: cameras, microphones, the latest in interior house paints that actually absorbed sound and translated it into audio that could be transmitted up to fifty miles away.

So why did he suddenly feel he should follow after Christine? Because as far as he could tell, he was the only CIA agent aboard Swissair 3309 and it was his job. It was as simple as that. Jacques Lemoneux was a patriot and in the moments he watched first one then the other of Christine's seat mates follow her off the plane to Russia and certain huge problems, his patriotism overwhelmed his good sense and he was suddenly transported up out of his seat and into the Jetway. He caught a glimpse of Angelina Sosa—he didn't know her name, of course—disappearing into the terminal at the far end of the passageway.

His step quickened and a million thoughts flooded his mind, the most pressing of which was, how would he contact Langley?

For a split second his heart missed a beat and he considered returning to the plane. What had come over him? What the hell, exactly what the hell, did he think he was doing?

For one, if he didn't follow her and get some details he wouldn't have anything to report to Langley. So, there was that. For another—and this one was a bitch to admit—he had always wanted to operate in the field. Despite his best notions about his best fit within the agency, he had always wanted to know what it felt like to wear the raincoat, as the field operatives called it. Now, he was wearing that raincoat. Not literally, of course. Literally he was wearing soggy suit pants and a rumpled suit coat and a day's worth of beard. He felt somewhat like a fool and in equal parts he felt somewhat like a hero. Now to see which would top the other.

He made the far end of the Jetway and stepped across that invisible line dividing no-man's land of the airplane-Jetway configuration from Russia. He found himself swept down upon by four Russian operatives, front, back, left, right, and moved along in a new direction. There was a side door without lettering and they were guiding him toward it. He drew a deep breath and gave himself over. It hadn't lasted long, his rogue state. In fact, it had lasted less than a minute before he too had been swarmed and taken into Russian custody.

He suddenly had the loose-bowel feeling that he should

have contacted Langley before swimming ashore, as it were. Shoulda-woulda-coulda the pop-psych phrase bounced through his head.

Last thought, then the door opened wide and he was pushed inside.

18

K arli and Yuri couldn't have been more accommodating. The GRU had trained them well.

Would she like tea, coffee, bottled water? Did she need to use the ladies'? Was she hungry? How, exactly, could they help?

She refused all offers. She knew her cell phone and iPad were in Russian custody undergoing analysis, and she knew her passport identity was undergoing an intelligence autopsy of its own.

The CIA was clever, of course. All personal data about Ama Gloq—address, date of birth, husband's name, kids' names, graduation dates, marriage dates—all of it was taken from Christine's own actual yearbook. Try as they may, the agents couldn't ask her one innocuous question that wasn't instantly and correctly answered by Christine.

Yes, Sonny was her husband and Chad and Missy were the offspring of the union officially formed at the United Methodist Church on June 6, 2002 in Orbit, Illinois. Yes, there was military service in Afghanistan and, yes, father was Afghani and yes, she was on her way to Afghanistan to visit family when the plane was hijacked. No, she had never wanted to come to Russia, had no reason to be there other than as the survivor of a crime, and wished to rejoin her group on the plane and leave immediately.

An hour into the "interview" they said they would like to take a break. They left, locking the door behind them.

Christine was left alone in a comfortable enough room: Danish furniture, minimalist abstract art on two walls, no windows, polite track lighting, bottled water unopened on the table, a small refrigerator which they said contained juices she could help herself to, and an insulated pitcher of black coffee surrounded by pink and white packets she could only assume were sweetener and creamer. A restroom extended in a doorway off the third wall and the fourth wall was the main entrance, beyond which lay a large room bulging with cubes and workers speaking nonstop Russian into throat mikes.

As she peered into the restroom, the main door to the interrogation room suddenly flew open and a female worker wearing spike heels and silk slacks with silk shirt came flitting into the room. She opened the file cabinet and flipped through to the D's, where she found her file, pulled it free, and turned and left the room.

This time, though, Christine listened for but did not hear the sound of the deadbolt sliding home. Had that woman actually left the door unlocked? Christine's pulse quickened.

She stood and walked around the table. She was keeping her cool; she had attended the Army's SERE class and knew all about interrogation techniques and how to button-up and wall-off the enemy. For she did consider them enemy combatants, having grown up with the Cold War in recent memory and having witnessed Russia's Piotor Irunyaev's ceaseless invasions of neighboring countries—especially Ukraine—and his despicable treatment of Chechens and their country. She had no use for anything Russian and could only hope her stay there would be brief.

But it came down to one question, in the end: why me? she thought. Had they made her real identity that fast? Had something given her away? Did she look like CIA or give off some CIA vibe she didn't recognize in herself? Otherwise, how in the world had they picked her out of three-hundred-some Swissair passengers? Ama Gloq. I am a Glock. Had they seen right through the false moniker, picked up on the homophone?

She plopped back down in her chair, sighed heavily, and helped herself to a mug of coffee, which was steaming and smelled friendly.

She figured she was being watched by CCTV, so she made a small drama out of pulling the chair next to her away from the table, turning it ninety degrees, inserting her legs and feet into its seat, and sitting back and closing her eyes as if terribly sleepy. That was all they were going to get out of her, she decided with no small jolt of determination. That picture was it.

At the other end of the airport the militia quarters were housed. The two remaining hijackers had been taken there and were being introduced to Russian pain while Christine sipped the strong coffee and kept her eyes closed. Feigning sleep deprivation she slowly rose and crossed to the light switch. She flicked the lights off, setting the room in black-grey tones, and she resumed her semi-sleep position on the two chairs.

Now she was free to look around and make a decision about cameras.

Were they watching her or not?

At first, she had figured they were.

But then she found the door had indeed been left unlocked.

WHY?

Would Russian GRU officers actually leave a prisoner in a room with third party access? Truth be told, this was the airport, not GRU headquarters where every door came outfitted with a lock and every room had a coded keypad and glass eyes peered out of every crack. Yegeny Yetesh-enko, the head of Russian intelligence had lobbied long and hard for a separate building for GRU activities at the Moscow Airport. But government revenues had dropped into a black abyss with the recession of 2008 and Yetesh-enko's request was ignored.

So, they worked out of the interrogation room and two others just like it. Adjoining the three GRU lairs, the cubed room was filled with airport employees hard at work managing the business of the airport. J2 jet fuel was being ordered, 3000 roast beef dinners secured, workers for the third shift conveyer trucks rousted and confirmed, pilots and co-pilots managed from the other side of the globe. Commercial workers, not intelligence workers. Had she walked right through them they wouldn't have noticed, much less cared.

Yuri and Karli were less than fifty feet away, on the other side of the wall. They were fully underway planning their assault on Ama Gloq.

They sat side-by-side at a commandeered desk, laptop computer tuned up and networked to GRU/Moscow, where preliminary GRU abstracts of Ama Gloq's intelligence dossier were coming up on the monitor. Karli followed the display over Yuri's forearms.

First, they had to rule out possible mis-identifications. This would be the case where other people with the same name as a subject under scrutiny would be mistakenly intercepted.

"Ama Gloq out of Finland," said Yuri as he scrolled down. "No."

"No," agreed Karli. "Not even close."

"Ama Gloq RSA," Yuri said with a hint of interest. "But what's South Africa doing on a crossover to Zurich? Doesn't compute."

"Agree. Wait! There's one out of New Zealand. She bears some resemblance to our lady."

"She does. But keep going down. She died in an auto-mobile accident two years ago."

They then scrolled through twenty or more "Ima's." But no other "Ama's."

An aide brought hot coffee to the men.

"She says she was accompanied by her friend, Thaddeus Murfee. He was traveling on business and would turn back in Zurich. She would then go on to visit relatives in Afghanistan."

"What do we know of Murfee?"

"The usual. American lawyer, based out of Chicago, four-attorney firm, nine assistants, primarily criminal and personal injury—birth defect cases."

Karli pursed his lips. "Anything political or governmental?"

"Says here he sued the State of Illinois. Wow, he made off with a truckload of rubles."

Karli sipped his coffee and narrowed his eyes at the screen. "I'll say. Millions of American dollars."

"But there's nothing in his history to indicate any connection to the government. Never worked for them, never clerked for them, has only sued them and that was a territory—a state."

"I say we contact the husband. Check out her name, for openers. See if he even exists. And if he does exist, what name he goes by."

Yuri nodded. "Completely agree. Have Mavick call him?"

"She can. Call him at work, when he least expects it."

"His name is Sonny. Sonny Gloq."

They both sat back and sipped coffee for several minutes. Then Yuri extracted a pack of Belomorkanals and lit up. He offered the pack to Karli, who declined. Yuri puffed out a series of smoke rings and absently poked his index finger at his smoky art.

"I'm thinking something," Yuri said at last. He stubbed out the half-smoked cigarette.

"What might that be?"

"I'm wondering if this entire hijacking was some kind of plot to bring spies into Russia. Maybe Ms. Gloq is not who we're after at all? Or maybe she's not the only one."

"That's paranoid. You really think the CIA would set up a fake hijacking to bring people to Moscow?"

Suddenly both men stood up.

It had come to them: she was alone in the room.

They ran from the office suite and back through the cube room. When they arrived at the interrogation room their worst fear was confirmed.

Ms. Gloq had left the building.

———

ONE HOUR EARLIER, Thaddeus and Angelina scored temporary visas, finally surrendered up by an exhausted customs agent who gave in to Angelina's insistence that they needed to enter the country for one night only. She warned him their aircraft had been hijacked and soon three hundred others would swamp his station, all of them in need of temporary accommodations. Take us first, Angelina pleaded, we got here first. Somehow her childish plea made the agent smile, at least the corners of his thick mouth twitched, as he stamped two hastily printed documents and extended his arm in the universal, "Pass on through."

An hour later they had searched for Christine with no luck. Last place to look, outside. So they found the exit and went out to the taxi stand, for a final look around.

19

T haddeus and Angelina caught up to Christine at the main taxi stand.

Christine had trotted along the walkway between Terminals D, E, and F, and the Aeroexpress railway terminal on the public access side. As did all passageways within the huge airport, the walkway eventually opened on the main taxi stand, above which extended the pedestrian bridge to short-term and long-term parking and car rental lots. She stepped into the sub-zero air and absorbed the alarming freeze of Russian winter on her exposed skin. She needed more outerwear than the tan sheepskin jacket she had brought along to manage from taxi to hotel and hotel back to taxi in Zurich. Of course, Zurich. She shivered. Zurich was a long-ago dream. Now she was in Moscow and she had no idea what came next.

Whereupon she felt a hand on her shoulder and reflexively dodged down and away. She spun in her low heels and stopped. Then she slowly came upright, a smile spreading across her face.

"Thaddeus Murfee. So glad we ran into each other."

"Where the hell did they take you?" he exclaimed. "We've combed the entire airport twice."

"Did you find me?"

"Don't, please. We need to move fast."

Angelina held out a wad of bills. "I changed a Benjamin at the currency exchange. We've got rubles galore. Let's grab a cab."

Christine looked at Thaddeus, who shrugged. "We need to get some place and let me make some calls."

"No, I need to make some calls," Christine said. "This is already turning into an international incident. Uncle is going to be very upset."

Angelina walked to the nearest cab. The driver lowered his window.

She returned. "He will take us to the airport Holiday Inn for fifteen hundred rubles."

"Do we have that much?"

"Easy-schmeezy. Aren't you glad I'm here?"

Thaddeus and Christine exchanged a dour look.

"Away we go," said Thaddeus, leading the trio to the cab. Christine went in first, followed by Angelina and Thaddeus.

Angelina spoke to the driver and instantly they lurched into the flow of traffic to their left.

"And away we go," said Angelina. "I told him the Holiday Inn would be perfect."

"Do they speak English there?"

She shrugged. "Does it matter? As long as I'm here, what difference does it make?"

"You learned Russian in college? Your family is Russian?"

"Right, Spanish-Russian. Duh. Of course college. I

minored in Russian and had a second minor, almost a major, in Russian literature. Which I read in the original Russian."

"I'm impressed," said Thaddeus.

Christine stared coldly out the window. She heard none of it. She was only considering how she would exit Russia quickly without her presence there amounting to anything more than a minuscule blip on the screen of Russian intelligence. She was here briefly but now she's gone. That's what she wanted them to say about her. Period.

The taxi headed north away from the airport, wending its way through Moscow suburbs to the Holiday Inn on Dmitrovskoe Shosse.

They passed by sullen parks where the plows had constructed their mounds, small lakes that lay aching and cold cupped against rolling hills, and suburban stands of timber, primeval and hellishly snowbound, tight in the grip of Russian winter under cloudy, starless skies.

The drive took all of twenty minutes. Christine expected to see red lights and hear sirens closing in from behind, but none came.

The hotel portico lay two hundred meters off the main road, set back between two hillocks, where the familiar green and yellow Holiday Inn neon pierced the gloom like a sedative from home. At last, something they all recognized, an American corporation that had somehow been uprooted and landed in Moscow and flourished.

Check-in took fifteen minutes while ID's were checked and credit cards confirmed. They opted for a double queen with a rollaway and a separate living area for those alarmists who couldn't sleep.

The room was large by Russian standards; small by Chicago standards, but they were exhausted and fell across beds and lay studying the ceiling for five minutes or more. Angelina called the front desk. There was no restaurant in the hotel but a pizza chain delivered, as did the Thai Palace four kilometers south. Singha Thai was ordered times three, chicken, beef, and shrimp, along with egg-fried rice for Thaddeus and chicken-fried rice for Angelina. Christine shook her head. She didn't need a side of rice. She would take the plain rice.

Three hours later they sat two on the couch and one at the desk while the TV featured Russian newsmen talking endlessly about what Angelina could only explain was a citywide election in which terrible voting fraud was rampant. Sleep was all but impossible. At the desk, Angelina was compiling screen upon screen of notes and captured dialogues in preparation for crafting her best seller.

At 3:15 a.m. she asked them to describe how they were then feeling in a sentence or two. They both stared blankly at the screen, simply ignoring yet another plea for feelings updates.

Then Christine mumbled, "Scared. Just scared."

"Why? You haven't done anything wrong."

Christine shook her head. Tears came to her eyes but they were swept away with one swipe of a muscular fore-arm, forbidden to return. She was having none of that, not tonight.

"We're all emotional," Thaddeus said. "With good reason."

"Are you two keeping something from me?" Angelina said. She had collected her thoughts, made her notes, and had pressed them about why Christine had been hurried off the plane by the Russian wearing the business suit when everyone else was left to the militiamen. So far she had only run into closed doors. No one was talking. Funny looks and shrugs; that was how she described it in her notes.

"Let me just ask it point blank, then," Angelina said. "Are you two spies?"

Thaddeus let out a deep groan. "What the hell, Angelina? Everyone's trying to settle down and get some sleep. Just let it go for tonight, okay?"

"That settles it. I'm thinking you're spies. At least Ama Gloq or Christine is. She's the one who got dragged off."

20

The next morning found Angelina awake and hard at it in the living area. She was seated at the desk, her hands and fingers flying over her laptop keyboard. She sat back and smiled. She had the first chapter of her *New York Times* bestseller. Most of the information was gleaned from a late night interview with Thaddeus before he turned in. The rest of it was purely fictional, straight out of Angelina's brain. She reviewed her work:

FROM: Thaddeus Murfee: A New York Times Bestseller

Thaddeus
by Angelina Sosa

The light in a child's eyes is in direct proportion to adult voices. When the adult messages are loving, the light burns brightly. Reports will have it that the child is a delight to have in class. Judo instructors will comment on the child's enthusiasm. Piano teachers will gush about notes and chords played beyond the child's years. But when the adult messages are hateful, the light dims, even extinguishes. Membership in

Scouts is terminated over infractions. Eyes are blackened and noses bloodied in fistfights. Case workers hammer at the door. Police are called. Juvenile halls bulge with the unwashed and the unwanted swept inside on the high tide. Judges admonish. Families fly apart, disarticulating host from offspring.

Thaddeus found himself, at ten, anxious in the visitors' seating of the home. He was alone and unguided, his appearance there arranged by Mrs. Mounce of the Department of Children and Family Services.

Thaddeus made a conscious effort to hide his hands and feet from the visitors and staff. His fingers were spatulate, either hand able to hold a regulation size basketball from the top, with blue veins risen across the backs of his hands like a map of the secondary roads in Phoenix, where he found himself. Likewise, his feet were disproportionate; ten-year-olds weren't supposed to be wearing 14-C's, but Thaddeus' feet would accommodate nothing smaller. When he walked, other children teased him, for his feet flopped like those of a frogman clapping their way into the surf. Surely, some thought, there was a grace awaiting Thaddeus at the end of a flat dive into a coming wave, where the flippers suddenly transform from absurd to powerful.

His usual posture, then, in places like the waiting room of the home for homeless children, would have been arms crossed on the chest, hands buried in the armpits, and feet crossed and scrunched back beneath the green Naugahyde chair. Camouflaged in this manner, Thaddeus became Sonoran. In a word, he imagined himself a Sonoran Desert Gila Monster—he had discovered one when he was hiking, and he had been wholly impressed with how the lizard deliquesced into the sandy arroyo, his beaded hide mixing with the sand. Transformed as Thaddeus was, his posture sent bored eyes elsewhere than on his extremities, where they could seek out the curious slant of light or splash of color or abstract shadow for the brain to consider, instead of contemplating the disproportion of Thaddeus' overdone extremities. Thaddeus had become a native son, adapted like the giant Gila lizard to a desperate landscape. In short, the parents were engaged in a death spiral and the children lost to the system.

Mrs. Mounce returned to his side from the reception desk. He had watched her mouth move and arms and hands gesture as she molded Thaddeus's life in the air for the receptionist to ponder. He knew she had done that; he knew Mrs. Mounce to be an all-out advocate for the cast-off child. He had even begun to believe her—or at least there was the possibility he might.

"The Administrator wants to meet you," she said, taking the chair beside Thaddeus's with an outward rush of air as she collapsed onto the Naugahyde. "He wants to ask you questions for himself."

Thaddeus continued Sonoran. But his mind raced ahead as he considered what the Administrator might want to ask. Had there been violence? Were there domestic crimes? How did he feel about other children? What did he want to do with his life?

"You'll have to answer his questions, of course," Mrs. Mounce pronounced, her face a tight disk of discomfiture at Thaddeus's maddening silence.

He thought he might speak, but then realized, in a quick plumb of his own intellectual state, he had nothing to say. So why say anything? If there was a social equivalency bestowed by casual talk, then mark him down as failed. Frankly, he couldn't have cared less. For the bottom-line was evident: they wouldn't just turn him loose in the street. There was a safety net and even now he was flopping about in its springy depths like the blind albino fish no one really cared to touch. To hell with them, he thought. Just let me be eighteen when I awaken in the morning. Eighteen and free.

Then, at the last moment, he blinked.

"Oh, so you are in there," his escort said. "I saw your eyes move. There's hope for you." She stopped, then slid a pleat of her navy skirt through her chunky fingers, thinking. "Wait, the lady's waving us over. Our turn. Come along, Thaddeus, off we go. Time to meet the wizard behind the curtain, young man."

Heaving herself out of her chair, she gave him a harsh look as if to say his Sonoran had run its course with her. Hands and feet clumsily emerged, and he stood. Unfolded, actually, for Thaddeus was six feet tall. Six feet tall and ten-years-old.

She turned to him and pressed the front of his shirt with the palm of her hand. She lifted upward on his button-down collar, freeing it from the neckline of his blue coat. Turning her head to the side as a water colorist concerned with a first wash, she slowly nodded. "It'll do," she said. "I've seen better, but it'll do. Now go like this," she said, and flicked her tongue around her lips, wetting them, then wiping thumb and forefinger dramatically at the corners of her mouth. "You've coffee in the corners."

He did as he was told. She held out a tissue to his wet fingers. He took it and wiped, then placed it in a front pocket of his khakis.

"Come, then."

She led him to the reception desk, where the lady pointed at a closed door behind her. "No need to knock," she stated. "He's waiting for you. Watch out for his questions," she said, directing this final comment to Thaddeus. The boy's heart fell. Inquisitive adults, he thought, are acquisitive adults. They look to gather the feelings and thoughts of children and file them away to retrieve for reference when there comes the slightest buckle in the air. In a word, they wanted to define you and own you by it. He knew the drill and he hated his near future for it.

He followed her into the large blue and orange office. The air smelled of cigarettes and stale coffee. Neither was evident on the man's desk. He remained standing while the administrator went back around his visitors and shut his door. With only the mildest curiosity, Thaddeus sized up the master of these halls.

The administrator was dressed administratively: blue serge suit, shiny black shoes, white shirt and thin blue necktie with a series of wavelets marching across the fabric at nipple level. Eyeglasses suspended from a coral-onyx chain around his neck, wedding ring of white gold nervously twirled by an obsessive thumb, and a sallow complexion beneath bushy eyebrows and permed black hair. Thaddeus saw a costume, a getup, giving face to a bureaucratic enterprise which, finally, failed its customers one and all. Places like this one always did. So many other kids telling the same story of failed hopes couldn't all be wrong.

This is what the child saw.

For not only was Thaddeus tall, but his IQ was unknowable; it exceeded 165 and, like Thaddeus, wasn't done growing. Which gave the child a certain slant on the world, an unequalled view of his fellows' transparency, and an inquiring mind that was never still. So he looked over this man, this administrator, who held some of the answers to his near-field life, and he saw, sadly, a shill. The man was paid by the state to fill beds in the home he administered, to keep the inmates fed and dry and to expose them to the underbelly of a skimpy in-house educational system. In return he was paid less per month than he could have earned selling Cadillacs. Great, Thaddeus thought, it will be a struggle, but one day I'll hit eighteen and be done with childhood. On cue, he forced a smile and shook the pale hand thrust toward him, the connective tissue to his loco parentis—the State of Arizona.

Angelina read back over her writing. It was sufficient, a little stilted maybe, a little too imaginative here and there, but good enough for now. Especially considering the circumstances under which it was written, hiding with a fugitive from the Russian authorities.

She heard Thaddeus moan in the next room. Across from him, in the second queen bed, was Christine. She had already used the bathroom twice that morning, once around four and again at six.

Then Angelina heard voices. They were talking and she needed to get right in there and watch her story develop.

She loved writing a *Pulitzer*. She loved writing a bestseller.

It was the best job she'd ever had.

21

K arli located the cab driver before the seven o'clock shift at the airport. Three passengers without luggage, one of whom spoke shaky Russian, were instantly recalled and their destination established.

By 7:20 a.m. Karli stood in the Holiday Inn lobby, having just been handed a pass key and room number.

He considered calling for backup; the one going by Gloq was definitely CIA, but the other two reported as missing from the passenger manifest, Mr. Murfee and Ms. Sosa, these two were definitely amateurs. Airport video followed them for a good forty-five minutes the night before, dodging and dashing through the airport, into this room and right back out, looking high and low. Their dress and manner at the taxi stand was likewise videoed and a still of them easily ID'd by the cabbie. Karli had no doubt they were holed up in the Holiday Inn; he would have them in hand within minutes. In the end he decided against backup because they were unarmed. That didn't mean they weren't dangerous, it simply meant they were no match for the nine mm. machine pistol he carried inside his coat.

Fifteen minutes later the trio sat handcuffed together in the back seat of Karli's ten-year-old Lada Samara. They were cramped back there, he noted in the rearview, and he was glad for it.

He had some English, so he spoke to them as he headed for the metro.

"What are your names?" Karli asked. He was smiling his friendly getting-to-know-you smile. The smile was standard issue, GRU.

"Thaddeus Murfee."

"Angelina Sosa."

"Ama Gloq."

Karli smiled at this last and waggled a forefinger, "No, no, Ms. Gloq. I believe you are really someone else. Am I right?" He smiled at her in the rearview.

"I don't know what you mean."

"Yes, you do. Tell me your real name and we'll put you right back on your plane. Did I tell you it's been cleared this morning to continue to Zurich? Would you like to be on that plane?"

"Definitely," said Thaddeus.

"What agency do you work for?" asked Angelina, ever the storyist.

"I'll ask the questions, please."

The silly smile had vanished.

"We would like to be taken to the American Embassy," Thaddeus said. "Please."

"Certainly, happy to oblige," Karli replied. "But first I need you at my office. We need to fill out some papers, a question or two, then we will go. All right?"

"No. We demand to be taken directly to the U.S. Embassy. We have that right."

"You do? Where do you think you are, Chicago?"

"I'm a lawyer. I know a little about international law."

Karli found him in the rearview. With a wink he said, "Did I tell you we don't have international law in Russia? Did they tell you that before you obtained the courtesy of our overnight visa?"

"No one told us that."

"Oh, but they should have. No, no international law here. We follow Russian law. Did you hear of it?"

"Please take us to our embassy," said Angelina, as if the weight of their plight had suddenly settled over her. For the first time in the twenty or so hours Thaddeus had been in her presence, she actually seemed frightened. Not much, but there were signs.

Karli sensed it too. "Young lady, are you recording me with that phone in your hand?"

"No. Yes. I'm a reporter, that's all."

"What kind of reporter?"

"Newspaper."

"Are you reporting on me?"

"Yes. No. I'm following a story. I'm living a story. I think."

GRU headquarters is located on Khoroshevskiy Highway in Khodynke. The main headquarters is more a campus than a single building, but just inside the main entrance, embedded in the marble floor just like the CIA embeds its emblem in its marble floor inside its main entrance—is the icon of Russian Intelligence, a bat-looking graphic in white and black marble spreading its eight foot wings. It's not wholly unlike the graphic bat beaming in the sky on nights Batman is called out.

Moving through the long, curving halls, Thaddeus noted how all office windows looked down on a courtyard where there was a covered garden, fountain and wooden bridge over a stream. The fitness center and swimming pool on the building's first floor were noted. Thaddeus moved along the corridor with his handcuff-mates, walking ahead of Karli, their captor, as the grim reality of GRU captivity set in.

"This is GRU," Thaddeus whispered to Christine.

"Roger that," she whispered back. "Not so good."

"Where are we?" said Angelina, who had been distracted by the young men working out in the glass-walled fitness center. They were buff, she would have termed it, and looked like young, tough men anywhere in the world.

What they couldn't see, of course, was the plethora of high-cost secrets the building hid away from view.

"These walls can withstand an American M1 Abrams tank," said Karli, as if reading minds. "We know because we have tested."

That same morning the Russian President, Piotor Irun-yaev, had landed on the building's roof in an Army helicopter. He had heard about the Swissair skyjacking and the possibility of the capture of an American CIA agent. The president understood the young woman's introduction into the motherland seemed to some as more than coincidental. Already there was a growing undercurrent inside the GRU that the skyjacking was a ruse for placing the young woman in-country, where she would mount an assassination attempt against the president himself. The rumor was started by none other than the president himself. He had his reasons.

Said Irunyaev, this spy he would see for himself.

Out of character? Not for this president, the man who publicized his virility with shirtless photos on horseback and

Speedo pictures entering the surf at the freezing Barents Sea. Photos of the great man personally overseeing the interrogation of the assassin at GRU headquarters guaranteed a ten-point jump in approval ratings. He never missed an opportunity and today was no different.

Two hours later, when the president climbed back aboard his helicopter, a press release was making its way around the government news service. New footage was appearing on the country's TV screens, radios were playing statements, and public affairs officers were all issuing the same stunning report: A young woman traveling as Ama Gloq, whose real name was Christine Susmann, a CIA field operative, had early that morning made an attempt on the life of Russian President Piotor Irunyaev as he made his way from his private residence to his staff car in preparation for the commute to the Kremlin. The young woman, the talking heads reported, had gained access to the President's compound while wearing the uniform of the Russian militia. She was fully armed, and attempted to draw her sidearm and assassinate the leader. The captain in charge of the command that morning had noticed the young woman, immediately realized the ruse, and taken her down to the ground where she was jumped and taken into custody. The CIA had been notified and complaints filed with the White House. The American president had denied all knowledge and maintained the U.S. had absolutely no interest in seeing the Russian premier dead. While there were differences, those were always ideological, not military; America was not at war with Russia and had sent no assassins.

But the point had been made. Russia had a new chip in the game. GRU decided Mother Russia could improve its position by obtaining a confession from the prisoner. President Irunyaev was advised he could expect a video at the

Kremlin within thirty-six hours. They promised it would contain a full confession by the young woman.

At a composite door lettered in Russian, three additional officers joined them. The three Americans were separated. Thaddeus and Angelina were uncuffed and forced to stand apart from Christine. They rubbed their wrists while Christine, still cuffed, looked at them helplessly.

A Russian with shaved head and no eyebrows stepped between Thaddeus and Christine. He faced Thaddeus full-on, his back to Christine, and seemed to dare the American lawyer to speak. Which he did.

"What the hell, Karli," said Thaddeus with alarm. "We go wherever she goes."

Karli waggled a finger at Thaddeus. "No, no, we need your friend to fill out some papers. It won't take ten minutes. Your new friend Ruskov will offer you breakfast next door. You will be fed and allowed restrooms. Thank you."

With that, Karli turned his back and faced Christine. He grasped the short chain running between her handcuffs and jerked her through the door. She turned and gave Thaddeus one final look before disappearing inside. Her eyes said it all: Christine was scared. Thaddeus had never seen her scared. Which caused a bolt of anger to surge along his spine.

"This is bullshit, Karli!" he called after the agent.

But to no avail: the door had abruptly closed.

Ruskov stuck a meaty finger in Thaddeus' chest and motioned him to move on down the hallway. Angelina had attracted her own escort, a tall, willowy man wearing a chocolate brown suit and orange and black necktie straight out of the 1970's—a tie six inches wide and heavily knotted at the throat, so its length was no more than twelve inches. He tentatively pushed Angelina's back to move her with

Thaddeus and she turned and gave him a dour look. He took one step back and smiled. "Please," he said in English, and indicated she should turn and follow Thaddeus. Which she did, her point having been made.

One hour later, Thaddeus and Angelina were shown through a side door and suddenly found themselves standing on Khoroshevskiy Highway, the street that fronted the GRU campus. In the mid-morning light they blinked and shaded their eyes against the sun just above the skyline of the headquarters.

"Must be thirty below out here," Thaddeus said, wrapping his arms around himself.

Angelina was the only one of the three who had taken her winter coat when departing the aircraft. It was a sturdy Northface, guaranteed to seventy below. She pulled the drawstrings at the cuffs and throat and jammed her fists into side pockets.

"At least thirty below. So what now? Where are we?"

"We're in Russia. We've been dismissed. The question is, where's Christine?"

"We could go around to the main entrance and ask about her."

"Good idea. We'll use your Russian."

They walked a good four hundred meters east, coming back to the main entrance of the intelligence enclave. Thaddeus followed Angelina up a double staircase, hoping against hope someone would tell them something. Better yet, that Christine would somehow miraculously be waiting for them to come for her.

They pushed through the double glass doors and walked across the huge GRU graphic of the bat.

A woman sat behind a bulletproof window, half-smiling in welcome. She was wearing a red sweater with animal fur around the neck and reminded Thaddeus of pictures of his mother out of the 1950's when sweater sets and animal furs were in.

Angelina spoke through the mike embedded in the Plexiglas. The woman spoke back.

Thaddeus understood no Russian, so he fought to remain patient while the conversation went back and forth at least a half dozen times. He did hear "Ama Gloq" said both ways.

At long last, Angelina turned to him.

"Well?"

"They know nothing. She's never heard of any Ama Gloq. No record of anyone being brought there by that name."

"Did you tell them about Karli? That he brought the three of us here?"

"She said they are hundreds of Karli's in the bureaucracy. She asked for a last name but of course I didn't have one for him."

"Great. So what did she suggest we do?"

"She said we couldn't loiter here. We need to leave the building at once."

"You're kidding. That's it?"

"Seems like it."

"Bullshit. I'm not leaving."

"The militia will be called, at least she hinted."

"Then we'll go back to our room and make some calls. I have a name in Langley, Virginia. Somebody back there needs to get all over this."

"Let's leave, Thaddeus. She made it very clear we had to leave at once."

"All right."

They retraced their steps to the front entrance.

Ten minutes later they had a cab and Angelina gave the destination.

And so they left Christine alone with the Russians.

Had they known what was about to happen to Christine, maybe they could have done something differently, Thaddeus would later think. But as it was, they knew nothing except it was urgent they get in touch with someone who could help.

That someone was in CIA headquarters, Moscow. It was located at Bolshoy Devyatinskiy Pereulok 8, the location they gave the cab driver.

———

THADDEUS WAS uncomfortable but managing in the back of the cab when it suddenly came to him: Katy. He had to let her know what was going on. She had been talking non-stop about getting pregnant, about a sibling for Sarai, and now, maybe more than ever, she needed him around. In more ways than one.

He pulled out his cell. It was international, it was worth a shot, so he hit speed-dial 1.

Moments later, her unmistakable voice came over the phone.

"Thad? I thought you would be in Chicago today. Where are you?"

"We're not coming home today. We've been...delayed."

"Is anything wrong? Tell me you weren't on that plane that got hijacked. That wasn't you, was it?"

The alarm in her voice tugged at him. He needed to be with her putting his arms around her. Instead, he was stuck in Moscow with no idea where he was or what was going on with Christine, the second most important woman in his life.

"Yes, it was my flight. I'm in Moscow."

Long silence. Then, "Not Idaho?"

"Afraid not. Russia is right outside my window. I'm in a cab with another American from the flight. We've hit a snag."

"What kind of snag?"

"Christine has been hauled away by the Russians. Something about her passport, I think," he said, though he said it without enough conviction even to convince Sarai, truth be told.

"I don't believe that for a second. What's really going on? This trip came up too suddenly. I knew there was something else going on here."

"That's what's really going on. She's been hauled in by the police and they won't let us see her. We're on our way to the American Embassy right now, for help."

Another silence. "We? Who are we?"

"She's a reporter from the *Tribune*. She's covering the hijack story and covering the Christine story."

"How old is she?"

"Please, Katy."

"No, just tell me. Old? Young?"

"The latter. Nothing to worry about there. You know I'm thinking about you and you know how much I want to get back to working on our little creation. Don't ever think otherwise. Not even for a second."

"You can't talk. She's sitting right there beside you."

"Now you've got it."

"Okay. Well, I trust you. Please call me after the Embassy. I need to know what's going on with Chris."

"Will do."

"And stay out of trouble. Try not to shoot anyone."

"No need to worry. I'm a guest here and no one's after me. It's all good."

"Just don't let it be too good. You read me?"

"I do. Okay, so long for now. I'll call after the Embassy."

"I'm thinking about you. In fact, I'm going to be worrying about you. Don't tell me not to. It's my nature and you know that."

"Okay, all my love, goodbye."

"Bye, Thad."

The phone went silent and Thaddeus turned in the seat. "Wife," he said.

"No shit, Sherlock," said Angelina. "You sounded like you were getting the third degree."

"No, nothing like that. My wife totally trusts me."

"Sure she does. I'm absolutely certain of that. That's why she asked you three times about me."

"You could hear that?"

"Thaddeus—Thad—it's crowded back here. Just let it go, okay?"

"Fine."

He faced forward and looked to his left.

He had been right. It was Russia outside.

22

They shot her up, she lost consciousness immediately, and they drove her to a dacha thirty kilometers north of Moscow. The building was set back off Caushkov Road in the Seshovkovich Mountain foothills. It was a long, low building built in the 1950s with river stonework to waist height across the front, above which was fastened redwood paneling in dire need of a new stain. The curtains were drawn and the ficus tree and small pine on either side of the entrance were dying for lack of water, although none of this was seen by Christine as she was carried inside from the Volga Sedan by two burly militiamen. Two others had come along, one of whom was Karli, and he looked not to be in a good mood at all.

Interrogation back at GRU had not gone well, as Karli had predicted. The young woman maintained a steady, calm composure and the usual threats and promises produced no admissions and no cooperation. So Karli elected to elevate to Stage Two—the dacha experience. The Caushkov dacha was selected primarily because neighbors were at such a distance that screams couldn't be heard coming from the interior.

The room was a good twenty feet by sixteen feet. It housed the wooden table used to restrain the subject, a side table of stainless steel, a utility sink with hot and cold water, and a small generator—vented to the outdoors—capable of producing voltages from as low as five volts to as high as 220 volts. The generator sprouted a set of four wires capped off with alligator clips to carry the current from generator to subject. There was also a glass cabinet on the south wall. In it were the various serums, syringes, dental appliances, pliers, and small cutting devices to hasten cooperation.

First they stripped her clothes away. Even her wristwatch and wedding and engagement rings were removed. They wanted her to know the terror of having every inch of her body exposed to their methods. As far as GRU was concerned, the time for talk had passed. Now it was time for persuasion by physical—first—and then mental means.

When she was nude, they cuffed her wrists and ankles to the wooden table. She was prone with the electric tilt keeping the head six inches lower than the feet so that upon regaining consciousness she could be easily water boarded. A broad leather strap was fastened across her chest and tightened so her breathing would be constricted. They wanted her to feel like she was suffocating.

Finally they secured a razor strop to either side of the table. It was drawn across her forehead, pinning her head to the wood. She could move only her eyes and mouth when they were at last ready.

They administered a smelling salt of ammonium carbonate. Her head jerked but was restrained. Her eyes opened, watery against her dark Middle Eastern/Italian skin.

"Welcome back, Ms. Susmann. Yes, our operatives have purchased your true ID. Even your CIA secrets are for sale. But you knew that."

He made a small production out of going to the wall cabinet and selecting a small taser. It was perhaps two inches longer and eight ounces heavier than a militiaman's Grach sidearm. It was colored light gray. Two silver darts produced out the muzzle end to violate human flesh. He held the Taser so she could see.

"I know you know what I'm holding. I am going to set it on low energy and dart you. We are finished with words, so no need to reply, no need to beg or suddenly become cooperative."

With that, he aimed the unit at her upper thigh, the fleshy part, and pulled the trigger.

She was instantly stunned by the shock, her back arching upward against the restraints and her mouth cruelly opening in a long, aching scream.

"NO NO NO," she cried, and tears flooded her eyes and she wept.

Karli released the trigger and the shock ceased. The darts remained embedded in her flesh.

"So. You didn't like that."

"UH UH UH!"

"I see. No one likes the Taser. But it is unavoidable."

"Please."

"No, no please. We are not negotiating. I thought I had made that clear."

"Please, don't. Not again."

"Oh, you mean this?"

He jerked the trigger and she again arched upward against the electricity rushing through her body. Again, the scream, "NO NO NO NO!"

Thankfully, it lasted but five seconds this time.

"Now. That is the first rule. Each time you ask me to stop, it will happen again. Like I said, we are not negotiating. The time for that has passed."

A brawny militiaman stepped to the head of the table. He wore the gray uniform of the Russian militia—the police authority in Russia, responsible for investigating crime and keeping the peace. His role today was to support the GRU and to supply certain items they would need. His name was Iganamov or "Moffi."

Moffi reached down and swept his hand across Christine's breasts. He said something in Russian and looked at Karli with a smile.

Karli barked something back at the man and the hand was instantly removed. Moffi hung his head, looking childishly contrite. With thumb and forefinger he wiped spittle from the corners of his mouth. Then he wiped his fingers on his tunic.

"I apologize for my friend, Ms. Susmann. He is rushing to the end of where we're going. We have much to do before we give you to the militia."

"UH UH UH," she moaned. She flexed her thigh, attempting to shake loose the darts. They remained in place, as designed.

"We are going to take pictures of you today. You are going to do exactly as I order. Now, we will begin by dressing you. Moffi!"

Moffi went out to the Volga and returned within minutes, a bundle of clothes wrapped in his arms.

"Ms. Susmann, I am going to release you now."

Karli stepped on a floor pedal and the wooden table inclined to ninety degrees, fully upright. The third man, a tired-looking militia private with white hands, neck and face jutting at odd angles from his uniform, unbuckled the restraints. He slid his hand beneath Christine's lower back and helped her stand away from the table. Unsteadily at first, then feeling her footing, she was standing upright.

Moffi extended a pair of gray militia pants to her. He indicated she should put them on.

Christine dangled the pants at arm's length.

"What? I'm to put these on?"

"Please," said Karli. He recoiled the Taser wires into the gun, dislodging and retracting the two silver darts. Christine lurched against the pain but said nothing. Her leg was burning but that was the least of her troubles just then, her mind told her.

She stepped first one leg then the other into the trousers. She pulled them up and zipped the zipper. A good four inches of extra material bulged forward at the waist.

Karli looked at Moffi. Moffi again went out to the Volga, returning quickly with a belt and shoulder strap. Christine took the belt and worked it through the pant loops. Then she fastened the shoulder strap to the front and back of the belt but left it hanging to the side, much as one would do with suspenders before putting on a shirt. Which came next, the white shirt. She slipped it on, buttoned up, and then received the militia tunic. At that point, Moffi placed the shoulder strap properly and clipped a holster to her utility belt. The holster contained an MP-443 Grach standard-issue militia semiautomatic pistol. She had no doubt it was unloaded and didn't bother to check. Her own military and police training would have dictated she eject the magazine and work the action on any sidearm handed to her, but at this point she knew already. It would contain no bullets.

They produced ankle boots that she slipped on even

though they were several sizes too large. She had the feeling that perfect fit and presentation was not going to be the issue. No, they were moving in some other direction, something she didn't yet fully understand. Was she going to be killed wearing the uniform? Brutalized? She had no idea; except she knew her life was totally out of her control. She was their plaything and she determined that she'd best come to grips with that and begin to plan how this all should end.

She trusted herself enough to know she would eventually take the initiative and eventually achieve the upper hand, she just didn't know how.

At least not yet.

23

T he U.S. Embassy in Moscow was housed within nine stories with two walls of glass and two of concrete. Anti-eavesdropping circuitry was built into the building's bones, as the construction of the embassy was performed by Goudanov Brothers Construction out of Queens, New York. The Goudanovs were experts in premises security and, just coincidentally, close relatives to the chair of the House Ways and Means committee from around the time the bid was let by the government.

The address was Bolshoy Devyatinskiy Pereulok 8, centrally located in the Presnensky District in the city center of Moscow. This was a noisy, smoggy area, full of panhandlers and street vendors selling everything from bronze castings of the Kremlin to maps leading to the president's home. Other embassies were located within a two-block area as well, including British and Swedish and Republic of South Africa.

Angelina told the cabbie where to pull over and, in the high-speed traffic flow, exited the cab on the sidewalk side.

Thaddeus followed out the same door. They were both carrying small bags and Thaddeus hadn't shaved in over a day. Both travelers looked grim and both looked exhausted.

The past twenty-four hours had been more than anyone could have anticipated. In addition, Angelina had adopted the unnerving habit of constantly speaking notes into her phone and providing a narrative of every move Thaddeus made. "He entered the cab at the Holiday Inn, looking unshaven and haggard...."

They pushed through the rotating door. The lower seven floors were all official U.S. State Department offices and trade and governmental representatives. The upper two floors were intelligence and security services. Thaddeus guessed the top floor was ruled over by the CIA. This was pure guesswork; there was no indication of a CIA presence and the lobby listings mentioned nothing. Still, from all he had heard and read, and from the many movies he had watched, Thaddeus was of the opinion that he would find the CIA in the building.

"This is Spycraft 101," Thaddeus told Angelina as they looked over the building directory. "I can smell CIA from down here in the lobby."

"Is that what that is? I thought it was the smell of bureaucrats."

"Well, that too, I guess."

They entered double glass doors and found themselves inside a large reception area. It was laid out in a U-shape, with courtesy windows along both legs and a windowless office at the base. A row of American flags stood at attention around the room. Windows were marked "Immigrant Visas," and "Non-Immigrant Visas," and "U.S. Citizen Services," and "Administrative," plus other, apparently lesser services.

Thaddeus and Angelina automatically stepped up to the Citizen Services window and waited for the svelte young woman on the other side to hang up her phone. She gave them a broad smile and held up a finger. Strangers in a strange land. Thaddeus immediately felt welcome and smiled back at her. She put the phone down and greeted them.

"Welcome to the Embassy of the United States of America. Are you citizens?"

"I'm Thaddeus Murfee and this is Angelina Sosa," he said. "We're Americans."

"I hear you are," the young woman smiled. She held out her hand. "I'm Sandy Gillette, Sacramento, California. How can we help you today?"

"We were passengers on the Swissair that was hijacked. We're here involuntarily," Angelina said.

"Oh, my, you should be back at the airport. That flight has been cleared to leave Russia at—"—viewing her computer screen—"one p.m. today."

"We're not leaving," said Thaddeus. "There's a third member of our group and she has been kidnapped."

Sandy Gillette's smile relaxed. "Oh? How did this happen?"

"She was whisked off the plane by two men. They stormed the plane and made off with her. She was the only one taken. We followed her to see if we could help."

"Uh, how did you enter Russia without visas?"

Thaddeus pulled the yellow carbon page of the visa issued the night before.

"We were both given one of these."

"These are emergency visas," said Sandy, scanning the receipt. She looked over Angelina's copy as well. "You'll be in the country illegally if you stay past ten o'clock tonight. They're only good for twenty-four hours."

"I think we knew that," Thaddeus said.

Angelina stopped dictating notes long enough to agree. She said, "We knew that."

"Okay, how can we help you?"

Thaddeus leaned into the window opening. He spoke confidentially.

"I was on this flight because my friend, Christine, was traveling under CIA orders. I was along just to provide cover for the first leg of the trip."

"How does that work?"

"I'm a lawyer. Christine is my paralegal."

"So you're here because—"

"I need to speak with the CIA. I know they're in this building. Please set that up for me. Us," he said, nodding at Angelina.

"Let me step away and speak to my supervisor. She'll know how we can help you—if even we can."

"All right."

Thaddeus turned and placed his back to the service window. He watched as Angelina thumbed her tablet's keyboard.

"What are you writing down?"

The young woman didn't look up. "Just getting down the conversation. And the look of this place. And the smell —god-awful."

"Sir?" he heard from behind. He turned and found himself facing Sandy and an older, huskier woman with thin black hair combed severely back on the top and sides. She was wearing redder-than-red lipstick and small diamond earrings—studs. She gave him a cold once-over and nodded. "I've got this," she said to Sandy, who stepped aside.

"Sir, you can't expect to just come in here and ask to speak to the CIA and have doors open up. That's not how it works."

Thaddeus winced. "Then tell me how it works."

"You need to give us your name and your local number. Information will be relayed and contacts made if appropriate. Please just give Sandy your contact info and someone will get back to you."

Thaddeus shook his head violently. "Sorry, but that's not good enough. Our plane is leaving in three hours. In eleven hours we're here illegally. We need to speed this up."

"Can I suggest going to the Russian visa office and seeking a visitor's fourteen day visa? Would that be something you'd be interested in doing? We have addresses and directions we can give you. We've made a small map."

"I need to see the CIA now! Maybe I haven't been clear. The person we're here about was kidnapped last night by Russian agents of some sort. She's missing and was taken away by GRU officers this morning at GRU headquarters. We need help now and we're not leaving until someone sees us!"

"Again, I'm afraid it doesn't work—"

"Look. You can either help me right now or I'm going straight to the AP and CNN and I'm going to tell them how the CIA has abandoned one of its own agents here in Moscow. Is that what I'm going to have to do in order to cut the red tape?"

"One moment, please," said the supervisor. She ducked back inside her windowed office. Sandy remained at her post, idly writing on an intake sheet of some sort while they waited. Thaddeus looked at Angelina and rolled his eyes.

She gave him a thumbs-up and whispered, "Don't forget, you have a representative of the press right here at your service."

Which was when it came clear in his mind. She was absolutely right. Angelina had immediate entrée into those news services thanks to her role at the *Chicago Tribune*. For the first time, he was glad she was along. Maybe this could be worked to their advantage. To Christine's advantage.

Five minutes dragged by. Sandy offered them each an eight-ounce bottle of water. They quickly accepted. They hadn't eaten that morning and had missed their customary coffee and liquids. Two more bottles were produced after the first were all but inhaled.

Finally the supervisor returned. She was holding two red visitor badges. She handed them to Thaddeus.

"Keep these with you. Sandy will key the elevator. You'll be taken to the top floor. Good luck."

"Wait, is the top floor CIA?"

The woman, walking away, turned and looked at Thaddeus. She nodded and her ruby lips glowed.

"CIA."

24

A gainst his will, Jacques was dragged from Russian customs into a small, windowless office the same night Christine was abducted. Four agents assisted him into a chair when he refused to sit and made it clear he wasn't going to be answering questions.

The largest agent, dressed in a rumpled gray suit and white shirt with collar flapped up on one side and spattered navy tie, came around behind and forced the Frenchman's chair up to the table. Jacques drew a deep breath and looked around. He knew far better than to struggle with these hoodlums from the GRU.

The room was mustard yellow with white ceiling, two fans overhead, and a sullen picture of the president on the wall. The four Russian agents sat one on either side of him and two across from him. He inhaled the strong odor of garlic and fish and knew they had been eating the Russian cafeteria standby of white fish in white garlic sauce with beets and hard rolls on the side. The fragrance lasted beyond even the next meal.

The largest agent reached from behind Jacques and placed a bottle of vodka on the table inches from his hands.

"Drink," said the agent. He added a drinking glass and reached and began pouring. Two ounces-four-eight—Jacques quit counting.

"I can't drink all that. It will kill me."

"What do you think our plans are for you? Do you think you're going to walk out of here and go running back to your CIA? Is that it?"

To the right of Jacques sat an agent with the largest forehead Jacques had ever seen. He immediately named him Cro-Magnon Man. The man behind him—someone called him Ivan, so he became Ivan the terrible. To his left was a man who looked more Asian than Caucasoid so Jacques named him The Mongol. And the fourth agent, across from him, was a fortyish woman wearing jungle fatigues bloused into combat boots. A small hat covered most of her head but Jacques could see she was starting to show a gray stripe above either ear. She was smoking and exhaling huge clouds of smoke directly at him. She became known as Smoky. Now he had them all, Ivan, Cro, Mongol, and Smoky. He played this little naming game because his colleagues at the Agency would want full descriptions of his captors and he didn't want to leave out any details.

Ivan pushed his back. "Drink. Drink the glass."

Jacques shook his head. "No. I don't drink alcohol."

"Nonsense! The French drink wine in the crib. Drink!"

He pushed again at Jacques' back, this time harder, more insistent.

Jacques relented. He picked up the glass and sipped a half-inch of the liquid. It burned his mouth and throat going down. "*Merde!*"

"What is shit? What of it?"

Jacques replaced the glass on the table and pointed at it as if warning of snakes.

"But do you have any hairs left on your balls?" Ivan laughed. "That is the true test of Russian vodka. Maybe we should look."

"It will do."

"Drink down the glass. Or else we shall have to look at those balls and I promise you that won't be pleasant."

"No. No more."

"Shall we?" Ivan said to Mongol and Cro and they turned in their chairs and seized his arms while Ivan, from behind, jerked from under his chin, pulling his head back so he was staring at the ceiling. The two fans lazily lopped the air, creating a downdraft. With his other hand, Ivan brought the vodka bottle to Jacques' mouth and inserted the neck halfway inside. He lifted the bottle and poured.

Jacques choked and sputtered and vodka flew out of his mouth, though a good inch or two made its way down his throat.

"There's no need for that! I'm not going to discuss anything with you. You know that."

"Who is this Ama Gloq? Mr. Lemoneux, we know about your employer. We know you were both working for the same employer. See how easy it is? There's nothing to hide. There's nothing we don't already know about you. So help us with her. Why did she come to Russia?"

"Now there's a stupid question, or did you fail to see the hijackers when you rushed the plane?"

"Again!" Ivan commanded and again he seized and poured. This time a good two fingers of the glass entered Jacques' throat, emptying the glass. Smoky reached across the table and refilled it. Jacques shook his head violently.

"No more. If you make me drink more I'll be useless. My tolerance is very low."

Ivan grimaced and made a fist of his huge right hand and slammed it with all his power against the back of Jacques' head. The Frenchman's head flew forward and slammed against the table, spilling the vodka and opening a split in the skin. "*Vas te faire enculer!*" cursed Jacques, and the Russians, fluent in many languages, seized his head and again slammed it against the table. This time blood spattered and Jacques' blow-dried hair flew forward and mattered in the wound. With his hand he drew the hair aside. He held up the same bloody hand. "Enough. I'm not a field agent. I haven't been trained to resist."

"What do you do for the CIA?"

"I bug rooms. Sometimes I follow people, but only once before."

"Did you follow Ama Gloq?"

"Briefly."

"And her real name is Christine Susmann?"

"I don't—yes."

"Why did Christine Susmann come to Russia? Was the hijack a ploy to bring her here? To embarrass the president? To establish her martyrdom in some fashion? What do you say?"

"The hijacking was real. We were supposed to fly to Zurich. I was to leave off there."

"Where was she supposed to go?"

"I don't know. Pakistan, maybe."

"For what purpose?"

"I honestly don't know. With them it's all need-to-know."

Ivan reached around and poured another glass of vodka.

"Drink it down," he commanded.

This time, Jacques did not resist. He drank down the entire eight ounces. Eight shots of vodka.

In minutes he could feel his breathing rate slow and the room begin to spin. Alcohol is a central nervous system depressant, he told himself. Don't lose consciousness. Stay awake!

Again Ivan poured. Again Jacques drank. He held up a hand. "No more."

"I will decide that."

"I can't take anymore. I will pass out."

"You will wish you had, when we're through with you. Now, let's back up to where you first became aware there was a person named Christine Susmann."

"Christine who?"

"Susmann."

"Never heard of her."

"Maybe we can help you remember. Gentlemen?"

They lifted him out of his chair and splayed him on his back on the table. His arms and legs were pinned by Mongol and Cro. Ivan leaned across him so his face was inches away.

"Take and drink so we don't have to hurt you."

Jacques opened his mouth.

Over the next ten minutes he drank down the entire bottle.

Then he told them everything. They slapped him and sat him upright several times, bringing him around, but then he would slump to the side and pass out again.

Then he was driven out of the underground parking garage. The car twisted and turned through Moscow traffic, making its way due west. They pushed him out of the car in an alley on the west side of downtown Moscow, the high crime area. This part of town belonged not to President

Irunyaev; it belonged to the Russian Mafia. Even the GRU officers were uncomfortable driving through those forbidding streets where doors were hammered over with plywood and windows barred and sealed from the inside.

Something or someone would finish him. If nothing else, he had swallowed enough ethyl alcohol to kill him. It always did.

Neat, simple, and very Russian, death by alcohol poisoning.

"*Vas te faire enculer, toi aussi!*" cried Cro-Magnon as he pulled the Volga out of the alley and back into traffic.

"*Vas te faire enculer, toi aussi!*"

25

T he elevator doors whooshed open and Thaddeus looked above for a floor number. There was no light glowing, no floor number. Nine was the highest number possible, but they had gone past nine. *Now what?* he wondered.

Angelina stepped past him, exiting the car first.

Thaddeus followed close behind and found they were in a very small reception area consisting of four chairs and a Plexiglas window with no one behind it. Thaddeus walked up to the window and pressed a black button set into the stainless steel counter. He heard nothing and assumed that it had buzzed or beeped somewhere back behind. They shrugged and took a chair. Oh yes, Thaddeus thought, they will definitely come looking to see what the tide brought in.

Five minutes slowly ticked by. There were no magazines, no TV screen, nothing. And there was no identification anywhere to be seen. They might be at any company quarters in the world, the young attorney thought. But they weren't; they were at the CIA's Moscow office.

A voice came over speakers embedded in the ceiling, speakers neither of them had noticed before.

"Can we help you?"

"Thaddeus Murfee and Angelina Sosa. We were keyed in from the Embassy downstairs."

"State your business, please."

"We came in on the hijacked Swissair. Our friend was traveling under CIA cover. She was going someplace for you. I never knew where," Thaddeus responded.

"Do you have a name?"

"Christine Susmann. Traveling as Ama Gloq. Look, I know they called you about this from downstairs. How about a real person coming out here and talking to me? Your agent—our friend—desperately needs some help."

Silence followed by more silence. The minutes ticked by.

At last, the door next to the reception window buzzed violently.

"Please enter."

Both Thaddeus and Angelina headed for the door.

"Wait, who is the second person?"

"Angelina Sosa. She's a reporter with the *Chicago Tribune*."

"She stays out. Only you, Mr. Murfee."

Angelina let out a huge sigh of disgust and returned to her chair. "Never mind," she said, "you can fill me in. Will you do that?"

Thaddeus ignored the question. "If I'm not back in two days, come looking."

"Funny man."

He twisted the doorknob and went inside.

There was a short hallway and at the end of it he found he was looking at cubicle heaven. It was impossible to see how many cubes were occupied. He stood at the entrance and waited for instructions.

Minutes later a black woman wearing a yellow knit dress appeared and held out her hand. Two gold bracelets encircled her wrist. She was medium height and looked to have powerful arms and shoulders. Thaddeus guessed her to be at the top of her physical and strength game. He shook her hand and smiled.

"I'm Thaddeus Murfee."

"We know. I'm Nancy Empress. Real name, honest. Welcome to our office. Follow me, please."

She led him through the first row of cubicles and at the far end another hall ran perpendicularly. They turned left and walked past three closed doors. At the fourth, Nancy stood back and motioned Thaddeus inside.

They entered and Nancy Empress closed the door behind them.

"Please take a seat."

It wasn't the usual executive chair-desk-visitor chair setup. In the center of the long room was a teak table maybe twenty feet long with six chairs to a side. Thaddeus selected the end chair and Nancy sat beside him. There were no papers, no files to be seen, and he had noticed his hostess wore no badge. So far, nothing had identified the suite and the workers as CIA, so he asked.

"You are CIA?"

"We are—I am. I am a group leader here and I know about Ama Gloq and her mission. The entire incident is regrettable."

"You mean the hijacking."

"Yes. The hijacking."

"What do you plan to do to get her out of Russian custody?"

Nancy shook her head. Her short hair glistened under the harsh lights in the room. A sorrowful expression came over her face.

"Nothing. There is nothing we can do."

"Why not?"

"Well, consider. If we go to the Russians and ask for her return, we as much as admit she's one of us, she's CIA."

"You can't do that?"

"Can't and won't. Agents are never identified as agents. Rule One of the spy game."

"So what am I doing here? Why did you agree to see me?"

She smiled. "We would like to ask for your silence about all this. We ask you to board your outbound Swissair flight and return to Zurich."

He winced. "You mean you want me to leave Christine here while you won't even confirm she's one of you? You can write this down: that isn't going to happen!"

"Look, Mr. Murfee. I understand you're upset. You have every right. But Ama—Christine—knew what she was getting herself into. Her family will be provided for. That was the deal if she didn't come back."

"Okay, okay, let's back up. If you do nothing and I go away quietly, what's the usual outcome in cases like that?"

"The agent is sent to a specialized prison. A work camp."

"And you're willing to let that happen?"

"Mr. Murfee, we're guests in a foreign country. We have no say or right of approval to anything that happens here. If the shoe was on the other foot, if this were America and we had captured a Russian spy, we certainly wouldn't just turn them loose. We would first question them, interrogate fully and then encamp them."

"Encamp them means what?"

"There are black ops camps. All spies know this going in. Christine was no different. We also have to trust her to maintain her silence. If we said anything to indicate we had an interest in her, they would become that much more willing to torture her to find out the connection, find out the mission. We don't do that. It can only hurt the person in custody."

"So you're not going to do anything?"

"Exactly. We're not going to do anything."

"What about the Embassy downstairs? Can they help?"

"They have already lodged a protest with the Russian government. Standard operating procedure."

"But that protest is only *pro forma*?"

"Afraid so, Mr. Murfee. Will that be all now?"

"No, I'm here to demand help. If it's not forthcoming I plan to go to the press."

"Really now, think that through. You go to the press and reveal you're Christine's employer and that she was carrying out a mission for the CIA. That connection only increases your believability, which confirms her identity as an agent. That makes the Russians that much more interested in finding out what she has to say."

"You're saying I'll get her tortured for certain if I go to the press?"

"That's what I'm saying. That would be the worst thing you could do for her. So, will you and your friend be on the Swissair flight?"

"I don't know about my friend. But I won't be. I won't leave Christine here."

"We figured you wouldn't. But you'll be on your own whatever you decide to do. We will deny all knowledge and information."

"Sure you will."

Nancy Empress stood up. She spread her hands. "I believe we're done here."

"Yes."

"Thank you for coming to see us."

"I would thank you but that would be tacit agreement to your position. I won't give you that. So I'll just say goodbye."

"Goodbye, Mr. Murfee. Godspeed."

Thaddeus and Angelina took the elevator back downstairs to the Embassy offices and walked out onto the sidewalk.

"Did you get it? Did my phone do the trick?"

Without a word, he pulled Angelina's phone from his inside jacket pocket. "Voila."

"It's still on record. There, I've shut it off."

"Good thinking, my friend," said Thaddeus.

"So you've got it all recorded. Now what do we do with it?"

"Honestly? I haven't gotten that far yet. Let's get lunch and talk. I'm starved."

"I'm right behind you, Thaddeus."

"Thaddeus? Really? What happened to Mr. Murfee?"

"He left the building. When he recorded an interview with the CIA he became just another one of us."

"Us?"

She smiled. "American citizens. Nobodies. Strangers in a strange land."

"All right then. We've only just begun. Angelina."

"See, first names aren't so hard."

Thaddeus waved over a taxi and they climbed in back.

26

P resident Piotor Irunyaev lived behind four-foot-
thick walls that were six-hundred-years old. Novo-
Ogaryonov was an estate in the Odintsovo District
of Moscow Oblast to the west of the city, by the Rubiyovo-
Uspenskove Highway. It was the official residence of the
President of Russia and first recognized as such in 2000.

A six-meter-high wall surrounded the presidential residence, consisting of indigenous stone four feet thick, later
reinforced with steel rebar and electronic listening devices.

The residence was overflown 24/7 by the Russian Air
Force, which operated three levels of aircraft beginning with
helicopters closest to the ground, a layer of Mach 2 fighter
aircraft, above which flew aircraft stuffed with electronics
capable of listening and watching in one-hundred-mile
sweeps.

The president was divorced in 2012. Two of the three
daughters of that marriage still resided with him; the third
—the oldest—was away at school at an undisclosed location
thought by many to be Moscow University, where she would

have been attending under an alias. Photographs of the children and the president's other family were never allowed and Muscovites really had no idea what the others even looked like. On the other hand, photographs of the president were issued in a constant stream: riding horses, surfboarding, surveying the Black Sea from aboard a Russian submarine, piloting a Russian bomber, relaxing with a Russian writer before an open fire in the presidential residence, coming from and going to work in his beloved Volga Gaz 21—all of it designed to impart a complete picture of who the accomplished man really was.

The capture of Christine Susmann—the Russian GRU no longer clung to the "Ama Gloq" ID—a known agent of the CIA, presented other photo ops proving the prowess of President Irunyaev. In the end, it was decided there would be a set of stills taken during the takedown and arrest of a CIA assassin caught inside the Russian president's compound Novo-Ogaryonov. Now all that was needed was a CIA agent to do his or her part. The capture of Christine Susmann was a timely gift from the gods no one officially believed in. Whatever, they decided to make the whole affair a sum much bigger than its parts.

First they would need pictures. Karli and his aides were contacted. Was she ready to play the part? Was she cooperating yet?

Karli had excellent news for the president.

27

S he was fully dressed and armed with the unloaded semi-automatic Grach. She wore gray militia trousers and tunic, held together at the waist by a black utility belt from which extended the black shoulder strap common to militia uniforms, ankle-high boots and holstered MP-443 Grach sidearm. When she was dressed and had regained her balance, Karli stepped back from her and admired his work. Then Moffi seized her arms from behind and held her.

Suddenly Karli feinted and threw a hard right hook that caught Christine fully on the left jaw, knocking her to her knees where, in total shock, she closed her eyes and drifted into unconsciousness. She sagged to the side and lay in the fetal position on the floor.

"Just so you know, this is the end for you," he said, he drew back his booted right foot and kicked her with all his weight directly in the stomach. He swung and kicked her again, this time in the chest. All the air could be heard rushing from her lungs even while she lay there unconscious.

Then the three GRU agents sat down and talked about possible pay increases while they waited for her to come around.

Fifteen minutes crawled by.

Christine hadn't moved. Karli broke a smelling salt and passed it beneath her nose. She groaned and rolled onto her back.

"That's a good girl," said the Mongol, who had arrived at the dacha an hour earlier. His report had pleased Karli: the Frenchman was alcohol-poisoned and taken away. He had confirmed their suspicions about Christine on his way out. They had been right all along: she was CIA and the CIA was not responding to inquiries. Which meant the agents were free to do with her as they pleased.

The smelling salt was held below her nose. Her eyes blinked open. She immediately touched her hand to her chest. "My God," she moaned. "What?"

"What?" said Karli. "Just softening you up, my dear."

"What?"

"What? What? What? Is the CIA the one asking the questions here? I don't think so."

Karli motioned to Mongol, who leapt to his feet and approached Christine from the side. He drew back his booted foot and sent a shock of a kick into her side. Another, this time to her ribs. She immediately passed out. Which called for another fifteen minutes of discussion about pay grades, possible GRU cars being lent for personal use, and better apartments in the city. If nothing else, the Russian agents were always hopeful their situations would improve even though deep down they knew they were dreaming. It was what it was, being GRU, and what it was wasn't all that bad, compared to the average Russian citizen who rarely was able to buy beef or poultry, while the GRU agents could buy such items and much more almost at will. Something to talk about while Christine moaned and cried out in her unconsciousness.

But they weren't finished. Not yet.

Another smelling salt. Eyes open but glassy.

"Stand her up."

Moffi obeyed Karli, dragging her to her feet from behind. She wobbled; he held her arms and steadied her.

Again Karli drew back and hit her, this time with a left hook that caused her to slump all the way to the floor. Karli nodded at Moffi, who kicked her fiercely in the back of the head.

"Careful!" said Karli. "We don't want fractures. We'll be taking pictures and she must stand upright on her own."

Karli went to the kitchen cupboard and returned with a bottle of American whiskey. Glasses were passed around and the agents drank off several shots. The whiskey warmed bellies, inhibitions were lowered, and more kicks were delivered to the unconscious woman.

"Hey," said Karli, "I'll wager you cannot break a finger using just two fingers of your own."

"I'll take that bet," said Mongol.

He knelt at Christine's side and took her left index finger between his thumb and index finger. Swiftly he bent her finger back, back, until the sound of the bone snapping was clearly heard. Christine moaned and tossed, but her eyes remained closed.

"Again. Same hand."

Mongol complied. Another snap and another moan and fuss.

"Good. Now we won't be pulling any triggers for a long

time, Ama. Ama, Ama, Ama. You are a Gloq? We'll show you something more powerful than a Glock," he said, referring to the armor-piercing rounds fired by his own sidearm. His own 7N21 Russian 9 mm. gun featured an armor-piercing bullet that generated a massive peak pressure. Karli fully intended to see one of his own rounds penetrate the skull bone of the CIA agent. The Russian president would weigh in on her disposal, of course, but Karli hoped the final disposition would be left to him and him alone. He had his own plans for her before she was shot.

"Good. Now take her to the car. Each of you on either side of her in the back seat. She'll probably still be unconscious when we arrive. But we'll give her a sniff and find she's happily cooperative, even bowing and scraping before the president."

Mongol and Moffi carried her out to the car. They opened the back door and all but threw Christine inside. A trickle of blood was found under her nose and issuing from her left ear, now that she had been moved.

"Wipe that off," Karli growled. We won't want blood in our pictures."

Karli drove with the militiamen and Christine in the back.

The presidential residence was twenty minutes toward Moscow.

He hoped she would come around before then.

The president would be merciless if she were still unconscious.

28

J acques Lemoneux dreamed a dog was eating his leg.

Wait. There really is a dog, and it's—

His eyes came unstuck and he contemplated in those first sore moments of coming-to with a hangover. Inches from his face were bricks, a pattern as in masonry, but up close, in-your-face up close. His eyes closed.

He contemplated. Bricks. And the dog.

Again, open eyes, pounding head, dog biting leg. Son of a bi—!

"There really is a dog and it's chewing my ankle!" he shouted against the masonry.

He kicked the beleaguered leg and the animal's mouth rose and fell with the effort. And what was this with the bricks? He tried separating himself from the wall. Lying on his left side, on cement, damp, pushing hard against the wall to get separation. Then his back squeezed up against something hard. He turned his head. If his eyes were working properly—and he could only hope they were—his back was wedged against a Dumpster.

That was it. He had come to between a Dumpster and a brick wall, lying on cement, dog biting his ankle. He kicked at the dog's head. Connecting, the dog yelped and backed off. Now growling, now closing again, another kick and the dog again separated.

Jacques placed his palms and knees against the brick wall and pushed away with tremendous effort. There. The Dumpster rolled back on its little wheels. *Who would have put such tiny wheels on such a big box?* He shook his head. *What did it matter, the wheels?*

He pushed again and was able to turn over onto his back. The sky looked down at him, obscenely gray and overcast. It was a hopeless sky to a man coming-to, hung-over, mouth filled with foul-tasting bits of vomitus, side of face streaked with same; a hopeless sky bereft of sunshine and blue. Gray, like his soul.

Then a memory. *Those sons of bitches got me drunk!* he said to himself. *They forced alcohol down my throat. Tried to kill me. Damn near killed me. Kicked me out in this alley to die.*

Placing his hands on the cement alleyway, he drew up his knees and forced himself upright onto his feet. *There, I survived.*

He felt his pockets. Wallet missing. Wedding ring missing, watch gone too. Stripped of all ID, all money, no idea where he was.

Moscow. He was in Moscow and he had to get to the U.S. Embassy before the Russians discovered he had survived because he knew them. Knew them and knew they wouldn't fail if they had another chance to kill him.

He walked a hundred meters to the near end of the alley and peered out. Sidewalk traffic, heavy vehicle traffic flow. All street signs were in Russian. He slumped against the brick wall. He had no idea where he was and no way to ask for help. You didn't just walk up to a stranger on a Russian street and ask for directions to the CIA. That wouldn't play. And certainly the cab drivers wouldn't know.

Hold that thought. If he could get a cab flagged down and communicate U.S. Embassy. He didn't know Russian for "U.S. Embassy," so he could only hope that the destination was a common enough one that the cabby would recognize the words.

No time like the present to find out.

He crossed the sidewalk and stepped between two parked cars. Looking left, surveying the oncoming traffic.

Finally a cab trundled up and closed the distance.

Could it be?

Yes! He was actually pulling to the side in order to transport Jacques.

He opened the back door and clambered inside. The driver immediately wheeled into traffic and spoke Russian into the rearview mirror.

"I speak English and French," said Jacques in English. He repeated it in French.

The cabby shrugged at him.

"United States Embassy," said Jacques. He repeated it in French.

"Oui, monsieur," said the cabby.

Jacques flopped back against the seat. His head rolled to the side. He felt carsick but fought down the urge to vomit. That would be the end of his ride, so he swallowed hard, keeping it down. He tried to focus on the driver's photograph affixed to the back of the seat with his name and registration number below—all in Russian, of course. It didn't matter who or what or where—he could've kissed the guy.

"Wait here," he told the cabby at the Embassy.
He ran inside and returned with cab fare plus tip.
And just like that, his life was spared.

29

V olga Gaz 21—the Russian president's favorite car. He had plenty to choose from, but the Volga was the Mercedes of Moscow.

The video was shot. It showed the Russian president Piotor Irunyaev coming out of his residence on Rubiyovo-Uspenskove highway. He was dressed for winter weather in stout lace-up brogans, a smart brown suit, heavy topcoat, gloves, and Russian ushanka winter hat, ear flaps up. He was smoking a thin cigarette and exhaled a mighty presidential plume of tobacco smoke and steam.

He approached the rear passenger seat of the Volga, an aide waited to open the door, when suddenly, from stage right, appeared a running figure.

The figure was wearing the uniform of the Russian Militia.

The figure was brandishing a Grach semi-automatic pistol in her right hand. Just as she reached the president and leveled the gun at his chest, the president ducked and lunged for her.

The camera panned back ten feet so the entire scene was captured: he wrestled the assailant to the ground, wrested the gun from her hand, and triumphantly placed a knee against the back of her head, pinning her to the circular driveway of Novo-Ogaryonov, the presidential residence in Moscow.

Militiamen dashed in from either side and the assailant was dragged to her feet. The camera panned in for a close-up of her face and there she was, no doubt about her identity, identified that night on Russian state TV as Christine Susmann, a CIA operative from America.

"Why does she appear to stagger?" said the president after Take One.

Karli shook his head. "Cooperation training, Mr. President. She was unwilling at first."

"So is she drugged?"

"See the purple bruising on the left side of the face? Beneath the face powder?"

The president waved for her to be brought to him. She was half-dragged before him, where she wobbled and her eyes glassed over.

"Can you hear me?" the president asked in perfect English.

Christine fought to focus her eyes. "Can I have— coffee?"

"Darling girl," said the president, "you need something much stronger than coffee. Karli, walk her around the drive once or twice. Deep breaths. I want her looking like she's really charging me, not stumbling at me."

The cameraman piped up. "That was a giveaway, I thought. She looks punch drunk."

The president nodded. "Indeed. Karli, here's a better idea. Take my phone and ring the house physician. He's listed on the speed dial. Get something brought out here for her."

Karli did as he was told. Within minutes the physician appeared carrying a bag, his coat unbuttoned to the wind.

"She's unsteady, Dimitri," President Irunyaev said to his personal physician. "Fix her."

The physician examined Christine's head. "No wonder. She's been brutally assaulted. Her ear is bleeding internally. And her nose is probably broken."

The president gave Karli a sour look. The pugnacious Russian GRU man shook his head. "She was very uncooperative," he said. "Sometimes easy, sometimes not so easy. She was not-so."

"I have something for her," said the physician. He held a finger between Christine's eyes and moved it right and left, attempting the horizontal gaze nystagmus test. Her eyes broke off tracking much before forty-five degrees and the physician sadly shook his head. "Damage to the optic nerve or worse. Brain damage, perhaps. She needs medical treatment."

"Nonsense," said the president. "She has assaulted me. She needs to be taken to prison."

The doctor backed away. "You have my opinion, Mr. President. Would you like me to medicate her?"

"Certainly."

The physician selected a small bottle from his bag and inserted a syringe through the rubber opening. He half-filled the syringe and again approached Christine. "Arm," he said, and Karli pulled up the sleeve of her militia tunic. The doctor turned her forearm upright and inserted the needle into a vein. The plunger was quick to deliver the medication and Christine gasped as the amphetamine worked its magic. In less than a minute she felt euphoric and she felt her pain halved. She was quickly coming around. Karli explained her role in the scene again. She nodded, ready to do what she was told. She was alert, understanding that these same men would attack her again if she failed to cooperate. She had no intention of anything other than complete cooperation.

They ran the scene again. This time the president clubbed her with his fist and knocked her to the cement driveway. She rolled on her side and vomited before he could press his knee against the side of her head. He stood up and spread his arms. "What?" he said to the physician. "What happened?"

The physician responded, "Too hard. The slightest concussion and she is gone. This time pull your punch, as they say."

Karli said, "What about if you step aside as she lunges and she goes sprawling? Then you can overpower her."

They ran it as Karli suggested and this time it was a perfect take. Christine lunged for the president, who spun away like he had seen American football players spin, and followed up with a knee to the head. This time there was no struggle. His quarry was unusually still, unresisting.

"Stop," the president told the cameraman. 'I think I've killed her."

"Probably," said the physician. "Her head struck the concrete and at the very least concussed her again. She'll likely be unconscious the rest of the day. Maybe longer. I recommend hospitalization."

"Nyet," spat the president. "Prison for this one."

By nightfall she had been charged with trespassing, assault, attempted murder, and violent aggression. She was taken to maximum-security prison Matrosskaya Tishina in Moscow, where it was said she awaited trial.

AN UNIDENTIFIED CALLER brought that night's News at Seven report to Thaddeus' attention.

"Have you seen her?" asked the female voice.

Thaddeus alerted. The voice was familiar. But why?

"Seen what?" he said.

"Watch the ten o'clock news. Your friend has been found. We will call you tomorrow."

The phone clicked off.

Thaddeus and Angelina had moved their belongings back into the original Holiday Inn. They had opted for two bedrooms, and she was in the shower "washing off the day," when the phone had beeped.

Thaddeus immediately dialed the front desk. He asked if they could give him the calling number of his latest incoming call. The desk clerk said they could not. Russian phones do not have that feature, he was told.

He knocked on the bathroom door when the shower stopped.

"You're going to want to see this," he shouted at the door.

"What have we got?"

"Ten o'clock news. Christine has been found."

"OMG!"

30

"It wasn't even like her," Thaddeus said to Nancy Empress. "It was her body but she was heavily medicated. Her face looked swollen. Her nose was clearly broken. What in the hell are you going to do!"

The woman from the CIA slowly shook her head. "We cannot get involved with this, Mr. Murfee."

"They're killing her!"

"She knew the risk going in. She knew she might not be coming home."

"That was a totally different thing. That was the Middle East. She didn't sign up for Russia. She knows nothing about Russia. She's never been here before. She doesn't know the language and knows nothing about surviving here. They're going to kill her. Now what are you going to do to help her?"

This time the woman's back stiffened. She gave him a hard, cold look. "We can offer nothing. Everyone in Russia believes that phony video is real. We can't have the CIA dragged in the mud by making that connection between the Agency and your friend. I cannot allow that."

"Then we're going to come to blows. I won't let this go."

"No, and you shouldn't. You're a smart man. File a lawsuit. You'll think of it. Maybe one of the humanitarian agencies can step in. Sometimes they're very useful in negotiating releases on humanitarian grounds. The Russians sometimes go for that as it makes them look honorable and sincere about human rights. Good PR."

Thaddeus scowled and shook his head. "I don't think we have that long. She's injured. Maybe mortally. The woman they showed wasn't the Christine I know."

Something stirred behind him and Thaddeus turned in his chair.

"This is someone we think you should meet, Mr. Murfee. His name is Jacques Lemoneux. Jacques, meet Thaddeus Murfee."

The man had been summoned into the meeting room.

Present now were Thaddeus, Nancy Empress, and Angelina—whom Thaddeus had insisted on bringing in this time because she was team translator back out in the world. And now Jacques Lemoneux was standing across the table from Thaddeus, his hand extended to shake.

Angelina beat Thaddeus to it, taking the man's hand and shaking violently. "I'm Angelina Sosa, *Chicago Tribune*. I'm doing a story on the kidnapping of Christine Susmann and hijacking of the Swissair flight."

"I was on that flight," said Jacques.

Thaddeus shook hands and everyone took a seat.

"Now," said Nancy Empress. "Mr. Murfee requested this second meeting following the television news story about Christine Susmann."

"And you asked me here why?" asked Jacques.

"The Agency cannot be involved officially. However, given your recent imbroglio with these people, I thought you might be able to offer insights."

"Unreasonable. Mean, hard people who live by the lie. If they can figure out how to use her to hurt the U.S., they will. And they won't give a damn what it does to her."

"How do I get past them to Christine?" Thaddeus asked. He was leaned back in his chair, arms crossed over his chest, looking to all the world like he was ready to go ten rounds.

"I don't know that you can get past them. This is their turf, their jails, their legal processes."

"Do they have anything like *habeas corpus* here?"

Nancy Empress shook her head. "In a prior life I was a lawyer so I know a little about Russian law. There is no *habeas corpus* here, no right to have her brought before the court to decide whether she should be held."

"What about a civil action? Is there any leverage to be gained by filing some kind of civil action against them? I'm aware they don't have civil rights laws like we do, but something else?"

She looked down. "Not that I know of. You might want to go talk to a Moscow lawyer and see what a member of the Russian bar might come up with."

"I like that," said Angelina. "I'll make some calls when we get back to the hotel."

"All right," said Thaddeus. "Now let me get down to the real deal. Tell me about this jail where she's being held."

Nancy responded. "We have confirmed that she's been taken to a maximum-security prison known as Matrosskaya Tishina."

"Located where?"

"Right here. Moscow."

"Has anyone ever escaped there?"

"Not since I've been in Moscow. We know nothing about its layout, security issues, or anything else."

Thaddeus looked exasperated. This was going nowhere fast.

"All right," he said, "I'm going to ask you for the name of a guard inside the prison. Someone who might be willing to work with me."

"That we can do," said Nancy. "I'll call you later today with that. Holiday Inn?"

"Perfect. We'll be back there in an hour or two."

"How can I help?" said Jacques.

"Do you speak Russian?"

"I don't."

"Then let me put you on hold," Thaddeus said. "But I'm sure something will come up."

"Hold that thought," said Nancy. "Jacques is one of us. We can't allow him to work this case with you."

"But I want to help," said Jacques. "I followed Christine. I feel like I owe her. And I owe those bastards big time for myself!"

"Appreciate that," said Thaddeus. "I believe you owe as well."

"That may be, but the answer is still no. He doesn't get involved," said Nancy. She wasn't angry, she wasn't unfriendly. But she was firm and cleared up any remaining doubt.

"I need a gun," Thaddeus then said. "Will you help me?"

"You can help yourself. Russian law allows foreigners to acquire guns on Russian territory. The grace period for foreigners awaiting a license from the Interior Ministry for firearms has been increased from five to ten days."

Thaddeus only stared blankly at her. "That's nice information for the record—I assume we're being recorded in here. But you know and I know that wasn't what I was asking. I wasn't planning on going through channels to obtain a gun."

"What do you need a gun for anyway?"

Thaddeus uncrossed his arms. "Let's just say I'm going to pay a call on a certain GRU agent. I think he might have had something to do with Christine's medical condition."

"Don't tell me any more."

"I'll try to help with that," said Jacques. He stared Nancy down, almost daring her to interfere. But she didn't. Evidently her unofficial feelings favored Christine too.

Nancy called an end to the meeting and thanked them for coming. Jacques walked Thaddeus and Angelina to the elevator. At the elevator door he leaned up to Thaddeus and whispered, "You'll have your gun by tonight. I'll drop by the hotel."

Thaddeus shook his hand and didn't otherwise respond.

There were just too many ears and too many eyes to do any real business there.

He followed Angelina into the elevator, glad to be done with the place.

A plan was coming into focus in his head. He would need the gun, yes. And he would need a certain address as well.

It was time to put on some dark clothes and find out about late-night Moscow.

31

After eight hours of waiting and begging and useless threats, Thaddeus and Angelina finally hit on the correct combination to make the system cough up two ninety-day visas. Money was the answer. What amounted to two thousand USD was the winning ticket number. The bribe was delivered by Thaddeus in a plain envelope stuffed with twenty American hundred dollar bills. Forty-five minutes later they had their visas and were walking out of the official office of the Russian State Administrative Secretary.

"That wasn't so bad," Thaddeus said to Angelina with a smile.

"They didn't even want to see my U.S. passport," she replied. "Jeez."

"I know. Once they had the two grand our bloodlines ran straight down from the Tsars. We were money."

"Hear that. I'm making my notes for the book. Problem is, nobody's gonna believe it."

"Oh, you'd be surprised what people will believe if it's found in a book. Surprising, I have found."

"I hope you're right. I really need this for my career."

"Done, Angelina. Just keep putting words together. We'll help you make that happen."

"My, you *have* changed."

"You've been very helpful yourself. I feel like I owe."

The next morning, Thaddeus retained the services of Moscow attorney Zialina Altedmivic. She would bring a *habeas corpus* case, which was a remedy under Russian law, despite what Nancy Empress had said.

He then made logistical preparations, purchasing four MacBooks and two printers and moving into a long-term apartment at the Execustay hotel ten kilometers north of Moscow, where he had a bedroom and two offices and Angelina had a bedroom.

The huge, windowless office furnishings consisted of a small wobbly table and Wi-Fi. So Thaddeus moved funds from Chicago to Moscow and sent Angelina on a shopping outing.

By early afternoon, the stores were delivering desks, phones, and supplies for the Moscow office of Murfee Hightower and Associates.

Two more computers arrived, networking set up, and a wide area network which joined the computers of Zialina Altedmivic Law Offices with those of Murfee Hightower, Moscow.

A husband-wife team of paralegals was hired. They would work out of their home in Zacharov Estates, north of the city. Their names were Eugeveny and Natalia Medeved. They were middle twentyish, childless, and into any kind of American rock music they could download from iTunes. Things were shaping up.

Early the next morning, Thaddeus, Angelina, Zialina and the Medeveds joined around the conference table to design their assault.

"First," said Thaddeus, "I want Zialina to discuss *habeas corpus* in Russia. As most of you know, *habeas corpus* is Latin for 'produce the body.' It is used in cases where you believe the authorities are holding someone illegally. It is filed in the court and requires the jailer or prosecutor to bring the arrested person in front of the judge so that the judge can review the reasons for imprisonment and decide whether those reasons are legal. The judge can also review conditions of release, in most jurisdictions. Zialina, what's the Russian take on *habeas*?"

She was a wide, rough woman with a farm wife's shoulders and stocky legs and a stony face that seldom smiled. But she had graduated first in her class at Moscow University and had successfully defended more criminal clients on appeal than any lawyer in all of Russia. She came highly recommended and Thaddeus was very grateful she had agreed to join them. "Agreed," as in twenty thousand American dollars later....

She nodded at the small group and brushed a comma of graying hair from her forehead.

"First, some history, because most Americans are surprised to hear what I'm about to tell you. The right to freedom and personal inviolability is guaranteed by the Russian Constitution. Article 22 of the Constitution states that arrest or detention shall be authorized by a judicial ruling. Without a judicial ruling no person may be subjected to detention for a period of more than forty-eight hours. The legal grounds for taking and holding a criminal suspect or an accused individual in detention are defined by the Code of Criminal Procedure, which entered into force on July 1, 2002"

"How many hours has Christine now been held?"

"I did some asking around and my staff reviewed the prison records. At this point she is ninety-six hours into her incarceration. So the case is ripe. We have—she has—standing to challenge the incarceration."

"Ripe, as in the law can be used to question her imprisonment at this time?"

"Exactly. So what we are going to do is put together a brief for the judge. The Medeveds will research it, I will write it and present it, and Thaddeus shall handle the testimonial aspects of the case. Meaning, he will question the witnesses in court."

"That's my call," said Thaddeus. "I had to be involved, not just turn it over to Zialina and walk away."

"Of course," said Angelina. "You would never just walk away." She smiled. "That's chapter two in my book. Thaddeus and what makes him tick."

"Great. Go for it. Zialina, please continue."

"Just a little more procedure, just to make sure we're all on the same page. Christine—meaning her lawyers—is allowed to provide explanations to the judge. After hearings, which last about twenty to thirty minutes, the judge decides whether to authorize the detention, to deny the detention request and release the individual, or to extend the detention for the next seventy-two hours in order to let the investigator build the case for the next detention hearings. The judge's ruling can be appealed to the higher court within three days."

"So this case go on for more than one hearing?" asked Eugeveny.

"That's right. And just because we might succeed in

getting her released doesn't mean they can't start the whole arrest and incarceration process over again."

"So we need something definitive," said Thaddeus. "We need to somehow make the underlying case go away."

Zialina looked at him. "We do. We need evidence that she's not guilty of the reported attempt on the president's life. Remember, they say they caught her inside the compound with a loaded weapon and that she made a move toward assassination. Wait—wait, Thaddeus. I know what you want to say. So let me say it for you. There's video and the video does tend to back up this claim. However—and this is a big however—my guess is that the entire production is a fake, from what Thaddeus tells me about Christine."

"She was on her way to the Middle East," Thaddeus said. He was unable to keep still any longer. "She was on her way to the Middle East at the request of the CIA. Yes, she had taken on a mission for the CIA, but it didn't involve Russia. It was ten thousand miles in a totally different direction. But Russia is using her relationship to the CIA to embarrass the United States and make it look like the mission was to take place in Moscow with the assassination of the president."

"How did she wind up in Moscow?" asked the paralegal wife, Natalia. "I'm sketchy on that."

"Bad luck, pure and simple. She happened to be on a commercial Swissair flight that got hijacked. It was supposed to land in Zurich, where Christine was going to change planes and go on to Turkey. Instead, it came to Moscow. No one saw it coming."

"And why are you here, Mr. Murfee," said Eugeveny.

"I had agreed to travel the first leg of the trip as cover for Christine. I'm her normal employer. She's my lead paralegal in Chicago."

"Okay, thanks."

Thaddeus said, "So, how do I make this go away?"

Everyone looked at Zialina. She raised her eyebrows and shrugged. "We need to talk about that. Off the top, I don't have any ideas."

"Natalia?" said Thaddeus.

"No."

"Eugeveny?"

"Afraid not."

"Angelina?"

"You need to have the Russian president recant his statement. Nothing less than what the Russian president can say will undo what the Russian president has already said. That's intro to journalism 101."

Thaddeus looked at the reporter.

"You know, you might have something, Angelina."

"Seriously, dude. Unless the judge hears it from the man himself it ain't gonna turn heads. This is Russia."

"Probably same would be true for America," Zialina said.

Angelina looked at her, then nodded slowly. "Agree."

"Okay. I can roll with that. So how do we get the president to change his story?"

"He won't change it voluntarily. That would be unthinkable," said Zialina.

"I'm not thinking voluntarily," said Thaddeus. "I'm thinking I force him to change his story."

"And you're going to do that how?"

"I don't know. All right. When can we get this *habeas corpus* on file and when can we have a hearing?"

Zialina fielded it. "I can have it on file before the sun goes down. Tomorrow will be hearing day."

"Then let's do it," said Thaddeus. "Everyone have everything they need?"

All said they did.

After the others were gone, Angelina re-heated pizza in the microwave and waved a piece at Thaddeus. He accepted and they both were chomping down, both in deep thought.

After several minutes, Angelina said, "Where is he vulnerable?"

"Family. Someone he loves."

"You're thinking going after someone?"

"I honestly don't know how else to do it."

"May I suggest we wait until after tomorrow's hearing. Maybe something will come up that gives us some new way of looking at this."

"Agree. We'll wait. But no longer than tomorrow. I can't get Christine's battered face out of my mind. How do we know that's not still going on?"

"Thaddeus, you're powerless over the Russian penal system. If it is going on, there's not a damn thing you can do about it. Except attend tomorrow's hearing and try to get her released on bail."

"Did I tell you I plan on being there?"

"I'm sorry. I sounded preachy."

"Hey, don't be. All ideas are welcome here. I'm just—scared. I love that woman and I can't see bad things happening to her. I already know I won't sleep tonight."

"I heard you up and around last night. Who were you talking to?"

"I called Katy just to check on her and the girls."

"Everything okay there?"

"Outstanding. Katy can handle anything that comes up. Pretty amazing lady."

"You must really love her."

She had said it almost as a question. Thaddeus knew he only wanted to turn it aside.

"Love her, adore her, worship her. She's everything to me."

Angelina looked down. She moved her pizza crust around with a forefinger. "I knew that. I wasn't testing you."

"What? Testing? I didn't think you were."

"No way, dude. You're like ancient."

"I'm thirty-one, thank you. If that's ancient, don't tell my dad."

"Tell me something about yourself. Something I can use in my best seller."

"I was born in Phoenix, Arizona."

"And? Go on."

32

F ROM: Thaddeus Murfee: A New York Times Bestseller

Marvelous Marvin of Madison Street
by Angelina Sosa

What good has ever come of abandonment? Abandonment can only happen where there is needful attachment. Attachment by itself isn't enough. It must be needful, the attachment, to cause the emotional difficulty associated with abandonment.

Thaddeus needed his mother. He needed his father. But he was abandoned to the system, the State of Arizona.

In place of the secure feelings that make most children sleep soundly, Thaddeus was filled with an anxious longing, a hope that soon his mother and father would be restored to him. But when it didn't happen the first year, and didn't happen the second year, he finally gave up and moved on.

That part of a child that knows the safety net of a parent ready to catch them when they fall was denied him.

Which made him more self-reliant than most. Self-reliant, because Thaddeus learned early on that he and he alone was there for Thaddeus. There was no one else to catch him. There was no one else looking out for him.

Sure, there was a custody arrangement with the state, but that wasn't the same thing as having a parent looking over protectively. And Thaddeus came to know this when he found himself in minor scrapes as a very young boy and had no adult to turn to. Custody and loving care were two totally different animals. The one could be judicially ordered; the other could only be given.

So he grew up faster than most, and one day just walked away from the school and the place where he had lived the last eight years. Just walked off, no good-byes, no requests for permission, no forwarding address or discussion of future plans, just gone.

Everything he owned was reduced to a back pack. Every penny he had saved from various odd jobs around the neighborhood was stuffed inside his shoe: $402.01.

At the 7-Eleven a block away he bought a bottle of water. It was May in Phoenix and the thermometer would top out that day at 104°. Hydration was key, in the desert. He drank off half the bottle then slipped it into his backpack.

At Central Avenue and Madison he took a seat on the bus bench. The bench advertised the services of a chiropractor who had eight locations in the Valley. Eight. He knew he didn't want to be a chiropractor. Something about touching other people that was a turnoff. There hadn't been physical closeness in his life and he unconsciously avoided it now. Which ruled out all the helping medical sciences.

Besides, there was something else that played around the edges of the mind where it projected the future. He had been to court no less than five times during his dependency. Usually modifications to custody terms. Once a change in homes. Whenever he had appeared in court with some court appointed attorney, he was always impressed with how much power a court could have over someone's life. He hadn't decided if that was a good thing or not. But he had decided that he wanted power over that power. In short, he wanted the state out of his life.

So when he was very young he decided he would be a judge. Or, at the very least, a lawyer.

The police stopped as he sat on the bus bench and asked some questions and got some straight answers. They returned him to the home.

Then he met Marvelous Marvin of Madison Street, the first hip, slick, and cool lawyer he'd ever witnessed up close. They were introduced in juvenile court.

MMM was a lawyer on the court's short leash and was doing probationary work in the juvenile courts as a predicate to having his law license restored after an ethics violation cost him his license for six months. It wasn't that big an offense, something about failing to file a divorce he'd been paid to file. Then turning off his phone and not responding to repeated inquiries by the client.

The State Bar had eventually served him with papers and Marvelous Marvin of Madison Street watched as his license grew wings and flew out the window for six months. But now he was working his way back in to the Bar's good graces.

One of his cases was as guardian ad litem for thirteen-year-old Thaddeus Murfee. The question had come up whether extended summer vacation with Thaddeus' mother was going to be granted on her petition. MMM had resisted her motion, arguing she hadn't yet proven to the court that she was able to maintain sobriety and provide the boy with a stable home environment. It had been a difficult hearing, one that left Thaddeus in tears when he saw his mother's disappointment over the disallowance of her motion to modify summer visitation.

Afterwards, MMM took Thaddeus to dinner at the Stockyards and bought him a steak and talked to him. Talked to him like a real person, which was the first time Thaddeus had ever known such intimacy with an adult. Marvelous Marvin listened to Thaddeus for over an hour and even cried with him at one point, after which he paid the bill and took the boy home.

Marvelous Marvin then applied to be Thaddeus' Big Brother. Big Brothers and Sisters immediately agreed, so MMM filed a petition in court to serve as Big Brother. The court appointed a DCFS worker to do a background; MMM was found to be a fit and proper person to serve as Big Brother, and the petition was proved.

Thaddeus officially had a new family member. A big brother.

A big brother who took him to ASU football games. And Phoenix Suns basketball games. Who took him to the Grand Canyon and helped him through two days of downhill skiing instruction on the San Francisco Peaks. Who bought him a guitar and enrolled him in lessons.

Soon Thaddeus was making his own music and with other kids in his group home formed a band. The Motherless Child, they called their group, and Thaddeus sang lead on some songs while Jeremy Lanier sang lead on others. Behind the scenes Marvelous Marvin Madison helped the band improve, helped with additional instruments and music lessons, and occasionally lined- up a birthday or Bar Mitzvah where the band could entertain.

Marvelous Marvin picked Thaddeus up most Saturdays at nine a.m. Marvin had petitioned for and been awarded weekend visitation with Thaddeus. They would go to Marvin's home in the Arizona Biltmore Estates off Twenty-fourth Street, where Thaddeus had his own room.

When Thaddeus was fifteen-and-a-half he was given driving lessons in school and Marvin allowed him to drive his Jaguar with Marvin riding shotgun. Then Marvin picked up a used Chevy pickup, stick, and taught him stick shift so his license wouldn't be restricted.

But most of all, Marvin spent time with his younger brother. They spent time watching TV, reading books, and talking about the Anasazi tribe of Arizona and visiting their cave dwellings in Northern Arizona.

When Thaddeus admitted he had his eye on a girl at the group home, Marvin made arrangements to drive the two of them to a movie *and pick them up after. The next weekend there was a dinner at Marvin's and Marvin had a date, Jennifer Rowley, and Thaddeus was given permission to bring Andrea Rodriguez, his first girlfriend. They gobbled down Marvin's spaghetti, drank diet colas and coffee, and played Monopoly before lapsing into a Netflix binge on Parenthoood.*

"So Thaddeus," said Marvin, one Saturday morning when Thaddeus was in his junior year of high school, "what do you want to do with yourself when you graduate?"

"Join the Army."

"No, come on. For real."

"I want to join the Army. Lots of the kids in my foster family go in the Army."

"You can shoot higher than the Army. What about college?"

"If I do the Army first, I get the GI bill. Then I can afford college after."

"What would you say if I told you I've set up a college fund for you myself? Would that help your decision?"

"What do you mean?"

"It's nothing great. Just that I settled this PI case a couple years ago and put a hundred and fifty grand into an irrevocable trust for you. You know how the stock market's been. Your fund is over three hundred grand now. You can go to college just about anyplace you want."

"Oh hell no, really? You did that for me?"

"Oh hell yes. You're my kid brother. I've got to make some arrangements for my bro."

"This is too much. I don't know."

"Yeah, you know. I've taught you how to receive gifts from the world. Just stand up and say 'thank you' like you deserved it. Come on, now."

"Well, thank you."

"So if you could choose any college and study anything you want, what are you thinking?"

"I don't know. What do you think I'd be good at?"

"Well, you're a likable kid—don't let it go to your head. I think—and I'm just dancing around this right now—I think juries would like you. I'm thinking law school."

"Like you? Be a lawyer?"

"Let me tell you something. Remember I told you my parents got divorced when I was eight and my dad left and my mom couldn't afford to keep me? Sent me to her sister's in Bisbee? Remember that?"

"I remember."

"Here's one thing I learned and I'm going to tell it to you. Because I think you're a cool dude and you need some ancient Anasazi wisdom."

"I'm listening."

"When a guy—or a gal—doesn't have parents, then you have to become your own parent. You have to meet your own needs. Start with financial needs. You have to get educated in something that will always provide for you. That's why I did law. Law became the parent with the bucks my own parents never had. It was always there for me. Bought me my first car, my first condo, rented me my first office—all the rest. That's how come I can afford to live in the Biltmore. Not because of what was given to me. But because of what I took. I reached out and took from the world. You need to do the same."

"Just take? I need to take?"

"Nobody is going to make a gift of anything to you, Thaddeus. That's because you got no parents. So you take what you need, leave the rest alone."

"Okay. I'll take then."

"So what about law school?"

"I wasn't that hot on the Army, tell the truth. I don't want to shoot anyone."

"There's nothing wrong with shooting bad guys. You just need to get that parent in place first. Tell you what. You go to college and law

school and if you still want to join the Army after, I'll drive you down to sign up myself. Deal?"

"Deal."

"So what about college?"

"You went to Arizona. You've done damn well."

"So you're thinking University of Arizona?"

"I mean, why not?"

"Deal. Let's get a catalog."

"I'll go online and order one."

"Deal."

Marvelous Marvin stuck out his hand. They shook.

One year later, Thaddeus arrived in Tucson, his pickup bulging with dorm room supplies, a keyboard synth and two guitars, including a Les Paul and a D-28 Martin.

All thanks to Marvelous Marvin of Madison Street.

Thaddeus went to college and MMM went on to his next project: a little kid who had lost his dad in a railroad accident and his mother to cancer.

"My name is Marvin," he told the little kid after the dependency hearing.

"I'm Ronnie."

"Ronnie, have you ever thought about having a Big Brother?"

33

K aty's Step 2 was a no-brainer. And it was connected closely to Step 3.

She read from the paperback she had picked up at Barnes and Noble:

The biggest secret to getting pregnant faster is knowing when you ovulate (release an egg from your ovary). Think of the egg as a bull's-eye and the sperm as arrows. One of the arrows has to hit the bull's-eye in order for you to get pregnant.

Since you ovulate once each menstrual cycle, there are only a few days out of each cycle when sex can actually lead to pregnancy. Knowing when you ovulate means that you and your partner can identify the bull's-eye and then aim for it, instead of just shooting a bunch of arrows and hoping the target happens to be there.

You can figure out when you ovulate using a few different methods. Our article about predicting ovulation walks you through them.

If you notice that you have irregular periods over the course of several months, pinpointing ovulation could be difficult. Ask your doctor for advice.

She sat back and considered what she'd just read. *Really?* She thought. *Bulls-eye and arrows? Who did they write this stuff for?*

Thaddeus hadn't called after the Embassy like he said he would, and the truth was she was missing his arrows. His quiver full of arrows, she thought with a smile. She loved her guy and she wanted him with her right then. Ovulating or not, she wanted to give it a try.

Why hadn't he called?

So, she called him. Speed-dial 1.

He answered on the third beep.

"Hey, Katy, sorry I didn't call when I said I would. It's been nuts here."

"Where are you and what are you doing? And who are you doing it with?"

"We're staying in an Execustay long-term hotel."

"You and the girl?"

"Yes, me and Angelina."

Katy held the phone away and frowned. Angelina. Now what?

"What do you call her, 'Angie?'"

He was sitting in the office area of his suite, and next to him sat Angelina, who was translating the Russian rules of civil procedure from a computer screen. He shifted uncomfortably, and realized he was feeling busted.

"I call her Angelina. That's her name. We're working on getting Christine brought into court. Hoping the judge will release her on bail."

"What's the official charge?"

"You won't believe it. They made up this dog and pony show about Christine attacking the Russian president. It's so ludicrous it's laughable. But they're serious. That's what has me so damn worried. They're totally serious."

"Why are they picking on Christine?"

He knew it was safe to tell her the Russian viewpoint, even though he had no doubt they were eavesdropping on everything he said. Their viewpoint was safe to recite.

"They're picking on her because they say she's a CIA plant, sent her on a fake hijack to kill the Russian president."

"My hell, how clever do they think Americans are? We couldn't pull that off if we tried."

"Thanks for your view of the CIA. I'm sure our Russian friends will be impressed."

"Russian friends?'"

"The ones listening in on this call. You can be sure of that."

"Well tell them I said to get over themselves. Christine is a paralegal and nothing more. If she was working for the CIA I would have known it. AND SHE'S NOT!"

Thaddeus pulled the phone away from his ear. He hoped Katy's scream had blown out Igor's hearing. Igor or Vladimir or Piotor or whoever was listening in on the call.

"Thanks for that. I'm sure your vouch for Christine will set her free."

"I just want my husband home. This is getting ridiculous. Turquoise said she saw something about a plot on the Russian president's life on CNN. She just told me. I don't watch CNN so I wouldn't know."

Thaddeus could hear Turquoise say in the background, "I wasn't watching. I was flipping through the channels and I thought I heard Christine's name. It was her they were talking about and my jaw hit the floor. So I watched."

"Did you hear that?" Katy asked.

"I did. Well, the Russian strategy is working then, if CNN is talking it up."

"Stupid."

"It is. Anyway, it's late here and I'm about to jump in bed and get some sleep. Big day tomorrow."

"Where does Miss Wonderful sleep?"

"She...has her own bedroom."

Thaddeus couldn't help it: he looked over at Angelina as he said it. She rolled her eyes and took a drink of a Russian Coke.

"But she's not under the same roof as you?"

"Yes, no. It's a suite. I have my room, she has hers. And we have an office too."

"My hell. You're shacking up."

"Please. Are you having a hormone thing?"

He'd no sooner said it than he knew it was the last thing he should have said.

"Hold it," he hurried, "you have to know that was a poor attempt at humor."

"Damn poor. And you're lucky you said that. I was just about to slam the phone down."

"Bad joke. I'm exhausted and the brain is on overload. Forgive me, please."

"You're forgiven. Just promise me you'll lock your doors at night."

"Of course. Wouldn't want Vladimir coming barging in."

"Or Angelina. Oh forget I said that. I'm sure she's a good person. Isn't she?"

"The best. Well, so long for now."

"I love you. I miss you."

"I love you and miss you too. Good night."

"It's morning here, but we're cool. Good night."

Katy hung up the phone.

She tried to ignore the mental image her brain was

forcing on her. The image of Thaddeus reaching over and taking some young woman's hand and looking into her eyes. She shook her head violently and told her brain to shut up.

Hormonal? She had to smile. She was enough of a physician to know he hadn't seen hormonal yet. Not like he would if she had to go *In Vitro* on him.

Now *that* would be hormonal.

34

I n Piotor Irunyaev's Russia, the judicial system was perceived as a means to curb the influence of figures that posed a threat to the Kremlin. In 2005, Yukos Oil CEO Mikhail Podeskayev was imprisoned on trumped-up charges of fraud in one of Russia's most controversial cases. In 2009 Sergei Amanovich, a lawyer who accused police officials of stealing $230 million from the government in a tax fraud scheme, died in prison after being held for a year without charge. And in April of last year, Russian prosecutors suspended a political group—unfriendly to the Kremlin —for three months, barring the Left Front from organizing or accessing their bank account until July 19. By that time they were out of business and bankrupt and the two leaders were imprisoned for failure to make good on group debts.

Two days after meeting with the *habeas* team, Thaddeus had learned the lay of the judicial landscape by making connections and asking questions inside the Russian legal community with those attorneys known to be less than friendly toward Irunyaev's Kremlin. It quickly came into focus for him, then, exactly what difficulties Christine faced in her upcoming *habeas* hearing.

The judge was Herbayevic Szeolben, a hard-nosed Communist who hailed from Leningrad and had made a name for himself doing the bidding of the Kremlin in disposition of political and religious cases. Where the Russian president was particularly upset with certain defendants, they would invariably find themselves placed on the docket of the Honorable Herbayevic Szeolben—a fast track to hell. The majority of those Szeolben sentenced wound up in the wilds of Siberia, spending daylight hours marking and cutting trees and breaking rocks for the Russian building industry. Nights were spent huddled around wood stoves, underfed and mind-numbingly deprived of all contact with the outside world. Letters neither came nor went, legal appeals and attorney visits were impossible two thousand miles from Moscow, and even family eventually moved on, knowing the Siberian prison camps were actually black holes where gravity prevented all escape.

Habeas team leader, attorney Zialina Altedmivic, was waiting for Thaddeus just inside the main doors of the courthouse in Moscow. Today she was dressed respectably if not fashionably, wearing a long woolen dress that brushed the tops of her black boots, a white vest that just did stretch across her broad, rough shoulders, and a distant smile that told Thaddeus she was already off in her own element, an element he recognized as what a lion must feel when she is going out to hunt meat to feed the pride. To some extent, he felt it himself. He wore his hastily-purchased and pressed ill-fitting suit of gray with heavy brogan shoes and a 1970's-wide tie that featured a fleur-de-lis in yellow against a field of black—a nod to some displaced French heraldry, he imagined.

All told, he was satisfied with his selection of Zialina. She had graduated first in her class at Moscow University, where she had served as editor of the Russian equivalent of the American law journal.

She extended her hand and they shook clumsily, knowing they were likely being filmed and watched on the security screens hidden behind high marble walls in the courthouse. Truth be told, Thaddeus hadn't *not* felt like he was being watched since de-planing in Russia and this morning was no different.

"Good, you have brought along a briefcase. This particular judge appreciates leather briefcases. Don't be surprised if he compliments you on it before ordering our client to return to lockup."

"Seriously, what are our chances here?"

She grimaced and led him to the security checkpoint before answering.

"Our chances? Nil. I told you that when we met. How do you Americans say it—the deck is a hard one?"

"The deck is stacked?"

"That's it. The deck is definitely stacked. Russian president, his second cousin sitting on the bench—"

"Wait, you're serious? The judge and Irunayev are actually related?"

"Oh, indeed. Judge Szeolben is the president's second cousin, mother's side."

The group ahead was waved on through security and Thaddeus set his briefcase down on the conveyor belt. It rolled through the X-ray and then he passed through the scanner himself. It buzzed and he was motioned back.

The security officer said something in Russian.

"It's your wedding ring. The scanners detect all metal.

Set your ring in the white tray and walk back through. Try again.

Thaddeus did as instructed. This time he made it to the other side, where he retrieved his briefcase and wedding ring from the conveyor belt. Zialina produced an ID card and was waved through without inspection. The two lawyers rounded a corner and came to a bank of elevators. They rode up to the twenty-second floor. The doors whooshed open and they stepped into a marble hallway, dimly lit with flickering neon bulbs. Down the hall were two doors on either side, both massive and both unmarked.

"Take the one on the right," Zialina said, and Thaddeus turned the doorknob.

The courtroom looked remarkably like American court rooms and Thaddeus immediately felt at home. This setting, he understood. Here was where he was accustomed to transacting the business of incarceration and conditions of release.

He found himself praying for a fair shot at release, which was all he asked. But, unlike American courts where one could have hopes, here, he knew, there was no reason to be hopeful.

With that thought, a sense of depression and isolation settled over him. He knew the isolation came from a feeling that justice wasn't present in the room, that he was shut off from justice even though he had come to the room of justice. He knew, without a word being said, that justice wasn't part of the day's pantomime.

A chill rippled up his spine and he admitted that the hearing was hopeless—that, and it hadn't even yet convened.

He felt a panic for Christine and tried to fight it down,

to maintain control of his emotions. Now more than ever she needed him cool and calm.

There were minor court officials working at the computer screens and setting up reporting tripods, none of whom acknowledged Zialina and Thaddeus.

With a stir and a rustle of chains, the second rear door opened and a hunched, chained, prisoner shuffled into the room. The prisoner was waist-chained and ankle-chained. Thaddeus looked closer. It appeared to be Christine's last known haircut, but the face wasn't at all familiar.

She was admitted to the prisoner dock along the right side of the courtroom. In Russian criminal proceedings, unlike American, the prisoners never are admitted into the courtroom where they are free to stand directly in front of the judge. Instead, they remain in the dock and interrogations for procedural matters are directed and received through vertical steel bars.

She sat on the low bench and hung her head. Thaddeus hurried to the bars and she looked up.

"Christine? Is that you?"

Two dark eyes passed over his face. There was no sign of recognition. The eyes again dropped to the floor.

"Christine!"

Again the head came up. Again the eyes sized him up. But there was no sign of recognition.

"Christine, it's Thaddeus! Are you all right?"

She looked and stared this time. Her face was swollen on both sides and her nose was mashed and spread on her face. One eye was almost swollen closed and the other appeared to fight for focus. She pressed her hands to the side of her face and he saw she was missing the wedding ring, engagement ring, and gold watch Sonny had given her on their last anniversary. Her knuckles were scabbed. Two fingers were splinted and Thaddeus knew they had been broken. She shook her head and he thought he saw tears forming.

"Thaddeus? Is that you?"

"Oh my God, Christine, what have they done?"

"Thaddeus? Are you here or am I dreaming again?"

"No, no, I'm right here. We're in court. We're fighting for your release."

"They said I killed the president."

"No, you didn't kill anyone. It's all a lie."

"Is that you, Thaddeus Murfee? I think it's you."

Whereupon the door to the judge's chambers, hidden in the wall without a visible seam, opened and a thick-chested, stumpy figure in a beige business suit mounted the judge's bench. He had a fringe of red hair around his bald scalp, a wide red mustache, and short fat fingers that twiddled and fiddled without surcease. It was as if he were knitting without yarn or needle. *Air-knitting*, thought Thaddeus, bringing himself back into the moment and turning away from Christine. Thaddeus proceeded to the left hand counsel table and took a seat next to Zialina. Her file was open and she was reading a pleading presented, of course, in Russian, so Thaddeus only knew what it said from earlier discussions.

The judge rapped a wooden mallet against the bench and called the court to order.

"You may proceed, Ms. Altedmivic. It's your motion for release."

There was no fanfare, no calling of the case, no case numbers spoken into the record—none of the usual precursors known so well in U.S. courts. Just, "proceed," and they were off and running.

Zialina climbed heavily to her feet.

"May it please the court and the Honorable People's Congress. Today we are seeking a cash bond for the prisoner Christine Susmann. As the court knows, the prisoner has been charged with various violations, including a charge stemming from an alleged attack upon the president. The issue of whether the attack happened or not isn't before the court today."

"It isn't?" said the judge.

"No, it isn't. What is before the court, according to the Habeas Statute, is whether the defendant should be held in jail without bail or whether bail should be allowed. In this case, it's the defendant's position that bail should be allowed."

"Absurd!" said the judge. "Why would I set bail for a defendant accused of making an attempt on the president's life? Especially a defendant not a citizen of Russia? Why?"

"Because justice requires it. And because common human decency requires it. Look at her, Your Honor, she has been beaten! Look at the swollen eyes, the broken nose!"

Avoiding even one look at Christine, the judge replied, "The defendant is accused of attempting to assassinate the President of Russia. Of course there would be injuries resulting from the intervention of the president's security personnel. Thank all goodness they were there and reacted quickly to stop her!"

"But she needs medical treatment. There are no medical facilities in prison. None. Her nose will knit and heal improperly. From here it looks as if her hands are injured. And a CT scan should be done of her head, as she has obviously been badly beaten. The court cannot, by law, ignore the prisoner's medical needs."

"I can order a doctor to look at her."

"She needs treatment, Judge, not a look."

"She's breathing and I am told she walked in here on her own. I am going to find as a matter of law there's no indication of ongoing need for medical attention. It is so noted in the record."

"What's he saying?" Thaddeus whispered to Zialina. "Give me a quick English translation."

"No. He's saying 'no.'"

"Is there a translator? Can I speak to him?"

"No. There's no translator."

"Why isn't there a translator?"

"My motion for a translator was denied."

Zialina returned her attention to the judge.

"Your Honor, you're making a finding of medical status without an inquiry into the facts. You're finding as a matter of law there's no need for medical care. You can't do that without taking testimony from the witness, the jailers—"

"Young lady, this is my court. We do what I say we do inside these four walls."

"But you're not following the law!"

"Then appeal my order! Bail is denied. We stand in recess."

With that—a quick crossover to the hidden door—he was gone.

Christine pushed up to her feet. She turned to her right to the opening cell door.

"Wait!" said Thaddeus. "We're not done talking."

The two jailers said something to Zialina and continued removing the prisoner from the courtroom.

"What? What did they say?"

"They said court is over. They're taking her back."

"To jail."

"To jail."

Thaddeus fumed. "I cannot believe what just happened! We didn't even get medical care for her?"

"No, we did not."

"Zialina, she didn't know me! A woman who's worked with me almost ten years didn't know me after four days in jail. What the hell! What can we do? Can we get a quick appeal?"

"Appeals take years in Russian courts. It could be five years before we found out anything."

"Five years? Are you kidding me? Okay. What else can we try?"

"Mr. Murfee, there is nothing else. *Habeas* is always a long shot in Russia. I told you that, going in. It ended like I tried to warn you it would end."

"There has to be someone else. Is there anyone we can call at the prison and beg for help?"

"There's not even a number."

"I feel like I'm in a time-warp."

"Well, welcome to Russia. You can't say you weren't warned."

35

After being put in the notoriously overcrowded Matrosskaya Tishina prison in northern Moscow following court, Christine was then moved to the prison's "Special Isolation Unit No. 4."

Since Christine's arrest, media interest in her living conditions, down to the minutiae of her daily routine and diet, her toilet facilities and bathing schedule, had been intense. Angelina was filing daily reports with the *Chicago Tribune's* Moscow office, and the articles were being picked up by AP and run nationwide in the U.S.

Based on the confidential statements Angelina procured from Justice Ministry officials and prison reform advocates, plus a varied roundup of the day's press reports, a day in the prison life of Christine Susmann was likely to resemble a day in Alexander Solzhenitsyn's *The Gulag Archipelago*, which is to say her incarceration was less than humane.

Christine's day began at 6 a.m. in a 5-meter-by-3 meter cell along with her three cellmates, according to Justice Ministry spokesman Boris Kalyagin.

The cell was equipped with two bunk beds.

A prison breakfast of fish soup, tea and bread was distributed, according to Kalyagin. Christine was then allowed a meeting with either of her lawyers or the physician Thaddeus had hired to assess her. At this point she still had difficulty recognizing faces and often struggled to remember who Thaddeus was. After a twenty-minute session she was returned to the cell, where she negotiated with her cellmates for a place to sit down and sometimes even to stretch out. Cigarettes were the currency of Matrosskaya Tishina prison, so Thaddeus made sure she was amply supplied so she could trade tobacco for favors.

Christine was served lunch from 1 p.m. to 1:20 p.m. and dinner from 6 p.m. to 6:30 p.m., *Izvestia* newspaper reported Tuesday, a schedule that Kalyagin confirmed.

Kalyagin said lunch consisted of meat-and-rice soup, a vegetable medley with rice, bread and compote, while dinner consisted of buttered kasha, or Russian porridge, tea and bread.

Christine was allowed to take daily walks in a closed-off courtyard for up to an hour a day. Thaddeus had it from inside sources he paid off that Christine struggled to make it even one time around the courtyard and that she often just ventured outside and stretched out on the grass and remained still and silent for her hour.

Overall, the Russian press did everything it could to make Christine's incarceration sound hospitable and humane, but Thaddeus disagreed violently.

The truth was, he proclaimed loudly to the press—as in all things Russian—a wholly different matter.

The physician who saw her twice a week at Thaddeus' request reported she needed CT workups, an MRI, and

other studies to try to assess the extent of her injuries—
none of which she was getting.

Thaddeus felt totally frustrated, alarmed, and often
went to bed only to toss and turn all night as he couldn't
stop worrying about her.

Something had to change.

He set about doing just that.

36

F

ROM: *Thaddeus Murfee: A New York Times Bestseller*

Bar-M Cattle Company
by Angelina Sosa

    Thaddeus was twenty-one, a senior at the University of Arizona. Three nights a week he tended bar at the Bar-M Cattle Company, a steakhouse out on Ina Road. One Saturday night, just before nine o'clock, voices were raised and two men began trading insults.

    They just didn't like each other. In fact, they hated each other. Hated each other's looks, heritage, speech, mannerisms, hairstyles and attitudes. The Navajo guy—he liked the Arizona Cardinals. The Russian guy—he liked the New York Giants. The Navajo guy—he wore his inky hair tousled with mousse. And he proudly wore the camo green of the National Guard weekend warrior. The Russian guy— oiled black hair and alabaster skin, he wore the shiny sharkskin of a Russian Mafioso. The Navajo refinished antiques in a small shop outside Flagstaff, the Russian had an oil company—heating oil—and ran a laundromat/beer hall called Duds&Suds. The one was married and true to his wife, a good father who took the kids to ball games on Saturdays and church on Sundays. The other was thrice divorced, abusive to his drug-peddling sons, and spent Sundays in hangover ICU.

It was a small lounge off the dining room where their paths crossed —a nothing joint in a mid-rent commercial strip, located in a building that had once housed Teamsters Local #4402 before they lost their lease. The Bar-M Cattle Company, Inc. was the official name on the legal documents, and it was owned by the same two-fisted-drinking lot as owned the Allstate Insurance Agency three strip malls north on Ina. This would be two brothers and two sisters engaged in a perpetual feud over the fair-and-square split of the net profits. These were the Nesbitt clan—Henry, Howard, Helga, and Hermione. The four of them drank and danced with the customers then pulled the shades and served freebies after hours, while Thaddeus tended bar, remained sober, and watered whiskey bottles per instructions.

But back to the two men sitting at the bar. The Navajo Guardsman's name was Billy Strawberry. The Russian Mafioso's name was Tony Folachnaya. Billy had arrived at the bar shortly after 5:15 PM; it was now 7:25. Tony had come off duty at Duds&Suds at 6:10 PM and arrived at The Bar M fifteen minutes later, at 6:25. Billy had put in his eight that day at a local armory, where he had filled out an inch of paperwork on ancient ordnance inventoried for the ten-thousandth time since Operation Iraqi Freedom. His rank was sergeant and his duty was Supply. He was drinking margaritas with three other guardsmen, two guys and a gal. The gal had won three arm-wrestling contests that night. Her handle was Mav, and like Billy Strawberry she too was a supply sergeant. Like the other three guardsmen she was dressed in bloused camo fatigues and shiny boots.

Tony Folachnaya had taken one nip of his neat Stoli when he witnessed Mav whipsaw arm-wrestler number three. He wished to buy her a drink. He also wished to bed her. The cordiality was a first step in that direction. When the bartender placed the fresh margarita before

Mav and announced it courtesy of the man three stools down, who should suddenly take offense but Billy Strawberry. "Keep your lousy drink," Billy muttered, and jerked it from Mav's hand. It was sent skidding back down the bar toward Tony Folachnaya, where it bit the lip of the bar and spilled into his lap. Billy, it seemed, had the same designs on Mav and the surge in competition among the lounge's habitués just pissed him off no end.

The hatred was mutual, intense, and spilled out of the men.

"Screw you," Tony muttered, and picked ice out of his lap. He flung the crystals at Billy, but they sailed right past and landed on Mav. She brushed them from her camo and ignored the disagreement.

Tony glared into the mirror and found Billy's twisted face. "It's for the lady," he said into the mirror. "What's it to you, anyway?"

"You just insulted the uniform of our country, grease ball."

"How's that?"

"Nobody here likes grease balls."

"Say what?"

"We don't like guineas. Wops. I-talians. This is the west, friend. I-talians find us very unfriendly."

"That's okay because I'm Russian."

"Russian mafia, I'm guessing."

"Well look at you," said Tony, again into the mirror. "If it ain't Running Elk all into his big self."

Billy stood up from his barstool and folded his arms. "One more word, mister," he snarled.

Tony shoved up from his seat and walked out.

Everyone left behind was amazed, most of all Billy, who was suddenly the new man what am, the top gun, king of the hill, badass mofo of the Bar M. Witnesses bought him drinks, clapped him on the back, and called him Sarge. He thanked everyone and headed for the restroom. "Time to drain the snake," he told Mav, and swatted her on the ass when she leaned over the bar to dump her ashtray. "Be right back, don't go away, pretty lady."

The cops would find it remarkable that when the Bar M crowd heard the "pop-pop-pop!" of the nickel pistol they might stampede away from the threat and huddle in the furthest corner. But no, that's not what actually happened. When the pistol barked, everyone went silent. But, three seconds later, the Bar M crowd rose as a wave and poured out the door into the valet parking slots. They went running to examine the ruckus. There hadn't been a barroom shooting in Tucson since 1997 following the Bob Dylan concert. They certainly weren't about to miss this one.

They didn't have far to go. Twenty paces south of the Bud sign over the Bar M's door they surrounded Billy Strawberry, who lay sprawled on his back, his right arm folded impossibly beneath his body, his eyes glazing over, a tiny red three-tap draining serious blood from his shredded aorta while his heart flopped about, sensing the morbid drop in blood pressure. The shooter, Tony Folachnaya cast a long shadow over Billy's failing body. The silver Colt dangled from his hand, muzzle still pointed at Billy. Jocelyn Conway would later swear she saw smoke wisp from the barrel. She would recite all this to Winston Warren of the Arizona State Police. Winston was a newly striped sergeant and this was his first 10-16 (homicide). "It was thick," she would say of the smoke. "You could smell it inside the bar, like firecrackers."

"I wouldn't say that," said Gloria, Jocelyn's drinking companion. "I couldn't smell it from the bar."

"I thought you said you were coming down with a nasty cold."

"Maybe that's it."

"See?" Jocelyn said to Trooper Winston. "I did smell it inside."

It took five minutes to Code 3 to the scene, but Trooper Winston hit the ground running outside the Bar M. He galloped to the valet stand. Trooper Winston asked the crowd to move back. He jumped down beside Billy. He tilted his head to listen for breath sounds. He heard none; rather, there was a falsetto gurgle. So he began CPR. "One-two-three—"he counted.

"He's dead," someone offered. "Call the widow."

"You'd best stay off the crime scene," said Jocelyn to the cop. "You already moved Billy's beer bottle."

Trooper Winston ignored the comments and continued giving CPR. He remarked to himself how thankful he was for his training and how he hoped to God it paid off now. While he compressed and released, compressed and released, he tried to shut out the chatter.

Jocelyn turned to Gloria. "See at the end of the movie, where Bambi's mother gets shot and dies, I cried." She pointed at Billy Strawberry's body. "Dead is dead. Deer or human being."

"I cried too."

"I always cry there. Then in the next scene Bambi's all grown up and he has a huge set of horns and he's looking down from a mountaintop."

"This badder than bad," muttered Trooper Warren.

It was Jocelyn's turn to ignore him. She'd had four Pink Ladies and was feeling no pain. She extended her arm. "Talk to the palm, officer."

"We got a dead guy here."

"So quit thumping on his chest."

Jocelyn turned from the cop back to Gloria. "See, at the end is when Bambi has made it. He's a full grown adult male and he's OK in the world."

"Except he doesn't have his mother."

"Bingo! No one ever taught me that I could be tough when I was all grown up, sure, but that I would still miss my mother."

"How old were you?"

"When she died? Eleven."

"That's young."

"I cried myself to sleep for a year. But I never let my dad know that."

"You couldn't."

Jocelyn leaned up against the hallway wall. "Woot! I've gotta slow down if I'm driving home. I love me some pink ladies."

"You said you didn't let your dad know you were bawling every night."

"Exactly. 'Cause there was nothing he could have done about it. Basically I was screwed and knew it."

"Which is what the Bambi movie doesn't get."

"It's what Disney doesn't get. So it's not 'til I'm an adult that I realize: I'm gonna miss her the rest of my natural days. It sucks but there it is."

"Like Billy Strawberry." She called across the crowd, "Is he dead?"

A male voice shouted back, "Well, he hasn't asked my wife to dance for nearly a hour now."

Jocelyn craned to see through the bystanders. "He's not moved since we got out here. My guess is yes."

"Dead?"

"Yep."

"Why don't they cover him up."

"Probably waiting on the detectives to do their thing. Don't you watch CSI?"

"Who has time?"

Jocelyn feigned a two-gun quick draw, and said, "All right you mothers, stay the hell outta my crime scene."

"I need another drink."

"Me too. It'll be hours before they get this mess cleaned up. Let's go back."

They retreated to the bar where they found their stools and ordered fresh drinks. "Bartender," said Gloria, "the whiskey pours like glue in here!"

"All right you mothers, stay the hell outta my crime scene!" shouted Jocelyn to everyone and no one.

By now Trooper Winston Warren had given up on the CPR. He stood up, wiped his bloody hands on his pants, and saw Tony Folach-

naya still standing there, patiently waiting. The murder weapon was still dangling from his shooting hand.

"Easy," said the trooper. "Let me have it, please."

Tony extended the gun and Winston gently took it away. He looked around and saw no place to put it. So he dropped it in his pant's pocket. Without a word he put Tony Folachnaya in cuffs. He steered the suspect over to the corner. He clicked on his cell's recorder and stuck it in Tony's face. Tony was calm and "looked peaceful," said those around him.

"So Tony, did you shoot Billy Strawberry?"

Tony nodded.

"Speak into the recorder, please."

"I shot Billy."

"Why did you shoot him?"

"He was going to throw me in front of oncoming cars. It was self-defense."

"One shot might have been self-defense, Tony, but you fired three times. How's that self-defense, number two and number three?"

"I wanna lawyer."

Trooper Warren pulled his Miranda card from his shirt pocket. "You have the right to remain silent..." he began reciting. His voice was a drone against the buzz of excited conversations ringing the decedent. Finally he finished, "...can and will be used against you in a court of law. Do you understand these rights?"

"Yes."

"And do you waive your rights?"

"I wanna see a lawyer. The cuffs are too tight."

Trooper Warren turned Tony around. His handling of the prisoner was rough. He checked the space between the handcuffs. "Feel loose enough to me."

"No the cuff part is cutting off my circulation."

"Mister Folachnaya, you cut off Billy Strawberry's circulation big time tonight and now you want someone to worry about your wrists?"

As he said this, Trooper Warren was glad the shooter was in cuffs. It was unlike him to talk smart to an arrestee and he didn't know why he did it now. Except everyone was watching. More or less.

"It was self-defense."

"Two and three weren't. That was an execution, you ask me."

"It happened so fast—"

A voice came up behind Trooper Warren. "Officer, when will you be removing the body from my parking lot? I'm Mr. Nesbitt, the manager. We need this mess cleaned up. Our guests are afraid."

"You want I should put the body in my squad car? Sit it up and belt it in?"

"I'm only thinking about the guests I'm responsible for."

"Do something with him, Winston," *said a gruff male voice from the crowd.* "Give Billy the dignity of a towel over his face."

"He's not allowed to move anything around," *a very intoxicated woman said.* "Ssshhush."

"No, you shush."

"No, you shush!" *she giggled.*

Trooper Warren was exasperated. He wasn't used to working homicide scenes. He said to no one in particular, "Do you see an ambulance out front? Do you see any EMTs checking for heart sounds? No, you don't. That's because the first responders are running Code Three to get here and take over the scene. You'll all have to wait."

Mr. Nesbitt shook his head and wrung his hands. "What do I tell my guests? Do they have to wait in the restaurant?"

"I don't want them mingling with the witnesses. Tell 'em to stay put. I have witness statements to take."

"And how long will that be?"

"Mr. Nussbaum—"

"Nesbitt." *He indicated the nameplate on his suit jacket.*

"Mr. Nesbitt, let's just pretend this part of the club isn't yours anymore. Pretend that I'm in charge now. In fact, don't let's pretend. I am in charge!"

"I'm not challenging you, sir. I'm only after information."

"Here's your information: one of your guests murdered another guest tonight after they were drinking in your restaurant lounge."

"It was self-defense!" Tony Folachnaya shot back.

"Why in God's name in my parking lot, sir?" Mr. Nesbitt asked the prisoner.

"He was charging at me. He was going to push me into traffic."

Overhearing this, Darnell Sykes, a thirtyish man wearing Army camo sidled over. His fatigues were bloused into his boots. The boots were desert tan. He pursed his lips and said, "He was chargin' him, officer," pointing at Billy then at Tony. " I seen the whole thing." Sykes was built like an ape and wore GI issue eyeglasses with a sports band. He crowded up to the cop and cocked his head. "The whole thing."

Trooper Winston fished his cell out of his breast pocket. He pressed RECORD. "State your name, sir."

"Corporal Darnell Sykes, United States Army. I'm over to Fort McDowell. I saw the dead guy charge your prisoner. Tell the truth, I woulda shot him too, if I was as slight a man as your prisoner."

"But he shot three times," Trooper Winston argued.

"First shot didn't drop the guy," says Sykes. "He kept comin' on like a raghead in Jihad week."

"See what I mean?" said Mr. Nesbitt the manager. "Corporal Sykes, I'm sorry you had to see this."

"Hell this ain't nothin'. Seen worse than this in Iraq every day. This is tame stuff y'all got goin' here." Corporal Sykes pulled a swig off a Bud he pulled from his fatigues pocket. "Ahh," he belched at the officer.

Trooper Warren turned away. "Listen up!" He commanded the crowd. They were mostly broken up in twos and threes then, chewing over God knows what. Some of them looked at the cop but most ignored him. He said in his police academy command voice, "Anyone who claims to know anything about this incident please come up to me one at a time and give me your name and phone number."

In response most of them turned back away and resumed their conversations. Except for Darnell Sykes. "Corporal Darnell Sykes. You want my cell or my old lady's number?"

"Here," said Trooper Warren. "Write it down on the back of this sheet. Use my pen."

Word traveled fast in the Bar M. When it reached Jocelyn and Gloria, Jocelyn announced she was going out and give her name to the cop. "I damn near saw the whole thing," she told Gloria. "You should come too."

"But I didn't see anything," Gloria shook a Marlboro from a hard pack. "We were in here."

"You saw as much as I did. We were almost the first ones out there."

"I did hear them arguing at the end of the bar. Before they went outside."

"Same here. Billy Strawberry was calling the little guy a fucking Italian."

"And the little guy was calling Billy Strawberry a gap-toothed Ape-a-zon."

Both giggled. "Stupid."

"Uh-uh. Men."

"Let's get our story straight."

"Let's."

"We're going outside to go home and we see—"

"We see the little guy flip off Billy Strawberry. Then he pulls a silver pistol."

"It was premeditation."

"And Billy laughs him off."

"Exactly."

"So the little guy starts walking directly toward Billy."

"Aiming the gun."

"Aiming the gun."

"When BLAM! It suddenly goes off."

"How many times, how many shots did we hear?"

"God, it must have been seven—six at least."

"He emptied it on Billy."

"Poor Billy. I went home with him once."

"You didn't! Tell me you didn't!"

"I did. Not bad. Nice enough guy. He bought me breakfast out at Zonell's."

"But he's married!"

"Not like you think. She sleeps in back with the door locked. He sleeps on the couch."

"Sick."

"They can't afford to get divorced. That's what he told me. So I went along."

Gloria shook her head. *"So Whosit shot Billy in cold blood."*

"Pretty much that must be what happened."

"Pretty much."

"Let's go tell the cop."

"Let's. We can get paid time off to go to court and testify."

"But Joce, we didn't actually see all this."

"But we heard it. That's damn close. Even a fool can fill in the missing parts."

"There's the point of it."

"There's the point. C'mon."

THE EMTS ARRIVED and made the pronouncement. They stood aside when the detectives arrived.

"All right, Trooper," said the detective in blue jeans and red windbreaker, *"you can stand down. We've got the scene."*

"Here's your prisoner."

"Did you get witnesses?"

"Names and addresses, right on the back of this fire exit strategy. I pulled it off the wall."

"How about you, sir," said the female detective to Tony Folach-naya. "Are those cuffs OK?"

"Too tight. I already told Andy of Mayberry."

"Whoa, hoss," warned Trooper Warren. "No need to get smart here."

"You're in no place to get smart, sir."

"Bull's-eyes!" Said the examining detective, who by now had unbuttoned Billy's white shirt.

"What do you have, Kent?"

"Look at this pattern. A three-tap, all in the heart."

"Some shooting."

"Where'd you learn to shoot like that, sir? That's pretty damn good."

The detectives were both up close and eyeing the bullet holes. They nodded and continued to make remarks about the terrific shooting.

"You gonna call next-of-kin?" Trooper Warren interrupted.

"Your arrest. You call," said Kent in the blue jeans.

"I'd rather not."

"Excuse me," said Jocelyn, who touched the female detective's elbow. "What's your name?"

"Miranda. Not to be confused with your Miranda rights."

"We saw the whole thing, Miranda. Me and Gloria."

"We saw the little guy almost run at Billy Strawberry," said Gloria. "He was holding the gun like this," she indicated a two hand grip. "Like the cops on TV."

"Did Billy have a weapon?" Miranda asked.

"Just his big dumb look."

"No weapon," said Trooper Warren. "I've already been over that."

"He was going to push me into traffic. Backwards," Tony Folach-naya muttered. "I didn't approach him at all."

"You didn't?" said Jocelyn. "That's not how we saw it."

"That's just it—you didn't see it. There was no one out here but

the soldier," said Tony. "And he was loaded down with his duffel and didn't stop."

"Right, ma'am, I had my duff on my shoulder. I wasn't about to get between those two."

"What did you see?"

"I saw the little guy gettin' charged by the big guy. He was runnin' right at him. Full on head of steam."

"Then what happened."

"Well...the little guy holds up the pistol sideways, like to show the big guy, but the big guy just sort of like laughs and keeps a-comin'."

"That's not what we saw at all," said Jocelyn.

"No ma'am," said Corporal Sykes. "Because you wasn't out here."

"Says you, Soldier Boy." To Trooper Warren she continued, "Truth was, Soldier Boy had his duffel bag hiked up on his shoulder. It blocked his view of me and Gloria. And I would have to say it also blocked his view of the shootout."

"You're saying it wasn't possible he was an eyewitness?" asked the trooper.

"Only with X-ray eyes. He don't look like no Superman to me. But he is cute."

"Sorry ma'am, but that's bullshit, all due respect. My duffel was in my hand."

"No, it was on your shoulder," said Tony Folachnaya, "but on your outside shoulder, the wall side. You could have seen everything."

"That's—"

"Now how the hell would you know," said Gloria, the less drunk of the two women. "You were aiming your gun, not looking around for eyewitnesses. You couldn't have seen Army."

Trooper Warren raised his hand for quiet. "Detective Ramos, here are your three eyewitnesses. Please statementize them now."

"When we're ready, Winston. If you hadn't tracked through our crime scene—"

Trooper Warren let out a long sigh. To the detectives he almost pleaded, "If you two have it under control, I'm taking my break. I've been on-scene nearly two hours and need a piss break."

"Got it Winston. Go drain the snake," said Detective Miranda. She tossed her head as she said this, just one of the guys.

The case made the Tucson Times newspaper every day for two weeks. In the end, the Russian was found not guilty. Thaddeus had testified how Billy Strawberry was the one who had started it all. It also turned out Thaddeus had gone on break just before the shooting and was standing five feet from the valet stand when the gun went off.

He saw the whole thing. And he was the only witness who hadn't been drinking. The valet would have seen it too, but he was running to retrieve a '59 Chevy for some AARP members.

Thaddeus' testimony set Tony Folachnaya free. Tony came up to him after the trial and told him if he ever needed anything just to call.

Thaddeus said he was sure he'd never need anything.

He just didn't know, at the time, that one day he would need a Russian. A Russian with strong ties to Russia. A Russian with access to certain government documents in Moscow.

A Russian Mafioso in a Russia ruled over by thugs.

37

J acques Lemoneux hadn't returned to the U.S. and his work at the French Embassy following the skyjacking. From Moscow he called his manager in New York and told her he was being delayed by Russian authorities following the skyjacking. She wanted the French Embassy to officially intervene, but he assured her he would be released much faster on an informal basis than if they escalated it to an international incident. In the end, she relied on Jacques' judgment and he promised he would be back in the states "within days." While she was an official at the French Embassy, she didn't know he was a CIA plant there. The French knew nothing about his dual role. So he was vague and ambiguous, telling her she could expect him "soon."

Whatever that meant.

Meantime, he had found an unused office in the CIA/Moscow. And he set to searching for the GRU operatives who had held him and poisoned him, particularly one who was called "Karli" by his fellows.

He was paging through snaps of GRU operatives when one stopped him cold. Karli Guryshenko. He considered his quarry: crewcut gray hair, long face featuring a boxer's flattened nose, and very tired gray eyes. There was a set of Russian alphabet characters below the picture, which Jacques could more or less make out. Truth be told, he spoke better Russian than he read.

Jacques studied the headshot. He wanted the man dead. There was no room inside his brain for any other form of resolution. Not after being poisoned. The man had sent him to his death—which had failed—and now Jacques wanted to repay the favor. But there was a problem with that approach: Jacques wasn't authorized to act in Russia. If he did, he would be considered rogue and the CIA would cut him down. Literally, they would terminate him.

So he considered other forms of revenge. Who else, he asked himself, would like to see harm come to Karli Guryshenko? He considered what he knew: the American woman Christine Susmann, working under deep CIA cover, had been taken captive, badly beaten—he could tell from frame-by-frame examination of the Russian video floated on Russian TV—and was now being held in a Russian prison, probably under less-than-humane conditions.

The answer was simple. Thaddeus Murfee, her customary employer, had the most interest in her of anyone, save, perhaps, her own husband. But Sonny Susmann was in Chicago and a civilian, which left only Murfee.

CIA Sheremetyevo had eyes on Murfee. CIA Sheremetyevo had picked up him the night he and the reporter and Christine had checked into the Holiday Inn. That would have been the night of the skyjacking.

Jacques caught a cab and headed for the Holiday Inn.

38

The guards agreed with Karli: the key to the practice was to elevate the prisoner's feet and legs above the torso and head so the immersion felt real. Then the Karminskaova rosebud towel would be laid across her face and water poured into her mouth and nose.

So they brought her into the windowless room with the dentist's chair in its center and strapped her in. Her forearms were lashed to the chair arms and her legs encircled from with a belt of Russian cowhide that was then cinched up as if a bull were about to be ridden. The electro-pneumatic chair adjusters were activated and her feet swung high above her head while her head and torso were lowered to Karli's knee level. Which made application of the towel and the water from the hose that much simpler.

Matrosskaya Tishina prison in northern Moscow had four such rooms; political prisoners were ever-abundant during President Irunyaev's reign and would be while he held office. Dissidence in the Russia of 2015 was dangerous and only the very brave or the very foolhardy dared tread there.

Captured foreign agents were an altogether different matter. They were brought to one of these four rooms, tortured for several days, admissions obtained, and then returned to the Russian prison system, usually Siberia, while their confessions were playing on CNN and *Isvestia*—wholly embarrassing to the agents' home countries and damaging to presidential careers. Which was the final aim of the Ama Gloq/Christine Susmann attack on the Russian president— the de-unification in the United States of the president from his base. De-unification meant destabilization and destabilization meant the implementation of Russian economic and military stratagems around the world.

They started in with the water. First, the towel placement: across eyes, nose, and mouth. Then the small hose with great velocity shot water into her nose and mouth. She began choking and shaking, violently jerking her head back and forth but unable to escape the flowing water.

"W-w-w—" she cried. "Wait!"

The water choked off the rest of it.

Her entire body spasmed as she lost consciousness. Then she was limp and the introduction of water into her airway was discontinued. Hands reached to administer CPR, her airway was clear, oxygen was force-fed to her lungs. Ever so slowly her eyes blinked open.

Karli leaned into her view.

He smiled.

"We would ask again. Will you give your full cooperation in front of our cameras?"

"Go to hell!"

Karli shrugged and motioned to the guards.

The water again flowed into nostrils and mouth. Immediately the towel was dripping wet and the prisoner was coughing and violently turning away. Again, the spasm and loss of consciousness. This time they were slow to revive her.

Karli watched the digits on his watch. At thirty-five seconds he motioned to his assistants. Again the airway was suctioned and oxygen administered. Again she slowly opened her eyes.

"Had enough? Will you give us your statement?" he asked.

Her eyes were glassy and refused to focus. She looked into a white disk and recognized its voice. Him again— Karl? Karli?

"Go. To. Hell."

Once again, he nodded. Once again the process repeated.

She opened her eyes minutes later. Water was trickling out her mouth and nose. She inhaled sharply and took in a rush of half-water-half-oxygen. She choked; coughing, a small lump of stomach contents ran out her mouth and down the side of her face. No one moved to wipe it away.

"Disgusting," spat Karli, and turned away.

"Help me," she said.

"Will you cooperate with the cameras?"

"Go to hell."

Karli sighed. He told the guards to repeat the process over the next two hours and then to place her in the box.

Two hours later, the three guards wedged her inside the box, which was a steel contraption the size of a coffin in which the prisoner could almost sit upright, but not quite. There was no light and no sound. She was soaking wet and struggling to breathe. She turned her head to the side and tried to sit upright, but the design just did prevent a full sitting position once again. She struggled to make it work but could not. So she laid back, head horizontal, which required that she pull her knees up to her chest.

They left her like that.

She cried, she prayed, she wet herself. Then there came the feeling of the box being moved on its wheels. She could just hear the electronic buzz as prison doors opened.

Thirty minutes later she was cold. Then shaking from the cold as her body heat evaporated.

They had moved her outside, into the prison yard.

And left her there.

She forced the faces of her children into her mind. She watched as she kissed them goodbye. Then she did the same with Sonny, her husband. She adored and admired that man, for he was a great father and a capable provider for his family. At the last minute she hugged him then turned away from the embrace of her family. She couldn't let them see her like this.

Nothing.

39

Tony Folachnaya kept a small, messy office at Duds&Suds, the combination laundromat/beer hall he had purchased for his two worthless sons. Their names were Viktor and Usurayev and they were gargantuan Cossacks who'd refused to play high school football, much to their father's disappointment, because, as they put it, they didn't want to "mess up their looks." They refused to attend college and refused to get jobs, so Duds&Suds had seemed the next best thing, to Tony Folachnaya. It gave them a place to work and earn their keep. Lamentably, they ignored the laundromat's open time of six a.m. and, rather than showing up ready to conduct business, they stayed in bed until ten. Which forced Tony to show up and open the business. Opening at six was never a futile exercise: the Pima Indian Tribe seemed to have selected the laundromat as its official laundry. There was always a line of two or three or four Indians waiting at the door, sometimes even as many as five. "One thing you gotta give those Indians," said Tony to his worthless sons, "they sure as hell wear clean clothes. It'd be nice if you two would help them spend their dollars with us."

Which fell on deaf ears.

So it was customary for Tony to unlock at six and be inside his small office five minutes later. Which he had done, the day Thaddeus called him.

Thaddeus had obtained Tony's number from the operator, calling all the way from Moscow.

"Hello?" said Tony.

"Tony Folachnaya," said Thaddeus, "this is Thaddeus Murfee. Remember me from your trial?"

"Of course. I'd be serving twenty years if not for you. Or worse."

"You told me to call if I ever needed anything from you."

"I remember that. How can I be of service?"

"My paralegal has been tossed in jail in Moscow. I need to get messages to her. And I need to make things all right for her. I also need a computer file from GRU computers. Do you still have contacts there?"

"I can't say over the phone. These lines are tapped. Can you fax me?"

"I can."

Tony supplied his fax number and Thaddeus created a message for him. The fax was received thirty minutes later.

Tony briefly read it over and then left for Wal-Mart. He made his way back to the electronics section and found help there. With the help of a clerk in a blue vest with gold lettering, Tony selected his phone. Except it wasn't registered in his name with ATT; it was registered in the sales clerk's name, using the sales clerk's credit card. Ten $100 bills made that happen. International calling was added for five dollars a month.

Tony left Wal-Mart with his new phone, which would remain in service for one month. After that it would be thrown away and the account canceled. If he needed more than thirty days, he would need to make arrangements with the kid again. For another thousand dollars. Tony was elated; it was a great deal.

Anything for the guy who kept him out of prison.

40

S he needed him with her.

Where was he? And what was he doing with that young girl who had attached herself to him? He had called last night to tell her they were still working on setting Christine free, but that things were looking dim for her. It was too bad; Katy had only the highest respect for Christine and actually loved her like a sister. But it had been good to hear Thaddeus' voice, even though she knew Angelina was close by, probably listening to every word.

And the new baby? Ovulation was probably three days away. So the time was perfect for Thaddeus to be home and trying with her. She had tried explaining all this to him when they talked last night.

"I think we're in the seventy-two hour period for ovulation. Couldn't you at least come home for a few days and work on Christine's case from here? I really would like that."

There had been a long silence, then:

"I can't leave her, Katy. I won't leave Russia without her. I owe it to her to do everything in my power to get her released. She's my best friend, outside of you and it would kill me to leave her here alone."

"What about the CIA or the Embassy? Can't they help?"

"The Embassy is very little help. I have met with other authorities and they deny any knowledge of her or why she was aboard that Swissair flight. Beyond that, I can't say much more because this phone is tapped."

Katy was frustrated, although she knew Thaddeus and she knew how much Christine meant to him. Still, it was hard not to act like the hurt little girlfriend even as the jealousy picked at her mind about the reporter who was with him every hour of the day. She wouldn't put it past the girl to try everything she could to get Thaddeus to wander in his marriage. Wouldn't put it past her at all.

"Well, my egg is coming and it only lives in the tubes for one day. Even if you just came for one day, the sperm can last much longer than that. They could go in now and wait for the egg. Is that asking too much, for you to come home, do your thing, and go back? That's not leaving her, is it?"

"It would be leaving her. We're getting ready to take the case back to court so I expect to have some good news in the next week or two. Please give me that much time."

"We need to hit the sheets, Thad. That's all I'm saying."

"Good grief. Where did you learn to talk like that? Hit the sheets? Really?"

She had laughed. "I know. It's something we said in med school. We thought ourselves very liberal back then."

"Oh, it sounds very liberal even today."

"If you do surprise me with a visit in the next day or two, please ejaculate first. Otherwise there's a buildup of dead sperm and that can't get me pregnant.

"Oh my God! I've got to get off here!"

"Please don't joke. I'm being serious."

"All right. Ejaculate it is."

"But not with you-know-who. Sorry, I shouldn't have said that."

"I've got to go. We can talk in the next day or two. Goodbye."

"I said I was sorry, please don't hang up mad."

"Katy, I love you and only you. I'm true to you because I want to be. You have no worries from me."

"I guess I knew that. I know I did. Well, thank you for saying that."

"Okay. Goodbye for now."

"Bye."

41

The text from Tony was short and to the point: "Karli Guryshenko. GRU. Torturing our girl."

An address followed in a second text.

"You ready to snoop?" Thaddeus asked Angelina.

"Ready as I'll ever be."

"We'll take the rental car and locate the address. You will leave me there and drive straight back to the hotel. Any problems with that?"

"You're going to make me miss out on the biggest story I'll ever land?"

"You'll get the exclusive. After we're out of Russia with Christine in tow. We cool?"

Angelina nodded. "We're cool. I can do that. Although I think I should stay in the area, in case you need me."

"Why would I need you?"

"Wheels?"

"Cabs. Moscow has more cabs per capita than any city in the world. Guess again."

"Translation? In case you need me to talk to someone for you?"

He slowly nodded. "That could happen. But I doubt it. No, you come back here to the hotel. Get ready now, it's freezing outside."

"No, it's thirty degrees below freezing. According to the news."

They stepped into the parking lot. Thaddeus was wearing black jeans, black turtleneck, and black watch cap. A heavy black goose-down coat, with hood and gloves completed his protection against the cold and against eyes.

Angelina got behind the wheel of the Lada rental. The car was like a million others in Moscow that night, made by Elvolka Motors of St. Petersburg. Light blue, no interior lights, halogen headlights that jiggled and threatened to go out as they entered the freeway traffic and gained speed. No radio, a half-hearted heater, and lap belts but no shoulder harness—standard Russian fare.

The city lay ten kilometers south of the hotel. In the distance it was a flare, a solar explosion, fireflies coming and going in the air traffic lanes above Moscow. Freeway traffic was heavy, but traffic was always heavy. Muscovites were always on the move, long, endless lines of them, an army of small, boxy cars, each with a mind of its own, moving, always moving, seemingly in retreat from the unfriendliest president and police in Eurasia. Huge B-Train double-trailer rigs blasted by in the fast lane, the entire rig coasting along at eighty-five feet, tip to tail. The huge trailers trundled along, spouting foreign letters and words along their sides and rear, letters that could have signified anything as far as Thaddeus knew.

A Volvo NH15 BP tanker road train blasted by, rocking the aerodynamically-challenged Lada in its jet stream.

Thaddeus realized for the ten thousandth time that he was a stranger in a strange land and if it weren't for Angelina's language ability he would be hopelessly lost. He revisited his decision to send her packing after she dropped him off in Karli's neighborhood. What if needed to take a cab? Would he even be able to tell the cabbie his hotel address? Even that was formidable to him. Maybe having her nearby was a good thing after all. He considered how the GPS guided the way—but in Russian. He was lost without her, he hated to admit. But it was true.

Guryshenko's neighborhood was cramped, trash-strewn, and reachable only by negotiating a labyrinth of dark, black streets after leaving the freeway. Thaddeus had warned Angelina not to slow down at the address, but to drive right by, which she did. Thaddeus turned his head to watch the apartment building pass from the side window to the rear window. The building was aglow with friendly incandescent lights in all but two upper windows, he noted, but reminded himself that, friendly or not, behind at least one of those windows lurked a deadly GRU agent who would gladly squash him. He shuddered and told her to go around the block but to stop at the far end as she came around. She wheeled the tiny car through three left turns, edged up to the stop sign, and pulled over.

"Here?" she said.

"Perfect. Turn the lights off and keep your foot off the brake."

She did as she was told.

"So, what's the plan?"

"The plan is, I want this guy. But for tonight, I'm getting the lay of the land. Then we'll talk to Tony about turning him, using him."

"Is he home right now?"

"I expect so. I'm just going to check out the building. I've reassessed and think you'd be okay waiting here. Just lock the doors and leave the lights off. Don't move the car. I should be back in ten minutes, max."

"That's good. I'll be fine here. Unless you think I should come with?"

"I don't think you should come with. Hold down the fort."

He opened the door and for a brief moment was caught in the yellow glare of the dome light. Stepping into the street he quickly closed the passenger door without slamming it. Then he paused and got his bearings. Up the sidewalk, back down the sidewalk, in front, behind: no one out and about. Great.

He slipped up to the corner and turned left. The building's entrance was a hundred feet down the walk. He said a silent prayer that a keypad or a card slot wouldn't control it.

Up to the door, where he pulled. Surprisingly, it came open and in a flash he was inside and headed for the bank of elevators. There was no watchman at the front desk as he passed by and he didn't come across any residents or visitors. So far, so good.

He hit the UP arrow and waited. Back inside the walls he could hear the elevator kick into life and begin rumbling down to meet him. As he waited, hair on the back of his neck stood up as he shivered and checked behind three times to make sure no one was coming or had seen him. He didn't like waiting at the elevator—too exposed.

The doors whooshed open and inside he scampered. Karli's unit number was 1504. Thaddeus pressed the button beside the 15 and the car began sliding upward as its brakes released and its cables turned.

On seven a young couple lurched into the car, slightly

out of control from the alcohol they had ingested. They looked him over and laughed together. Something about him had drawn their attention. He was clueless what prompted their mirth.

At nine the car stopped and the doors opened and the couple exited. He heard a murmur of laughter as the doors closed. Then he was alone again, headed for the fifteenth.

At fifteen, the doors parted and directly in front of him was 1504. Karli Guryshenko was somewhere behind that door and he held the key to Christine. Thaddeus pressed his ear against the door. The strains of ABBA singing "Dancing Queen" reached his ear. He pulled away. ABBA? The GRU listens to ABBA? For a moment his mind was disjointed as he tried to comprehend the unthinkable, that a murderous Russian secret agent would find such innocent music somehow attractive. He stepped to the side of the door and leaned his back against the wall. He closed his eyes. Now what?

He considered Christine, imagined her face in pain, and wished he had a gun with him. Should he leave and arm himself and then return? What would that solve? Well, at least he could blast away at the guy who had personally assaulted Thaddeus' best friend. How sweet it would be to knock on the door and shoot the bastard in the face. His mind worked through that scenario but it came down to the inescapable conclusion that killing this guy wasn't going to free Christine. No, he would have to be smarter than that.

Then it occurred to him.

He swung around and rapped his knuckles on the door. Time to talk.

Suddenly the music shut off and the doorknob turned. He knew he was being studied through the eyehole in the door. So he smiled. A huge, friendly smile.

It opened and he stepped half inside.

"Do you understand English?" asked Thaddeus, certain that a Russian agent in this day and age would be required to know at least some English.

"Who are you?" the powerful man growled. "You're American?"

"I'm American, yes. Can I come in and talk to you?"

"We can talk right here. What is it?"

"You're hurting a friend of mine. A woman named Ama Gloq."

"Christine Susmann you're talking about? What of her?"

"I don't want her hurt. It's that simple. And if you keep hurting her, I'm going to hunt you down."

The huge man smiled. "Hunt me down for what? So that I can squash you under my foot?"

"Hunt you down and shoot you. It might not help Christine, but it will help me. Maybe that's all I can do. But do it, I will."

"Let me tell you something, American. I know you. And I know your hotel. Should I call on you there? You and that girl you're living with?"

Thaddeus was taken aback, even startled. They had been watching him. But hadn't he known they would be? Why be surprised. Of course they would be watching him. This was Russia, after all. Everyone watched everyone.

"Anytime, brother. You can come snooping anytime. I don't give a rat's ass where you are when I pull the trigger. Here, there, anywhere. Just try me. Now let's agree, just us boys, that you're going to see to it that no one hurts Christine again."

"You agree. I don't agree to anything, American."

At which point, Thaddeus folded his fingers into a flesh gun and pulled the trigger in the man's face.

"Do you understand that? Do you?"

"Try me," grunted the bullish Russian. "I come for you. You have been warned. You have twenty-four hours to leave my country. Or I come for you."

He slammed the door and Thaddeus suddenly found himself nose-to-wood. He considered hammering the door again in his fury, but decided against it. He calmed himself, forcing himself to take slow, deep breaths. He stepped back, then stepped to the side, where he couldn't be seen. He leaned down and placed his hands on his knees and slowed his heart, slowed his breathing. He closed his eyes. Never had he felt so helpless. They had her and they weren't going to stop until they had killed her. Or worse.

Which was when he decided.

He was going to take her from them.

He didn't know how, he didn't know when, but he was going to die trying. That was it: he was willing to die trying. To leave it all on the table.

He turned away and jabbed the DOWN arrow of the elevator. The clunky system roared to life and within several seconds the doors swung open. It had been waiting there for him, as elevators do.

Inside and falling to the lobby, he leaned against the wall. He shut his eyes and tried to see Christine's face. Almost unbelievably, he couldn't picture her.

He had forgotten what she looked like.

42

L ater that night, Thaddeus was just climbing into
bed when the door buzzed jolted him from his
reverie about Christine. He went to the peephole.
A familiar face stared back at him. The man was wearing a
heavy winter hat pulled low to his eyes. Where had he seen
this person?

The security chain was latched, so he opened the door
and looked through the crack.

"Can I help you?"

The man lifted a wallet, opened it, and flashed a badge.

"Jacques Lemoneux. CIA. I need to talk to you, Mr.
Murfee."

"Hold the ID card up where I can get a good look."

The man obliged him. Thaddeus studied the ID, studied
the man's face, and decided What the hell?

He slid the chain free and stepped back.

"Have a seat," said Thaddeus, indicating the round
dining table. But the man remained at the door, waiting.

Thaddeus shrugged. "What does the CIA want with

me? I thought you people weren't going to involve yourselves with our friend."

"This room is bugged. Can we step outside?"

"How do you know this room is bugged?"

"You're in Russia on a visitors' visa. All visitors' rooms are surveilled. You're no different."

"Lead on," said Thaddeus, removing his winter coat from the door hook.

They stepped outside into the parking lot. Jacques led him to the rear property line, and turned to him.

"I have information for you. Here."

He handed Thaddeus a single sheet of paper, folded once.

"What is this?"

"Names you need. Christine's guards."

"How can I use these? They aren't going to set her free, no matter how much I offer."

"I don't know. I don't know your thinking. But I couldn't leave you twisting in the wind. Officially I'm not here. I would lose my position or worse if my employer knew I was even talking to you. You have the list. That's all I can do for you. Good night."

"Your name is Jacques Lemoneux. Real name?"

As he was walking away, the man turned.

"Honest-to-God name."

"How can I reach you if I need?"

"You can't." He moved a step closer. "I'm sorry."

"Talk to me, please. What would you do if you were in my shoes?"

"Really? Probably I'd do the wrong thing. Shoot someone, shoot the wrong person. Get my friend killed. I'm the wrong one to ask."

"I want to shoot someone."

"Don't. You need to arrange for Christine to leave the prison and snatch her away from them. Some pretense to get her away from there. You're a smart man, I'm sure you'll think of something."

"Are you saying—"

"You are going to receive a delivery. It will contain a passport with a false name. It will have Christine's picture inside. You'll know what to do with it. You're a smart man."

There; he had said it again: "You're a smart man."

What was that supposed to mean?

"What do you mean, I'm a smart man."

Jacques pushed the heavy winter hat back on his head. He rubbed his forehead.

"If I were you, I'd make a federal case out of it."

"Meaning?"

"Take her back to court. Another *habeas* petition."

"That judge is owned by the president of Russia. That gets me nowhere."

"True. But it does get Christine somewhere. Somewhere outside the prison."

"Well."

"Yes."

The man spun on his heel and walked briskly to a Volga parked several doors away. He climbed inside but the dome light didn't come on. With a long stream of exhaust pouring from the back end, the car accelerated and sped away toward the highway.

Thaddeus watched it go. He watched the taillights flare at the highway. It sped south, toward the city. Then he returned to his room.

He opened his MacBook and brought up a fresh Word document.

It was time to make a federal case out of it.

He typed until two o'clock in the morning. Then it was time to call Tony Folachnaya, the laundry man. It was true: back in the USA, Tony was a laundryman. But here, in Moscow, he was a powerful crime figure. And he owed Thaddeus.

It was a matter of honor, the debt.

And Tony, it turned out, was willing for Thaddeus to cash it in.

43

O leg Valadnikov was a wiry Russian from the Urals, trained as a guard while serving in the Russian army, with a deep-rooted hatred of anything American, a society he considered purely hedonistic and spiritually dead. He was short, with massive hands and feet, and more Asian than Europid in the face. He'd had his eye on Christine in Special Isolation Unit No. 4 for two weeks. She was known to be American, she was known to have resisted 150 attempts to water board a confession from her, and she was one of those prisoners whose eyes flashed with an intense hatred anytime a guard came near. Including when Valadnikov served her soup and bread through the slot in her isolation cell.

Valadnikov was one of the four-man detail tasked with moving the prisoner outside into the courtyard twice a day while she was locked in the isolation unit's cage. She remained outside for three to six hours each time, and each time they brought her back inside she was shivering so badly that she would buck and roll off the slab bunk where they placed her. Valadnikov was amused by her agony and thought she, the hated American, deserved no less for the attempt she had made on the Russian president's life. Were it up to him she would have been summarily dispatched and buried in the pauper's cemetery behind the prison.

On the day following Jacques' visit to Thaddeus, Karli let it be known among the guards that a known member of the American CIA had visited Christine's lawyer. Eyes had been in place, as usual, as the visit was observed with both close range and long range cameras and listening gear. When the duo had left the Execustay suite and gone outside to talk, the monitors had been unable to hear what was said, even though listening devices had been installed throughout the grounds and parking areas. Karli instructed the guards to maintain utmost care and utmost readiness for anything unusual, as he knew from Thaddeus' threats that the battle for her soul had really just begun.

Following the usual morning ritual, she was water boarded before lunch by Valadnikov, questioned by Karli, and water boarded again when she refused to give a statement implicating the CIA in a plot to assassinate the Russian president. Following that she was fed potato gruel through the slot in her cell, then hosed down with ice water, forced inside the isolation unit, and rolled outside into the courtyard. During all of this she was stripped naked and was totally nude when wheeled outside.

She was semi-conscious and suffering hypothermia when Valadnikov left his post at four-thirty that afternoon and crept into the courtyard. He removed the bolt from the hasp and opened the small cargo container into which they had stuffed her. He grabbed her by the ankles and roughly pulled her from the box and stood her on her feet. She promptly collapsed to the frozen ground, striking her head on the ice, and rolling onto her side, eyes closed, completely unconscious. Valadnikov moved around her and grasped her arm and began dragging her to the side of the building, where there was a slight overhang and several 2000 gallon drums where the building's heating oil was stored. He dragged her between two drums and arranged her on her back. Then he spread her legs and assaulted her.

When he was done, he left her there between the barrels, until he and two others came for her at six o'clock. She was non-responsive and wasn't breathing. They carried her inside and ran through the halls with her to the infirmary, where they roughly deposited her on the linoleum floor in front of the desk of the admitting clerk. Emergency help was summoned and examinations performed. She was found to have a pulse rate of twenty, unknown if breathing, and unresponsive mental status. Her skin was blue, and her rectal temperature was five degrees below normal. In a word, she had frozen to death.

Or just about.

Dr. Nedrava Bella evaluated the prisoner carefully before using anti-shock trousers. She had to be certain that inflation of the trousers did not expose the heart to a sudden rush of cold, acidotic, venous blood from the legs. She knew how sudden temperature and/or pH changes in the heart were causing cardiac arrest in severely hypothermic patients. Gentle handling was critical and the physician barked orders at her staff to use the greatest care. She knew that stimulating peripheral circulation would reduce the blood volume in the woman's core, so she took every precaution when moving her.

Two hours later the prisoner's heart rate had increased, the rectal temperature was approaching normal, but her blood gases were far from normal.

Further examination then revealed the woman had been sexually assaulted. At which point the physician set off looking for the prison administrator to register her complaints.

Prison administration officials knew a confession was required. So they ordered the prisoner held in the infirmary. If they allowed her to die—if they allowed the torture to continue—she wouldn't survive. Which would enrage the Russian president, who would be deprived of his confession. Heads would roll and re-assignments of key personnel made. None of the upper echelon was anxious to spend the rest of their careers in Siberia at a work camp, so the greatest care was taken to ensure the prisoner survived.

At noon the next day Christine opened her eyes. She found herself intubated and heard the sound of the ventilator breathing for her. Her eyes closed and she slept until nightfall, when she awakened again and found they had removed the breathing tube. She was fed a mixture of warm mashed potatoes and beef gravy. She managed to swallow two bites before vomiting on the hand feeding her. The nurses cleaned her up and she was fed again. This time she kept it down, four tiny bites in all. Fluids were still being transfused and pain meds administered on a drip. They increased the drip and she slipped away into unconsciousness, sleeping another six hours until she was again fed. The catheter was removed and she was helped into the restroom, where she was placed on the toilet and steadied by the hands of two nursing assistants. They helped her back into bed and this time she slept without chemicals.

The administrator was notified, and he notified the president's staff.

The prisoner had survived.

Excellent, came the president's reply. Now get me the confession I require.

The next morning, the water boarding began again.

44

B lack Monday was a Russian mafia.

It was comprised of three brothers from the Ukraine who had migrated to Russia and devoured the Russian underbelly. Guns and drugs were the mainstay. Militia workers smuggled guns, mortars and rockets out of the armories, transported them to Black Monday border stations, and sold them into the black market for use in Ukraine and the Middle East battles. Cash poured in the windows. It was easy money that the brothers were unwilling to share. Competitors were rounded up and airlifted to 3000 feet, where they were kicked into the night—always on Mondays, a trademark practice. The practice became known as black Monday and the mafia became known as Black Monday.

The brothers were Nikki, Fazi, and Kruzkov and they were all clear-eyed killers before they were twenty-six years old. They answered to only one man—their father's brother. He lived in America and ran Black Monday from there. Uncle Tony Folachnaya's management style was straight out of the American mafia's playbook, paying everyone off, militia and Kremlin alike. There was enough money to paper walls and Black Monday prospered.

Uncle Tony Folachnaya never forgot a debt. When Thaddeus Murfee called him and asked for his help there was no hesitation. The Russian GRU was holding a prisoner Thaddeus wanted freed. But there was a snag: President Piotor Irunyaev wanted Ama Gloq as a political pawn and he would never agree to her release. A huge invention would be required. "Can you do it?" asked Thaddeus. Uncle Tony's voice was smooth and mellow over the phone. It was as good as done.

Tony met with nephew Nikki on a subzero day in mid-January. Tony had arrived at Sheremetyevo Airport at six a.m. At six-forty-five the meeting took place aboard Tony's plane. Huge snowflakes were covering all runways, only to be bladed and pushed back by endless plowing and potassium acetate liquid de-icing.

"We owe a favor," Tony explained to his nephew. "A very big favor."

"What can I do to help?" Nikki said. He was a cool-looking, smooth-talking Ukrainian who had seen and done everything before his twenty-seventh birthday. Nikki was slender and wore his black hair shaved down to the scalp and a huge diamond earring in his left earlobe. He carried dual Austrian Glock pistols concealed beneath his leather overcoat and it was known he wouldn't hesitate to use them. Enemies withered and disappeared at the mention of his name. The last thing any hoodlum wanted was to have Nikki learn his name.

Tony knew he could rely on the young man for anything, which is why he was selected out of the three brothers to head up repayment of the favor Tony owed Thaddeus.

He sat across from his uncle at the onyx table in the Gulfstream.

"Who do we know in Matrosskaya Tishina prison?" asked the uncle.

Tony ran a pale hand back across his bare head. His eyes narrowed.

"We know everyone. What do we want there?"

"There is a prisoner. Her name is Christine Susmann."

"Do you want her dead?"

"Not at all. I want her freed."

"Done. Should I bring her to you this morning?"

Uncle Tony raised a hand.

"Not so fast. Our glorious president is holding her for political reasons. It must look like an accident. Or an escape."

"Done. We can arrange that."

"It must be done so there is no injury and no re-capture."

"What will she do after she's freed?"

"You will bring her to this aircraft. It is Russian registry and she will have false ID. There will be no suspicions when she leaves Russia for the United States. From this end it will look like a common business flight."

"Do I come with her?"

"No need for that. However, there are two others who will come along."

"They are?"

"Thaddeus Murfee and Angelina Sosa."

"Who are these people?"

"The man is someone who once saved my life. The woman is a nobody. A reporter."

"Then we must honor what this man did for you."

"Exactly. You will take the three of them to Chicago. After that, you're free to go."

"Consider it done."

"How will you set her free?" said Uncle Tony. He wanted to be clear on what Nikki had in mind. There could be no slip-ups.

"Did you ever hear of Oleg Topalov?"

"No."

"Oleg was a twice-convicted murderer. Small stuff to us, but a little bit crazy, his friends called him."

"What did he do?"

"He escaped this prison with a spoon."

"Explain that."

The men continued plotting and laying their plans for another half hour. After that, Nikki double-timed down the outside stairway and jumped in the back seat of his Mercedes. With a long plume of gray diesel smoke the black automobile pulled away from the General Aviation tarmac and departed through an open gate.

Nikki was already planning how he would get the spoon to Christine Susmann.

45

On the eighteenth day they didn't beat her. Nor did they water-board her. Nor did they subject her to sub-zero temperatures in the courtyard. Instead, the lone prisoner in the isolation cell received a breakfast of scrambled eggs and bacon, two pieces of toast, and a small carafe of American coffee. She was astonished. Astonishment turned to elation.

Then turned to suspicion. Perhaps they were going to take a new tack with her, try to influence her and obtain a confession by other means. Halfway through the breakfast she pushed it aside. That wasn't going to work with her either, any form of bribery. What the hell, did they really think she was that dumb?

She numbly looked around her cell. She was sitting on the edge of her bunk—rather, a flat slab of concrete extruded from the wall of her cell. It was just barely long enough for her to stretch out on, and even then the length of the cell required that she keep her knees bent. There was no mattress, no sheets, and no blanket. At the far end of the cell squatted a wooden bucket with wooden top and rope handle. She had used that for her toilet. The only opening, besides the steel door, was the overhead HVAC vent equipped with an ancient slide switch that opened and closed the antique vent. The walls were solid concrete, washed in a thin green paint that boiled and blistered along the seams where the concrete was joined to itself. The floor was the same concrete, but natural color.

Her mind was in the process of re-learning how to fashion together two consecutive thoughts on the same topic. It had been shattered in its usefulness by the pain and fear she had known for two weeks now. Torture inhibits all useful thought and that is actually why it is done, to break down the mental processes of the subject so information can be extracted from the unwary mind.

As her eyes played over the room, she realized she was no longer being held with the three cellmates she had started with. She was alone. She shivered and wrapped her arms around herself. So far she hadn't given them what they wanted. She had known they would come for her again and immerse her in water again, so the breakfast was mind-numbingly twisted. They would try anything, she finally decided, and for that she would have to remain on high alert.

Four hours passed as she sat and tried to join thoughts together. Almost alarmingly the slot in the cell door opened and a plate of food slid onto the ledge on her side. She retrieved the plate and sat down again on the bunk. She studied the food. Chicken with mashed pota-toes and gravy and what looked like cranberry sauce. She drew her finger through the mashed potatoes and inserted it into her mouth. It was warm and bore her away into dreams of what real food could be. Ten minutes later, she realized she had cleaned her plate. She stood, stumbled, and replaced the plate on the ledge. A hand swept inside and retrieved it. The plate was replaced in minutes with a gold and black carafe of coffee and a clean cup and saucer.

Was she dreaming?

She retrieved the hot liquid and got back up on the bench. This time she leaned back against the wall and prepared to enjoy the delicacy.

A sip and then she heard the lock on her door being turned from the outside.

The door came open and there stood three guards. Except on closer examination they weren't guards at all. Their gray coveralls meant they were maintenance men. They entered her cell and indicated she should move as far back on her bench bed as possible. She did, pulling knees to chin as she sat back. She still had her coffee and gulped down the last of the cup, fearing they would take it from her before she finished.

But they didn't take it.

Instead, they pulled in behind them a squat machine on wheels with a huge canister and electric motor. A thick black hose came off the machine and ended in a long silver spike. Next came a short ladder. The bald man opened the ladder and climbed up. He pressed against the ventilation duct then inserted a screwdriver and began removing screws until the duct had come free, whereupon he passed it to the youngest man. The third man, a bearded worker with thick black eyeglasses, passed the business end of the hose back up the ladder. A switch was thrown on the machine and a huge racket slammed Christine's heightened hearing. She recoiled, scrunching up against the wall with her side, and shut her eyes. Then the man on the ladder inserted the silver spike end of the hose into the open duct and began enlarging it.

For the next two hours they widened the duct and removed crumbled plaster and concrete torn loose by the tool. Soon the man on the ladder had half-disappeared into the enlarged duct and was still going at it with the tool. He came down twice for a bottle of water and Christine watched him closely. He was wearing goggles and ear protection and his wavy black hair was a matted white color from the materials he had shattered loose inside the duct.

She had to pinch herself to make sure she wasn't hallucinating again.

"What doing?" she managed to say.

The trio ignored her.

She asked again. "What doing?"

The youngest man made a circle of his arms and then enlarged the circle. He looked at her questioningly: did she understand?

"You're making the hole bigger. Okay. Thank you. Please leave now."

Ignoring her, they finished their water and the hole work restarted.

A word was swimming through her mind, a word she could claim. Then it surfaced.

Jackhammer.

The thing was a jackhammer and they were enlarging the hole in her cell.

When they were finished they cleaned up the mess and handed her a large, metal spoon, the type used to ladle gravy.

She accepted the spoon and watched as they closed the door behind.

They had taken maybe half of the debris from the hole

widening and stuffed it inside her toilet. She lifted the lid and looked in. Her heart fell: someone was going to be very angry with her for the mess.

What else was there to see?

She found that by standing on her bench bed she could see inside the ceiling hole. In fact, she was able to introduce the upper half of her body into the hole, as low as the ceiling was. She looked up and saw light at the far end, maybe five feet away. She reached, grabbed a warm pipe that passed through the hole, and tried pulling herself up into the hole. But it was no use. She was much too weak to pull her body into the cramped space. So she released her arms and found the bench with her feet and came back out and down onto the bench.

What in the world? she wondered. *What in the world?*

Somewhere between three hours and six hours crept by. She lay on her side the whole time, peering at the hole in her ceiling. She tried but couldn't make sense of it.

More food appeared through the slot. Pie and coffee. It tasted like her grandmother's rhubarb pie, sweet and tangy. The coffee was hot and received as the greatest delicacy she'd ever known. She had forgotten how much she loved a hot cup of coffee. For weeks all she had known was cold and now she clung to the warmth of the carafe and the luscious, warm liquid inside.

It startled her to realize she was actually having sequential thoughts again. She was stringing together several thoughts in her mind and weighing evidences of her existence and her situation. She didn't understand what was happening, but it was something. And so far it was all good.

Two guards came for her in the middle of the night.

They stood her up and held her so she didn't collapse on her weak legs.

They had left the door open—something the guards never did. Now they spun her around and helped her through the door, out into the hall. She realized she'd never seen the hall before, at least not that she would have remembered. Each time she had come and gone in her cell she had either just been beaten or water boarded and was out of her mind.

But this time she was alert and fully conscious.

They began walking her down the hall to a double door. It buzzed and they pushed through, helping her as well.

Another hall, this one off to the right and probably thirty meters long. It was much brighter than the first hall and she realized the hall outside her cell was darkened to allow sleeping inside the row of cells it fronted.

Another door, another buzz, followed by two more buzzes and an elevator ride that descended.

The doors opened on a very dark cell and the two guards helped her out and steered her to the left. Several meters down, they came to an open door and paused. Christine's eyes adjusted to the dark. She realized what she was smelling was the smell of death. She had smelled it before in Iraq. Once learned, the smell was never forgotten. Geometric shapes—long supine boxes—began to emerge out of the black and then it occurred to her as clear as any thought she'd had that day: morgue. They were in the prison morgue and it was death she smelled.

A third man came into the room. He wore the white lab coat of a medical worker and carried a small plastic bag and a small bottle, which he set on a shelf she was being pinned against. He tore open the plastic bag, removed a syringe, and inserted its tip into the bottle. He withdrew maybe 15 cc's and then turned to her. A Russian word was spoken and the sleeve of her jail coveralls was pulled up to reveal her bicep. The lab coat man inserted the needle into her arm and worked the plunger down into the syringe tube, expelling the clear liquid into her arm. He abruptly left without another word.

As she faded out of consciousness she became aware that she was being lowered on her back into a long box that was padded with soft foam.

When the lid began closing on her, she realized.

Casket. She had been shot up and put into a casket.

A deep breath and she felt a warm comfort flowing through her body.

Sleep, she thought, and dream no more.

Then she was out.

46

E *yes, open.*

The eyes obeyed.

She surveyed the immediate area. She found herself lying on a very soft bed. Except it wasn't a bed, it was something slightly less comfortable than a bed, but padded, still.

Eyes wide open. She was covered with a wool blanket and there was a pillow beneath her head. *Fair enough*, she thought. *I'm alive*.

She sat up and saw that she had been lying across two seats. Seats like they use inside buses or trains or—

Airplanes. She was sitting onboard an airplane.

Her eyes pierced the window and she saw dark outside. Dark and the blinking light of an aircraft wedging its way through the gloom.

Then a man stood beside her. He leaned down and wrapped his arms around her shoulders.

"Welcome back, Christine. You'll be home in about eight hours."

"Who?"

"Thaddeus. Your friend, Thaddeus."

Tears came into her eyes. At first she didn't dare believe it. But they realized. It was actually his voice. Thaddeus had her.

Which meant she was safe.

"Where we going?"

"Home. Here, let's recline your seat back and you can close your eyes."

"No. Coffee."

"Miss," Thaddeus called out, "coffee here, please. Bring two cups."

He stepped across Christine's legs and took the seat beside her.

"Where was I?"

"You were smuggled out of the prison."

"How?"

He smiled. "Friends in high places. Very high places."

"Okay. This plane can just leave Russia when it wants?"

"Whenever it wants. No questions asked."

"Why not?"

"No one would dare."

Coffee was served on a silver tray with a silver service. Nothing too rarified for the Gulfstream line of aircraft and their dining ware. Thaddeus nodded to himself. Tony had brought nothing but his best game. He owed Tony big time.

No, they were actually even now. At least they would be once it was wheels-down on O'Hare runway. They would probably never speak again.

An hour later, she leaned forward and stretched her back.

"They hurt me, Thaddeus."

"I know they did. Bastards."

"Bastards."

"What do you think we should do about that?" Thaddeus asked.

"We should sue them."

"Yes, there's always that."

"We don't have anything else."

He nodded. "You're probably right. Fine, we'll sue them."

"Sue that bastard president."

"President Irunyaev? Why not," he said, not as a question. "Why not."

"Get them for me, Thaddeus. Please get them."

He reached down and patted her knee.

"I will. Consider it done."

At refuel in Zurich an America trauma doctor, flown in by Thaddeus, joined them. He took Christine to the rear compartment of the aircraft and examined her. He gave her two Vicodin and returned her to her seat.

"Well?" said Thaddeus.

"Broken fingers, knitted without being reset. They'll need to be broken again and allowed to mend correctly."

"You could tell all that without X-ray?"

"You should see them."

"All right. What else?"

"Probably dehydrated. Keep the fluids coming until we can get her into a hospital and do a workup. I've also started a line in her arm. Ringer's."

"Thank you."

"Yes. I left her on the bed in the sleeping compartment. Five minutes later the Vicodin had done it work and she was out again. It's best, for now."

"All right."

Hours later they touched down in Chicago.

An ambulance was waiting. Christine was rushed off to the O'Hare Clinic, operated by the University of Illinois in Des Plaines.

Thaddeus stayed with her. While he waited bedside in her room, she was undergoing a full examination, including scans and X-rays and blood and urine panels. Three hours later, they returned her to the room. She immediately fell asleep.

Thaddeus pulled out his cell phone. He one-dialed a number.

"Albert. Thad. We're going to sue the president of Russia. Put Eleanor and Kit on it. Research jurisdictional issues. Put Paul on asset location—I want to know about anything owned or controlled by the Russian president inside the United States."

"She's out?"

"Sound asleep. They loaded her up."

"So we're suing the president of Russia? Can we even do that?"

"We can now."

47

A t the entrance to the great man's office stood two soldiers selected from the Russian army of 1,600,000 men. They were selected for their looks, their dedication, and for their ability with small arms. Each wore a shiny black holster containing a Grach semi-auto, and each held at parade rest a Kalashnikov automatic rifle. Karli brushed by and knocked twice on the door.

"Enter!" came the booming voice inside.

Karli found the Russian president at his desk, which was covered in files and maps. Behind him were two twelve foot oil paintings, one of Lenin and one of Piotor Irunyaev himself. Lenin had a serious, educated look on his face. The president looked as though he had just won World War III and was about to enter New York as a conqueror, standing erect, a sword grasped in his right hand and stuck into the ground, his left hand raised above his head as if to summon applause. His portrait had been rendered and placed on the wall almost the same week of his election in 2001 and had gotten raves from all visitors.

Greetings and salutations were traded and then Karli launched into the update on the prisoner Christine Susmann.

Piotor Irunyaev couldn't believe the wild story being relayed to him. He sat behind his massive mahogany desk—reputedly used by Czar Nicholas I—and slammed his hand down with such force it caused nearby papers to elevate. He slammed it down a second time. "How can this be!" he said, incredulous. "I gave no such order!"

Karli studied the president deferentially, only occasionally meeting his gaze. He tried explaining again.

"She enlarged a heating duct with a spoon. Just like Oleg Topalov."

"Where did the spoon come from?" the President Irunyaev asked Karli.

"Stolen from the kitchen. We don't know who helped her, but we're working on it."

"I thought she was with your group all day? Wasn't that my order?"

"She was, then your orders changed. They said to stand down."

The Russian president's jaw tightened.

"I gave no such order."

Karli spread his hands. "We were told you had ordered full meals and two days of rest."

Piotor Irunyaev shook his head violently. "No such order came from me."

"Let me talk to the guards. I'll get to the bottom of it."

"Do that. Bring me names of those who gave her assistance. All of them!"

"Yes, Mr. President. Consider it done."

"Now, then. Where has she gone?"

"That's just it. We have checked all hotels, trains, and airlines. There has been no evidence of her use of a room or seat on a train or airplane. No bus has sold her a ticket and no taxicabs have any record of an American woman unable to speak Russian. We know she doesn't know our language so she couldn't have gotten far without being noticed and remembered."

"What about private aircraft? What has happened there?"

"A plane registered to your loyal supporter Antonin Folachnaya. It came and went."

"Surely he wouldn't have anything to do with this woman. By all reason it wouldn't have happened because she was working for the CIA! What would a Mafioso have to do with the CIA?"

"Understood. There could be no connection."

"All right. So she's still hiding in Russia. Your orders: find her and return her to me. We have unfinished business with her."

"I will find her."

"You go and do that. Now."

Karli turned on his heel and left the president sitting at his priceless desk, a dark scowl on his face. The president was breathing heavily, trying to suppress his rage before it erupted against one of the underlings in his office. He trusted his GRU. He knew they would find her and end this nonsense, so he eventually relaxed and his breathing returned to normal.

He spoke directly into his intercom, which was always engaged and broadcasting all conversations to his staff. At the other end was Prime Minister Nuramov.

"Give it three days," he told the second-in-command.

"Then send Karli to America. That is where she'll try to go. If she makes it to America she will be shot and killed. We will have the original video to prove the Americans tried to assassinate me."

"Indeed, Mr. President," said Nuramov. "We will send the entire GRU if that's what it takes. She will be found."

48

F

ROM: *Thaddeus Murfee: A New York Times Bestseller*

Blackjack McDonough, the King of Torts
by Angelina Sosa

Blackjack McDonough taught torts to freshman law students. There was a balance to his professional life, his teaching: he held the study of tort law in highest esteem; he held freshman law students in lowest esteem.

Had he been in charge of the world, torts would be studied only in the third year of law school, "When the legal mind has overcome adolescence," he told his colleagues. Most of whom gave Blackjack a wide berth, both academically and socially—especially at the Friday afternoon keggers at Pius XII Memorial Law Library. For as the beer flowed, the more vocal and obstreperous the law professor was known to become. He had even invited Father Milligan to an alley brawl late one Friday after the beer—along with Blackjack McDonough's sobriety— was exhausted. Father Milligan clutched the rough Jesuit cross he wore and thrust it in the putative tortfeasor's face: "Get thee behind me, Satan!" he cried, which seemed to bring Blackjack to full consciousness of who-where-what and he immediately backed off and settled down. Later he returned to the party clutching a venti Starbucks, abashed and embarrassed, where he muttered apologies to the diminutive priest. But the damage to his own reputation was done. He was an intellectual profligate among the Jesuit community of the law school, and a blowhard, and colleagues avoided him.

Blackjack's interface with his freshman students was anything but apologetic. In fact, he was obtuse, and omniscient in the hide-the-ball dialogue that inhabited 1L lecture halls. The final word on the subject came from 1L Manny Magence. As he put it for his classmates when they were all but huddled in the corner with Blackjack towering over them, "the guy's a dick."

Pure and simple. A dick.

It was the first day of class when Blackjack's Socratic method battered 1L Angelina Sosa. It was done to frighten her off to the regis-trar's where Blackjack imagined her withdrawing from law school in favor of the master's program in primary education. While the law school might have viewed the loss of a freshman in the first week as calamitous, Blackjack would have counted it another notch in his gun.

"So, Miss—Miss—" he turned the seating diagram of the class roster north-to-south and east-to-west, but still couldn't come up with her name.

"Sosa?" she volunteered. "You seem to be looking at me, sir?"

"Angelina Sosa? What the hell kind of name is that?"

"It's a name on a birth certificate, no more, no less," she said, and gave him her best black-haired-dark-eyed beach-maid smile.

Which he found off-putting. There was no room in law school for great beauty and charm. Law school was a place of inquiry, a place of important Socratic discourse. Blond hair and blue eyes and sparkling smiles held no sway here, not to the dick.

"I get that. I get it's a name on a birth certificate. It just threw me. Now, let's get our little show on the road, Ms. Sosa."

"I'm ready."

"You're riding an elevator and the man behind you accidentally brushes your posterior with his hand. Can you sue him?"

"I can sue him," said Angelina Sosa. "Will I prevail? That's what I'm here to learn, isn't it. I didn't come here today for our first class already knowing the answer to that question, did I? If I was supposed to already know what you're looking for, someone should have directed me to sufficient reading material to allow me to prepare an answer grounded in the common law. As well as the statutory law of the state where the elevator operated."

"Good, good," said Blackjack. He plucked the Montblanc pen from his shirt pocket and made a chopping motion with it as he spoke, as if words alone weren't enough. His slicing jabs with the writing tool were reminiscent to the law student sitting to the right of Angelina Sosa. Reminiscent of Anthony Perkins playing Norman Bates in Psycho as he assaulted Janet Leigh in the shower. At least that's how 1L Thaddeus Murfee viewed the matchup. The psychotic law professor versus the unsuspecting, vulnerable law student who had just pulled in for a three-year stay at a deranged motel called law school. Thaddeus Murfee, with his classmates, waited while the bespectacled, slack jawed Blackjack continued his verbal foray, which ended with him saying, "—and so, if the stranger standing behind you on the elevator purposely brushes your posterior—is that actionable? Can a lawsuit be brought and won?"

Angelina Sosa was quick. "Same answer as before to the first part, different answer to the second part. Now I would say the law suit is winnable."

Blackjack nodded, quickly gathering his mental breath. "Why is that? Why is it winnable?"

"Because that intentional touching would constitute a tort. And tort

is why we're all here today, instead of outside in the quadrangle, sipping coffee and making weekend hookups."

"A tort. Tort this, tort that. What is a tort?"

"A tort is a civil wrong."

"What tort would be committed by our elevator passenger as he purposely touched your posterior?"

"Assault, I believe. Plus it would be a damn poor way to hookup for a drink."

The class erupted and Blackjack's mouth worked silently, the lower jaw grinding sideways, looking to all who knew about such things as a chewing rodent.

"Please. Spare me the humor. Torts is the most serious of all law school courses."

"Sorry. It just seemed funny," said the girl from Angelina named Angelina. Beside her, Thaddeus Murfee crossed and uncrossed his legs. He looked at her left hand. No ring, which was amazing for a girl of her beauty who would be twenty-one or twenty-two, because she had made it this far without being entrapped by some guy's $2500 .7 carat handcuff. His first feeling of admiration for her stirred in his chest. She had at least made it that far, as had he. No rings, no promises, no broken hearts, no expectations. Nor would there be rings, for him, as he was already committed to a three-year relationship with casebooks followed by marriage to a law degree. Remembering his promise to himself to stay above the hookup fray, he set his mind on IGNORE and barricaded his thinking against any interest in the beauty standing next to him, facing Blackjack on their first day of law school, first class of the day. He did have to admire her though. She hadn't flinched, her fingers weren't nervously picking at the skin on her thumb, her smile was professional and her posture unbowed and, to his thinking, probably unbowable. Blackjack had his work cut out for him.

"Well, we'll try to minimize the hell out of levity in my class," Blackjack assured Angelina. "We'll keep it turned down low. Now, which tort would you posit the posterior passenger had committed?"

"What tort did he do? Is that what you're asking?"

"Yes. Please."

"Assault."

"Is that all?"

"Battery?"

"Why would you say 'battery?'"

"Because a battery is an unpermitted, unconsented-to, harmful or offensive touching."

"My, we've done our reading, haven't we Miss—Miss—"

"Sosa."

"Miss Sosa. Admirable. Please take your seat. Oh, before I forget, the dean also requests introductions today. Please tell us where you're from and what your goal is in coming to law school, Miss Sosa."

She turned and smiled across the tier of students surrounding her.

"I'm from San Diego and my goal is to write a New York Times best seller."

"Indeed. A New York Times best seller. And how does law school figure into that?"

"Well—I don't know yet. Maybe it will come after law school is over. But I'm sure the story will present itself. It always does."

"Commendable, I'm sure. Let's move on to the gentleman sitting to your left. Please stand, sir, and give us your name."

Thaddeus stood and faced the inquisitor.

"Thaddeus Murfee, Chicago, Illinois."

"Mr. Murfee, are you afraid of God?"

Thaddeus gave him a dumb look—dumb as in dumbfounded.

"I—I—I'm not even sure I believe in God. Maybe we should start with that first."

"Please, sir. Answer my question."

"No, if there's a God, I'm not afraid of him."

"Or her," muttered Angelina beside him.

"Or her," Thaddeus repeated.

"Indeed. Well, this being a Catholic law school, our heritage is

replete with accounts of God coming to earth in the form of a man. So we needn't bother our heads about God as her, fair enough?"

Thaddeus sighed. "If you say so. Is this going someplace?"

"Let's make it go someplace. Like most one-L's, you won't be happy until it goes somewhere. So let's say this. Let's say I'm going to make you unafraid of God. Are you up for that?"

Thaddeus looked at the ceiling. He considered the next move on the board, and the next. Then all the pieces jumbled and he surrendered to the moment.

"I'm up for that."

"Do you know why we're going to make you so you don't fear God?"

"No I don't."

"Because most judges think they are God. They act like it and believe it. And when you go before them, I want no fear in you. Do you follow now?"

Thaddeus shrugged. "I guess I do. I can't argue with it."

"Well, thank you. Because, if you're afraid of the judge, you can't adequately represent your client because you will fear challenging the judge. Am I making sense?"

Several students around Thaddeus nodded. Including Angelina.

"You're making sense to several of us, yes, I can see that. So how do I get over my fear of God, who may or may not exist?"

"You do that by learning how to think like a lawyer. And that's my job. I'm going to teach each of you to think like lawyers, so there's no fear. There will be no fear because you will know how to hold your own in an argument no matter which side you're on. Sound exciting? I'm waiting for a show of hands."

All hands shot up.

"Then we have a quorum. Please take your seat, Mr. Murfee. And tonight when you say your prayers, ask God to help you get over your fear of him."

"I don't pray."

"You will want to learn. Because when you're a lawyer and you're facing your Goliath, believe me, brother, you will want to know how to pray. Sometimes prayer is all the lawyer has. It's an acquired skill. Which is why you came to a Catholic law school. We're holistic here. You will even get a course in prayer. It's called Torts, and that's my course, and you're going to be praying you pass this course before we're done. That's enough for today. Brief the first five cases for Wednesday. Come ready to recite. And pray I don't call on you first. Dismissed."

A sudden commotion erupted as students stood and plugged ear buds into ears, activated smartphones to grab the latest text from Barbie or Ken, and began banging books into bags and exchanging comments on what they had just witnessed.

"So you're not a praying man, Murfee?" said Angelina, as he was angling his torts casebook into his book bag.

"Can't say as I am. We didn't do much of that where I grew up."

"And where did you grow up?"

"West side of Chicago. Urban blight. You?"

She pulled a comma of hair up on her forehead.

"Ocean Beach. OB, we call it. Just off the ten freeway in SD."

"SD?"

"San Diego. God, man, get a map."

"Hey, I don't do California. I'm a Midwestern boy. And what are you doing clear back here anyway? California girls usually can't be pried off the beach, from what I hear."

She smiled and her perfect lips and teeth caused his heart to flutter.

"Didn't you hear? I'm here to write a New York Times best seller. You will be the star of my book."

"Me?" he smiled. She was quite good at games. And fun.

"You."

"Then I'd best do something to turn heads. Something best-sellerish."

"Just don't make it about sex. There's already enough of that on the shelves."

"How about justice? What if my story is about justice?"

"Make your life about justice, then. That will sell some books."

What Thaddeus couldn't have known was that a week later Angelina did drop out of law school. Not because of Blackjack McDonough, nothing like that. No, she dropped out because one night after criminal procedure, when she had stopped to put gas in her car, four men in a low rider sped past and one of them leveled his pistol at her and shot her. She was rushed to the hospital and treated, and three days later was released to her mother. Her rehab, however, took much longer. The rest of that school year and part of the next.

Angelina Sosa finally did return to school, this time at the University of Chicago, where she majored in journalism and minored in Russian.

Her classmate-for-a-week Thaddeus Murfee remembered none of that conversation.

But she remembered him. Within three short years he was making a name for himself around the state.

So she began stalking him. She told her editor she was off to Zurich to research a story about Nazi gold in Swiss banks.

Nothing could have been further from the truth.

Thaddeus Murfee was headed to Zurich and she knew it.

So was she.

49

I t was decreed Karli would take two agents along to America. This was decided after three days of combing Russian transportation depots and ticketing agents and finding no clue of Christine.

"She will be in America by now," Karli told the president.

"Then follow. And take your best men with you. That's an order," said Piotor Irunyaev.

Karli handpicked two agents to join him in the search.

The first selection was a woman, a thirty-five year old Afghanistan war veteran. Glynda Maximo had flown Russian Mil Mi-24 helicopters up and down in the valleys of Afghanistan, hauling soldiers to battle and returning the wounded to field hospitals. Her exploits and coolness under pressure were noted; senior officers recommended her for GRU school—a destination reserved only for the cream of the cream. GRU was interested; testing followed; admission followed testing. Then the training began. One month surviving the Siberian winter while living off the land, one month surviving the Gobi Desert summer with nothing more than the clothing she wore and a parachutist's knife, and four months of cloak and dagger in Russian cities where the game was to kill or be killed. It was a game all GRU agents played, but a deadly serious game. The environment was real, the weapons were real, and only the killing was make-believe. If you "died," you went back to the army. If you survived, you were accepted into undercover training, a regimen that lasted another six months in which she studied the CIA handbook and the GRU handbook and learned to kill. Finally she was ready. Glynda Maximo was ecstatic to be chosen. "But only if you allow me to terminate this Christine." She was dismayed that the first prong of the assignment was to return Christine to Russia. She much preferred to locate and kill her.

His second choice was Madi Petrovich, an ardent communist and a card-carrying member of the Party—unusual for one only twenty-five years old. Madi's father was a high-ranking Kremlin bureaucrat, who boosted his son's chances of getting into the GRU, but this was possible only after Madi had proved himself a worthy candidate while serving in Russia's police force. In his eighteen months in the police, Madi had put four members of Black Monday in the ground and in each case the killing had been ruled justified. In short, Madi was expert at crime scene preparation in the aftermath of a killing, making each one of his takedowns look like he had been attacked first. In hand-to-hand combat he was highly skilled in what the police called Back Alley, which was slang for street fighting methods to be mastered before going into service. Graduating from GRU Academy at the top of his class, Madi had outscored his Back Alley instructor three out of four falls in the final week of training.

His team populated with Glynda and Madi, Karli and his protégés scoured Moscow for any evidence of Christine's escape and disappearance. Two days into the questioning of those who had been in contact with her at the prison, it was becoming clear that Christine's escape had been aided and abetted by prison workers themselves, most likely acting on orders from Black Monday. Repeatedly they were told that the treatment of the prisoner softened and reversed on orders of President Irunyaev himself—a fact that Karli's team knew to be patently untrue. An intercessory hand had been played and, while there was no smoking gun to be uncovered by the end of the prison investigation, all clues led back to Black Monday, where they abruptly ended. A tight veil of secrecy had been drawn around Black Monday and Karli could only conclude that Tony Folachnaya himself was responsible for the escape. At least the orders had issued from the Mafioso kingpin.

Karli reported his investigation's conclusions to the president in person and was immediately ordered to leave for the United States, find her, and return the woman to Moscow. Karli bowed out of the meeting a hundred percent resolute and engaged. He would satisfy his president regardless of who tried to get in his way. He made that promise and the president was placated, if only temporarily.

"Mr. President, let me promise that I will bring her to you," Karli said as he reached across to shake the hand of the leader.

But Irunyaev wasn't in a handshaking mood. He brushed aside the agent's hand and said, "We will save our handshaking for the successful conclusion of this assignment. In fact, not only will we shake hands, I can see a private dacha in your future the day you return her to me."

Which electrified Karli and made him that much more

resolute. Dacha's—country cottages of beauty and elegance —were usually reserved for only cabinet-level leaders of Russian bureaucracy. For a mere field agent to come into ownership of such a treasure was unthinkable. Karli couldn't back out of the president's office fast enough and get to the task at hand. In his mind, it was all but done.

"All of the motherland's resources are at your disposal," the president told Karli as he was leaving. "Just contact our people in America and tell them what you need. Whatever it is will be instantly made available to you. Funds and manpower are unlimited. Bring this woman to me."

"My solemn promise," Karli replied. "I will not fail."

"No, you will not fail, Guryshenkoyash. Failure is not an option. You will not return here without her." The Russian president's use of Karli's diminutive name indicated the tender feelings he had for the people's servant. He was letting Guryshenko know that he would be personally following the assignment and that he held his soldier dear.

―――――

THE RUSSIAN TRIO entered the United States through New York on embassy visas. As far as their hosts were concerned, they were Russian Embassy workers, nothing more. The GRU enclave at the Russian Embassy outfitted them with American money and arms. Each agent received a Colt .45 pistol, a Remington Model 870 shotgun, and the Colt M4 5.56 mm. combat rifle plus all the ammo they could ever hope to shoot in one lifetime. They rented a Bronco and immediately left town. Next stop: the Chicago law offices of Murfee and Hightower.

Eighteen hours later, Glynda rode the elevator up to the eighty-first floor of the Citibank Building. She wore a gray wool suit and, in deference to her days as a pilot, Ray-Ban sunglasses perched on her head. She wanted to appear nonchalant, even haphazard, so as not to alarm Christine's co-workers.

The waiting area of Murfee and Hightower was sub-divided into four pods of two chairs plus loveseat plus Carrera marble coffee table, room enough for five visitors each. The idea was for clients to feel welcome yet enjoy some privacy while waiting to see Thaddeus or Albert Hightower.

The walls were taupe this season. A gold and white marble tile floor demarcated the waiting area, and at the far end a staircase to the second floor could be seen, back-dropped by six vertical windows, the upper three with lattice inserts. Beneath the staircase waited a wingback couch, flanked by end tables, fronted by a coffee table and surrounded by a flurry of wingback chairs. Glynda guessed that this particular area was reserved for the groups that would visit Thaddeus.

At the front desk, Melinda Mounce was working the phones.

Glynda strode up to the desk as if she owned the place.

"I'm looking for Christine Susmann," she said to Melinda, even though it was clear Melinda was still speaking into her headset. The visitor's English was perfect, without the hint of an accent—a requirement for all members of the Karli team.

Melinda raised one finger and smiled her million-dollar smile.

She said goodbye.

"How can we help you today?"

"I'm looking for Christine Susmann. I want to hire her."

"Hire her? She isn't a lawyer."

"I need some legal work done."

"By a paralegal? I don't think she's available for private jobs outside the office. But why don't you leave me your phone number and I'll get back to you about it."

"No need. I'll call back when she's in. Thank you."

She turned and left the offices.

Melinda punched a number on her phone.

"Rogert, she's coming to the lobby. Gray dress, Ray-Bans."

She punched another number.

"Thaddeus here, what's up M?"

"Russia was just here."

"Tell me."

"A woman. Maybe mid-thirties, looking for Chris. Says she wants to hire her to do some legal work."

"Did she just leave?"

"She did."

"Did you notify Rogert?"

"I did."

"Excellent. I'll check in with him."

"I can make that call for you, Mr. Murfee."

"No need. I'll use my cell. Thanks, MM."

"You've got it."

Thaddeus hung up the handset and leaned back in his chair. He stared out the window at Lake Michigan, roiling beneath storm clouds and two foot high waves. It was a gloomy late-January day and more snow was forecast. He shivered and hit speed-dial 8 on his cell phone.

"Rogert here."

"Thad. You have her?"

"Yes, we're headed for the Kennedy, I do believe."

"What's she driving."

"She's a passenger in a black Bronco. Two guys with her."

"Stay close and call me."

"Roger that."

"What do you know about Christine today?"

"XFBI has her. She's got two doctors' appointments, then back to her apartment."

"Your monitor that for me, please. Keep me updated."

"Done."

"Rogert, one other thing. Just check the guys at my place. No need to upset Katy and the girls. Just quietly check, make sure systems are up and people in place. Cautionary."

"Done."

They hung up and Thaddeus considered calling Katy himself. At first he thought he would leave it to Rogert, then decided against that. She was probably down at the homeless kitchen.

He pressed speed-dial 1.

"Katy here, darling boy. What's up?"

"Hey, girl. You down at the shelter?"

"I am."

"Turquoise and Sarai get off to school okay?"

"They did. Sarai complained of a scratchy throat. I think she just wants to skip school, though. She doesn't like numbers."

Thaddeus laughed. "I didn't either. I believe it was third grade when long division came crashing down on our heads. I was lost to math forever after that."

"I loved math. Anyhoo, what you doing?"

"Just being a little cautious today. Nothing to worry about."

"I don't like the sound of that. Tell me what's really happening?"

"Some woman came around asking for Christine."

"Came to the office?"

"That's right. Rogert is on her ass now."

"She didn't head out our way, did she?"

"No need to worry about that. If they come, they'll be looking for Christine, like I told you."

"What about Angelina Sosa? Does she need to be alerted?"

"I have XFBI guys watching after her. She's clueless."

"I think you owe her an update."

"I suppose."

"Hey, her help was priceless in Russia."

"Word."

"Word dat, my little rapper."

"Hey, what do you say we catch a movie tonight?"

There was a long pause. Katy could be heard talking off the phone momentarily. Then she returned.

"I'm sorry, did you say something about a movie?"

"I did. _American Sniper_ just opened."

"You and your guns. How about a nice romantic comedy."

"Never mind. I'll go see it with Albert."

"Come home after work. You know how I am when things flare up."

"Sure enough. But I've checked up on the people working your security. It's all good."

"I'm glad the girls are being watched over, but for me, I hate it."

"We've been over this, Mrs. Murfee. It's part of the job description for being my wife."

"I should have been told up front. When I met you you

were just some guy living in a cabin on my reservation. How simple things were then."

"But it's been good change. Lots of people being helped."

"Here comes another guy wanting a bedroll. I better go."

"Later."

"Love you."

Thaddeus clicked off and slipped the phone back into his shirt pocket.

He considered calling Christine but decided against it. She had enough on her plate already. Better to let Rogert and his guys run with it.

———

FIVE MILES west of downtown Chicago, as traffic was slowing on the westbound Kennedy, a buckle in the traffic brought Rogert's van to a sudden stop. Without warning, the eighteen-wheeler behind him kept coming and drove up and over the van. Rogert was killed instantly. The driver of the truck keyed his cellphone. "It's done," he said.

Up ahead, Karli smiled and nodded. He spoke into his cell. "Stay here. Make sure."

"Done."

Now they were free to find the woman. Thaddeus Murfee would soon learn that the old schema and devices weren't enough this time.

And at O'Hare, an Aeroflot jet was being serviced. It could be ready for a nonstop to Russia on a moment's notice.

Exactly what Karli intended to pull off.

50

They had shattered her jaw and it had knit improperly, leaving her able to chew only pasta and soft vegetables. An oral surgeon was called in. Work began.

They had amputated two of her fingers and she needed rehabilitation to learn to use that hand. Voc rehab was summoned.

Beatings around the head—the numerous times she had been punched and kicked—left her a victim of concussive syndrome and doctors' orders never to experience concussive events again, not unless she wanted to suffer permanent brain damage.

The rapist had transmitted syphilis and herpes. She was embarrassed by the canker sores on her lips. The antibiotic was slow to stop the syphilis' spread.

She was suffering from PTSD. Experts at the VA were called in.

But worst of all was the depression. It had come over her during her second week in isolation at the Russian prison and now shrouded her in its iconic secret: life was no longer worth living.

She didn't enjoy her husband and found her children noisy and needy. They were rejected; she felt she no longer loved them—which, thanks to the depression, was evidently true, as she simply had no energy for them or interest in them. Her own parents were viewed as hecklers and childish in their demands that she behave as she once did, such as coming by on Sundays for dinner, going for a beer with her brothers on Friday night, or attending the dance recitals and piano recitals of nieces and nephews.

Night held a special horror for Christine. They had often come for her at night and water boarded her in the dark room with the blackout towel smothering her face as she lay manacled to the dentists' chair. Now she awoke several times a night, sweating and panicked, oftentimes screaming, oftentimes certain that she was dying and imploring Sonny to dial 911 so that she might be rushed to the hospital.

Surgery on her mandibular fractures was delicate and was repeated four times, each one a major surgery. The VD spread to her ovaries and a hysterectomy was required.

She separated from her husband and children, renting a room above a print shop where she stayed in bed with the curtains and shades drawn. She refused to go to the office and resume work. Thaddeus missed her and felt powerless to help. Still, he came by to see her every day but she refused to allow him into her new home. Instead, she made him stand in the hallway while she refused to make eye contact with him and spoke in the deadened meter and tone of the emotionally damned.

Sonny sought marriage counseling; she refused. The kids called on the phone several times a day and cried and begged her to return home and mother them like she had before Russia. But the concussions and the depression took a terrible toll on her, leaving her at odds with Sonny, fighting and fearful, unable to cope.

She tried transcendental meditation; one of the VA doctors introduced her to it. She cried and blamed the therapist for her inability to maintain any ongoing mental state for more than ten seconds without thought intrusion. Horrible images intruded when she meditated: thoughts of suicide, of imminent torture, of gang rapes, of mutilation, of being beaten with hands and feet, of being electrocuted with Tasers.

The VA pastoral staff was introduced. She found their Bible and belief systems "crazier than bat shit," as she put it, refusing every attempt by them to put into prayer what her needs and hopes were. They were rejected and their God was rejected as "one angry dude," who made the lives of his Chosen People miserable and therefore untrustworthy. All religion was rejected and prayers left unspoken.

———

FINDING her home address in Schaumburg took all of five minutes: Christine and Sonny Susmann were listed in the White Pages. From a block away, the Russians studied the house. Madi was driving a rented Honda, Glynda appeared to be a mountain bike rider on her way through the neighborhood, and Karli was still driving the Bronco from New York. The Bronco's plates were Indiana plates, which was right across the border from Schaumburg, Illinois, so the neighbors took no note.

Sonny was usually picked up by a co-worker and gone by six-thirty a.m. Just as he was leaving, an older woman would drive up, leave her Impala in the driveway, and let herself in. They decided this was someone's mother, either Sonny's or Christine's. And it was clear she was there to watch the kids until they had left for school. Clear, because Christine was never there. After the kids left for school, and after the matronly woman drove off, Glynda would wheel into the driveway, skip around to the back of the house, and let herself in with a simple set of lock picks. She was very cautious the first two times, because Christine would be a very formidable opponent in a one-on-one fight and the kidnappers didn't know if she was inside.

From there the hunt became easy. A phone bill in the kitchen turned up numerous calls to Itasca, Illinois. Itasca was seven miles from Schaumburg. It was a tiny place. The Internet helped Karli reverse-search the phone number; within five minutes they had the address of the Itasca phone number. They had found her.

They went back to their hotel in Des Plaines and made their plans.

———

ON THE THIRD day of their arrival in the United States, they went for her. But first they purchased Amtrak tickets for four passengers, Union Station Chicago to New York City. The idea was to abduct her, drug her, slip her aboard the train in a wheelchair, and hold her in a sleeping car, drugged, while they headed east.

Her room was on the second floor of an apartment complex across from the train station in the center of Itasca. It took Karli less than fifteen minutes to drive there with Madi and Glynda.

Christine had just returned from the maxillofacial

surgeon's office. They had ground her teeth and taken dental impressions for a solid hour. Just sitting in a dental chair called up the water boarding in her mind. It was all she could manage to sit there and let the surgeon do his work. Sonny was called and he left work to help her. But she was only angry he had come. Still, Sonny stood his ground and insisted on holding her hand while the dentist and staff went about their work.

Then she returned to her apartment.

She had taken to sitting in the second-floor window seat and counting the trains passing through Itasca. The track was a Metra line, the daily commuter that ran from Harvard, Illinois to Chicago. At times she thought she would lie down on the tracks and let the train run her over; then at times she imagined herself on the train headed for Union Station and a cross-country trip to someplace she would never be found.

She didn't notice Karli from the upstairs window when he stepped out of the Bronco dressed in coveralls and wearing a seed corn cap. He looked like any other farmer and her eyes didn't linger. Nor did she notice the Bronco had dropped Madi and Glynda at the station, where they had disappeared into the ticket office.

The trio joined up in the lobby of the apartment building. There was no security as it was a $550 per month apartment with no security, plus it was right on the Itasca square where anyone could open the door downstairs and walk in. The elevator was also public. Karli punched the button for the second floor and the slow ascent began.

Which was when the XFBI agents positioned themselves on either side of the elevator upstairs. They had noticed Karli and his friends; they had seen them cluster in the lobby; they had a strong suspicion who they were. At the very least they posed a threat because they weren't usual tenants and because there were three of them together.

The XFBI crew was run by Matty Harroway, a retired FBI agent who stood six-feet-five-inches tall and packed a MAC -10 machine pistol hidden in his overcoat. He believed in being armed for bear and was poised on the button panel side of the elevator as it chugged upstairs. Across the opening from Harroway was Ronald "Big Mac" MacDonald, a retired FBI agent who had worked white-collar crime for twenty-five years while secretly yearning to engage in shoot-outs with bad guys on the street. XFBI's work had appealed to Big Mac, after retirement from the Bureau, because bodyguards found themselves in "kill or be killed" situations more than any other post-retirement work out there. And standing sentry at Christine's closed apartment door was Elise Marilynn Sullivan, a retired FBI investigator who had spent her entire career working federal crimes on two Indian reservations in South Dakota. Elise had found herself in no less than a dozen firefights during her twenty-two years behind the badge and counted Wild Wally Juniper among her kills, the crazy man who had led the police and FBI on a nationwide manhunt while he killed his way across the country in 1995. Elise had cornered Wild Wally behind a drugstore in Butte, Montana, while she waited in her Crown Vic for her partner to pick up a Vicodin prescription for his chronic back pain. Wild Wally had burst out the back door of the drugstore, guns blazing at Elise's partner, who was in hot pursuit after interrupting a robbery inside, and Elise had simply lowered her driver-side window and shot him through the temple with her left, non-shooting hand. A special Certificate of Merit was awarded, signed by the president, and now mounted in her kitchen where she spent her off-duty hours, cooking for the love of her life, a college professor named Wendy. Elise was quick to acknowledge that she was even better at the Glock with her right hand than she was with her left. So far, while working for XFBI, she hadn't found it necessary to prove that point.

When the elevator door opened on Christine's floor, the three XFBI agents were there with guns drawn. Glynda saw them and said, "Sorry, wrong floor," and punched the button for 1. The doors began closing but Big Mac managed to insert his foot into the crack before it completely shut. A shot was fired inside the elevator, a clean through-and-through in the agent's foot, and he cried out and jerked himself free then rolled to the floor, wincing in pain.

Matty Harroway and his Mac-10 stayed behind to give first aid while Elise headed for the stairwell. She beat the three Russians to street level but had to leave off the chase when her Glock suffered a hang-fire—an impossibility, most Glock aficionados would say, but still, it happened to Elise at the worst possible moment. Luckily the gang went the opposite direction and she didn't get the opportunity to give chase with the .380 semi she carried for backup in her ankle holster. The Glock failure had taken all the fight out of her; she'd seen enough for one day. Besides which she was totally outgunned and knew it. Even on its best day the .380 couldn't be counted on to stop an oncoming man under the best of circumstances, much less in a street shootout where it's usefulness was at a distinct disadvantage.

The Russians fled in their Bronco, which went unseen by any XFBI agent that day.

Immediately upon hearing the elevator round fired off, Christine had leapt for the front door to her apartment and the pistol hanging there in its shoulder holster. She drew the gun and placed her back against the wall, waiting. Finally the elevator could be heard chugging downstairs and Christine cracked her door. She knew the agents, knew of their assignment, and quickly hurried to aid Matty with Big Mac.

"Dial 911," ordered Matty as he struggled to wrap Big Mac's bare foot.

"Got it," said Christine, and she ran for her cell phone.

After Big Mac had been rushed to the hospital by the EMTs, Matty turned to Christine.

"You need to rethink this living situation, girl," he told her. "You're a target here in this building. Not good."

Christine gave him a hard look before answering.

"You maybe be right, Matt, but I've got a ton of baggage to work through right now and I need some space. I'm not going home to Sonny and the kids. Not yet. Maybe not ever."

"No, no, no, I wasn't saying you should go home. Far be it from me to stick my nose in there. I'm just saying the apartment is street side, which makes it an easy target from a moving vehicle, and there's no good cover for us in the event of shots fired. You were an MP, you know what I'm saying."

"You're saying it's dangerous for you here, and I can appreciate that. I'll look for something more secure."

"Yes, please. Well," he said, and his voice trailed off.

"I'm thinking of moving taking Thad up on his offer of a place downtown. It would be too expensive for me to make it work, but he's offered to find me a condo with good lobby security, pass cards, and so forth."

"Definitely worth looking into. These sons of bitches will be back."

"I'm sure you're right. I'll call Thaddeus tonight and make some plans."

"Thanks, Chris. Well, we'll be downstairs if you need

anything. I'm sure Elise has called for backup by now, so you'll be in good hands."

"Thank you."

She returned to her apartment and holstered her pistol. Then she sat down on her couch and waited for the tears. The tears that always came with even the slightest provocation anymore. Sure enough, a minute later her eyes were brimming and her vision glassy and she pressed the remaining three fingers of her right hand to her face. "Calm the hell down," she admonished herself. "You've gotta quit this."

At which point, her cell buzzed. THADDEUS said the ID.

"Hey, Thad. Guess they called you."

"Elise called me. We need to get you moved."

"Agree. This place isn't safe for your agents."

"Nor for you."

"I'm not worried about me."

"Well, while you're not, I am. So I'm going ahead with a condo for you, something on the near north side. Fair enough?"

"That's fine."

"I'll have the movers there tomorrow. In the meantime, please catch a cab downtown. You'll be registered in the Hilton under the name of Christopher Luckman."

"Sounds a lot like Christine Susmann. You going soft on me?"

"I'm just trying to make it easy. Right now we need to be very careful with you."

"Christopher Luckman it is. I'll be there in an hour."

"Matty and Elise are close-by. They'll follow you down and make sure you get registered okay."

"Please call them off. You know how I feel about being watched."

"No can do. My guess is the Russians are officially here. These are some very bad people."

"Well, I can be very bad back. Just give me the right gun and stand back."

"I have no doubt of that. But you're just going to have to stand aside this time. Besides, there are political ramifications here."

"How's that?"

"What I've been told so far is the three who visited you today are officially attached to the Russian Embassy. Complaints will be filed."

"Oh, screw all that."

"I know. But it is what it is."

She hung her head and studied the two stubs where once she'd had fingers. An anger at the disfigurement surged inside.

"Thad, I want first shot at the main guy, if it's who I think it is."

"Karli? He's one of them."

She felt her heart rate increase.

"I knew it. I knew they would send him."

"Of course they would. He has much face to save since he lost you."

"Well, you just made my day. I want that bastard. Want him in the worst way."

"Please, leave that up to me."

"What about the Agency?"

"CIA? They told you they would deny all knowledge. So far I can't get a callback from anyone in that entire division."

"Figures."

"Yep. So you start packing and we'll do the next indicated thing. Which is to get you downtown where we can all keep a closer watch over you."

"Roger that."

"Later. Get to it, now."

"Roger that."

They hung up and Christine started packing. But she was actually feeling positive for the first time since returning to the States, she slowly realized. Positive, as in, the entire drama was going to come to an end. And maybe she would have a leading role, as in, facing down Karli herself. On her own. One-on-one.

She couldn't wait.

Less than an hour later she was packed and waiting for Thaddeus' people. Who could tell? She might even call the kids and tell them goodnight. She was feeling better by the minute.

She might even talk to Sonny without biting his head off.

51

"Do you know what today is?" she asked him.

He looked up from his laptop. He was sitting in the family room, where Turquoise and Sarai were watching *Animal Planet*. Vaguely he knew the show was about an orangutan island or some such thing. It was good to be home, good to be feeling normal again.

"What is today?" Thaddeus asked. "I give up."

"Today is O day."

"I don't get it. What's O day?"

From where they were sitting, the kids couldn't see Katy when she pointed to her pelvic region.

"Ovulation," she mouthed the word to him."

"Got it. I'm up to bat. So to speak."

"Uh-huh. Tonight. So get ready."

He looked at her quizzically. "How do I do that?"

"You know—"

"Afraid I don't know. Wash my hands? Take a shower? I do that just about every night anyway." He was teasing her and she hadn't caught on quite yet. Given her serious look and intense feelings about the new baby, he realized how important it was to her and told himself to lay off. He had to honor her. "Just kidding, forgive, please. I'll be ready."

"You pitch, I'll catch."

Turquoise turned her head around, taking them in. "TMI, folks. TMI."

"Sorry, Turq," Katy said. "My bad."

Turquoise had turned back to the orangutans. She shrugged and let it go.

———

HE USUALLY WORE a T-shirt to bed. But tonight he didn't. The sheets were cool and soothing to his skin and exhausted muscles. Moscow had been much more than he had expected and he was still trying to come down from the ordeal.

Katy finally finished up in the bathroom and slid under the covers beside him.

She snuggled up, totally nude, and he was immediately aroused.

He kissed her. She tasted like Crest toothpaste and mouthwash. And, she had showered. He hadn't, and kicked himself. But she didn't seem to mind.

"Now. This is a very important night. My bulls-eye is waiting for your arrows."

"I think I follow that. C'mere and kiss me."

She moved closer, throwing a leg over his mid-section. He rose up to meet her and felt the cool inner thigh that he loved so much and always desired.

"Mmmm, feels good," she murmured.

"What feels good?"

"You know what."

"I'm glad. I've really missed you," he whispered. "Terribly."

"Good. Even Angelina didn't turn your head?"

"Not once. I'm not that way."

"All men are that way. Trust me, I know."

He pulled back and looked at the top of her head. It was dark, but he could see the outline of the head he loved.

"Well, *your* man isn't that way. I'm only interested in one bulls-eye."

"Thank you for telling me that. Now take your hand and put it right here, please."

She took his hand and placed it between her legs.

"That's perfect."

"You're right."

"Now. Let's get us a baby."

"I'm ready. Baby it is."

52

"I'm hurt and I'm angry!" Christine yelled at Thaddeus. "The fricking CIA wouldn't even acknowledge me over there!"

"I think they probably told you that going in," said Thaddeus.

Christine's pale blue eyes flickered. She was hurting and he knew it. He honestly didn't know what else to say to her. But something had to take away her pain. What was it? Shooting Karli herself? He knew she would do exactly that, given the chance.

"They told me just the opposite, going in. They said there would be helicopters to get me out, S.E.A.L. teams if need be—whatever I needed I would get."

Thaddeus held up a hand. "Whoa, you're talking about Syria and MESA, if I'm not mistaken. There's no way they could have promised that for Russia because they didn't know ahead of time the hijack was coming. Let's get our heads straight about this."

She slumped back in the visitor's chair in his office.

Outside the snow was swirling past the windows and seagulls were gliding and settling to the sidewalks far below. It reminded Thaddeus of a hungry world, of the World Vision kids he and Katy had adopted. So much need, so short of help. And now Christine. She was wounded beyond reason, beyond having clear thoughts about what had happened to her and who was at fault and who owed her. He tried again.

"I think you turned up in the wrong place at the wrong time. The Russians are in deep shit over the whole Ukraine uprising they've caused. The U.S. has seized assets and embargoed them to where it's really hurting. They needed a PR chance, a photo-op, and you showed up, a CIA operative on special assignment to the Middle East. You weren't supposed to even be in Russia. But that didn't stop president Irunyaev. He jumped all over you and used you. In a sense, you were innocent and just got caught up. Don't you see it?"

She shook her head violently. "I see the CIA refusing to help. If it wasn't for you and Tony, I'd still be strapped to a dentist's chair with a towel over my face and water flowing down my throat. Thank God for you, Thaddeus. And thank God for Tony. I'll never forget what you guys pulled off for me."

Just then the phone buzzed on Thaddeus' desk. He held up one finger.

"Yes?"

"Thaddeus," said Melinda, the receptionist. "I have Angelina Sosa out here. She says it's urgent and says you wanted to see her."

Thaddeus covered the received. "Angelina," he said to Christine. "I've got an idea for you and her. Let's get her in here."

Christine shrugged. "It's your office. Fine by me."

Angelina entered the room with Melinda's guidance.

"Hi, Angelina," said Thaddeus as he stood behind his desk. "I think you might remember Christine?"

Angelina smiled and took a seat beside Christine. She touched her on the shoulder and nodded at her. "I remember her grabbing my tablet on the plane. I remember trying to locate her. I remember one night at the hotel with her. But there's lots more I'd like to know. If she's willing."

Christine gave her a dour look and brushed her hand away.

"I'm not one of the willing. I don't want to see my name in your damn newspaper."

"Actually, you might," said Thaddeus. "Which is why I've asked Angelina to join us this morning."

Christine sighed. "Okay. What's up your sleeve?"

"Well, we're smarter than these people who came for you yesterday. Especially this Karli thug. So I'm thinking we bait a trap and then see who gets caught."

"And if someone gets caught, do I get to shoot them?"

Thaddeus shook his head. "Chris, I can't tell you how to live your life. You'll do what you need to do. You always have. My idea only goes so far."

"So tell us," said Christine. "What do you want me to do?"

———

AN HOUR later Christine and Angelina left the office together and walked across the hall to the elevator. A dark woman wearing sunglasses on top of her head was standing there, seemingly waiting for the elevator too. She gave the twosome a half-smile and returned her gaze to the numbers above the door.

Christine gave the slightest nudge to Angelina.

The doors opened and the three women climbed inside. It was a four-minute ride to the lobby, with two stops in between.

Finally the lobby doors opened and Christine guided Angelina toward the side exit onto LaSalle Street. The other woman went out the main entrance.

"Watch this," Christine said. "She's still back there."

"Russian?"

"Bet your booty, honey."

"Exciting."

They headed east.

"How did you get here?"

"Cab."

"Okay, me too. Let's grab one and see who follows."

Angelina was all in. "Are these the Russians?"

"Uh-huh. Near as I can tell. No one else is after me. Yet."

They stepped up to the curb and looked left at oncoming traffic. Several cabs sped by—middle lanes, impossible to get over. Until finally a white van with All-day Taxi written on the side pulled over. A man leaned down and caught their eyes. Turban, earpiece (why were they always on the phone? Christine wondered), and he was smiling. They climbed in back.

Christine looked behind. Coming up fast was a green and yellow taxi with a woman in the back seat. She was wearing sunglasses—that much could be ascertained.

So Christine began doling out nonsense directions to the driver.

"Turn left, up two blocks, go right, back down four blocks then pull over to the curb."

"Excuse please, what?

"All right, get in the left hand lane. Good, good. Now go two blocks and then right. Then go four blocks and pull over to the curb."

"I think I know."

"Fine, you'll do great."

Christine tugged to loosen the drawstrings on her purse and it was then that Angelina saw it: Glock pistol with sound suppressor.

"You have a gun!"

"I do. And I know how to use it."

"Are we in danger?"

"Lady, what movie have you been watching? See this," she said, and held up the hand missing two fingers. "This look like danger to you? Yes, I'd say we 're in danger."

"Good. I've always wanted to be in a thriller movie."

"Well this ain't no movie. This is my life and I'm not liking the opening scene one bit."

As she spoke, she swiveled in the back seat and peered out the rear window.

"Got you, lady," she said softly. She whistled. "Uh-huh, there's two of them now. She stopped and picked someone up."

"Can you see them?"

"Hang on. A white cube truck just pulled in front of them, they'll have to come around—yes, there they are!" She stretched and looked down the cross street. "But where's XFBI? Our guys should be on us now too."

"Can you see them? Anyone?"

"Driver, pop a U-turn and gun it."

The driver complied and in a brief instant the cab was across the centerline then speeding up to sixty-five and passing the green and yellow cab, which was trapped in the curb lane, headed the opposite direction. Christine waved at them as they blew by and the occupants pretended not to see.

"That felt good," she said to Angelina. "Wave at those sons-of-bitches."

She pulled her pistol from her purse and worked the slide. Satisfied she had one in the chamber, she slipped the gun back into the purse.

"When we get out, you hit the sidewalk running with me. I want us inside and out of sight by the time they find my street. If they even find it; I don't know they will. Okay, driver, right here then go four lights and left."

"Whew," Christine said. She comedically wiped her forehead. "Whew. Haven't had one that close since Donald Duck," she said in her best Bugs Bunny.

"Hey, that's the first time I've ever seen you smile."

"You're right. But you know what? I'm gonna enjoy this. I'm gonna enjoy taking these assholes down."

"I can see that. Well rock on, sister."

They did a fist bump and both exploded in laughter.

After the left turn, they went up two blocks and Christine told the driver to stop. They were right beside a well-known Chicago landmark consisting of a round tower of condos.

Christine tossed a twenty-dollar bill and a five dollar bill over the seat.

"Ready?"

"Ready."

"Let's go for it!"

They joined hands and ran into the lobby of the building. The doorman held the door and then stepped backwards twenty paces.

Angelina looked back. Why was he moving away from the doors?

Just as her mind formulated the thought, the green and white cab pulled up and double-parked next to the cab that Christine and Angelina had arrived in. Three people jumped out and came running for the building's front door. The woman with the sunglasses was in the lead, then Karli, then Madi. Guns were drawn and it was clear nothing was going to stop them. They clambered through the open door, held by Glynda, the sunglasses woman, now that the doorman had disappeared.

As they came through the door, a series of eleven gunshots blasted the quiet interior.

Thaddeus Murfee was there, waiting behind the information desk, and firing at the oncoming Russians. Glynda went down. Then Madi was spun around by a shot in the shoulder and one through the back of his head. Karli, halfway through the door, stopped and then jumped back for the first cab, which was still hemmed in by the green and white cab. Now the green and white moved on and so Karli, on his back in the taxi, calmly instructed the driver to flee the scene. The taxi lurched and picked up speed. By the time Thaddeus was on the sidewalk, it was too far gone and there was just too much traffic to risk a shot. So he went back inside.

Glynda was moaning, eyes half-open, a mortal wound in her neck. As Thaddeus toed the Russian named Madi, Glynda died with a long sigh. At the elevator, Angelina and Christine were stopped, frozen, and suddenly Christine was advancing with her own pistol trained on the two dead Russians.

Thaddeus brushed her pistol aside.

"We're good now, Chris. You can put it away."

SERGEANT BRANERTON of the Second Precinct Homicide was impressed with Thaddeus and impressed with the doorman, but most of all he was impressed by the CCTV video that undeniably showed the Russians charging the door with guns drawn. Clearly Thaddeus had saved the two women with his gunshots. Thaddeus knew his law: Illinois allows shooting to kill where done to protect the lives of others from imminent death. Sergeant Branerton applied the law and announced Thaddeus' shooting was a justifiable homicide. The shooting occurred just before noon. Just after midnight, Thaddeus was released. He was told not to leave town, that more questions would follow, but for now he was free to go.

XFBI had arrived on the scene and taken Christine and Angelina across town to Christine's real address.

"Serious," said Angelina. "We were bait?"

"We were. I taught Thad to shoot so I knew we'd be all right."

"But why _that_ building?"

"Thaddeus has a condo there. The doorman knows him, the HOA knows him, and the District Attorney's Office knows him. It was clever, eh?"

"I'll say."

"So now we're down to Karli. I wonder how I'll get him?"

"You want to fight him yourself, don't you?"

"I don't especially care about fighting him. I just want to torture him. I owe him big time."

"That's cool. I understand. But you won't get the chance, with all the cops and Thad and XFBI running around. They'll get to him first."

Christine walked across the gray carpet in the condo

Thaddeus had provided her. She slipped behind the bar and retrieved two Bud longnecks from the refrigerator.

"Here, have one on me."

"I don't ever drink more than one."

"Well, it's time to break that rule. You earned a second one."

"I'm going to drink this one and then I'm going to scoop this story to my editor. Inside info."

"Go for it. Just don't use our names. Not yet."

"I'll keep a lid on it."

"Exactly."

53

C hristine wanted to sue the Russian president. And Thaddeus needed no encouragement to agree to file the case for her. The president had fabricated the entire "attack" by Christine and Thaddeus was going to prove it.

But how do you sue a Russian president?

From her home, Christine did the legal research. She learned that in the United States the federal courts have adopted an important mechanism for acquiring jurisdiction over foreign defendants. She sighed: it was always about jurisdiction. The question was always, had he done something within the United States or to a U.S. citizen that would warrant the U.S. courts accepting a lawsuit? She read further. The willingness of federal courts to accept such cases was known as the effects doctrine. The doctrine says that if the effects of extraterritorial behavior harms citizens in the United States then jurisdiction in a U.S. court is permissible.

The first case to establish the effects doctrine was _United_

States v. Aluminum Company of America, 148 F.2d 416, a Second Circuit case handed down in 1945. The doctrine, it turned out, was well established. All of which meant, President Piotor Irunyaev could be sued in Chicago for the injuries he had caused to a citizen in the United States. The injuries in such a case would be the mental and emotional distress of being ambushed twice by Russian agents.

Then Thaddeus had an even better idea: he would go for punitive damages based on the injuries caused Christine in Russia. The theory was that the abuse was ongoing and that, while the injuries hadn't occurred in the U.S., the abuse in the states was part of a series of ongoing abusive acts and therefore the court should be allowed to consider the Russian torture and abuse when considering the amount of damages to award Christine.

Christine and Thaddeus spent the first weekend in March holed up in her condo. By late Sunday night they had drafted a complaint to be filed in the U.S. District Court for the Northern District of Illinois. The complaint alleged the Russian president was part of a conspiracy to injure and even kill Christine Susmann. The language of the complaint and the federal statute included the RICO Act: Racketeer Influenced Corrupt Organization Act.

Monday morning Thaddeus filed the complaint. Christine was working out of the temporary condo and XFBI was guarding her there and also watching over Sonny and the kids. Additional staff was needed; Thaddeus was quick to call in more agents, more arms, and more technology to keep eyes on the family. And also on his own family. For himself, he felt confident carrying his own gun, but, at the same time, he was accompanied and shadowed by no less than two XFBI agents wherever he went. Everyone knew that Karli was out there and that he would strike again. But no one knew where.

The lawsuit was then sent to Moscow for service of process on the Russian president.

"I'd give a thousand dollars to be in that room when he gets served," Thaddeus told Christine.

"Not me. I'll never set foot in that country again. Unless they disguise me and send me in to take down the son of a bitch. That I would do."

"Notch it down, girl, let me do it this way."

"Will it even bother him? Or will he just think it's a nuisance lawsuit and laugh about it?"

"I've got ideas about that. My guess is, if we walked away with a bunch of Russian rubles filling the bed of Sonny's dump truck then he won't be laughing. Especially if those rubles belonged to him personally. I've got some people looking into Russian funds in the United States, money we can get the court to give us."

"Sounds great. I'd love to really hurt them."

"You and about ten million Afghans, Chechens, Ukrainians and all the rest."

"Do you think RICO is the best way to formulate the case against him?"

Thaddeus thought it over.

"Well, the racketeering law is very sneaky. The Racketeer Influenced and Corrupt Organizations Act provides for criminal penalties and a civil lawsuit for acts performed as part of an ongoing criminal organization. Question being, is the Russian government a criminal organization? Our argument is Yes, it is. It's a novel idea, declaring a foreign government to be a criminal organization."

"Does it go against Irunyaev personally? Or just the government?"

"Good question. The RICO Act focuses specifically on racketeering, and it allows the <u>leaders</u> of a syndicate to be tried for the crimes which they <u>ordered</u> others to do or assisted them."

"So they can't avoid liability by saying it wasn't them personally who killed someone or stole someone's gold."

"Exactly. RICO closes the old loophole that allowed someone to be exempt even where he or she had told a man to murder someone, because he did not actually commit the crime personally. That was old law. This is new law—actually not all that new, but it's the law we get to use."

"I'm impressed. You've done this before."

"Remember when I sued the mob for coming after me and coming after Ermeline Ransom after I kicked their ass? I did that under RICO. Huge damages under RICO, too. Treble, three times. Beaucoup dollars can be grabbed."

"I like that idea. Someone owes me for these two missing fingers!"

"Not to mention the torture."

"And the—the rape. You've seen my medical records. Syphilis and an upcoming hysterectomy. That only came from one place. But I can't say who, because I was unconscious when the rape happened."

"Won't matter. It all relates back to what the president of Russia started when he kidnapped you and lied about you. I'm going to hang him by his nuts for that."

"God bless you, Mr. Murfee. Always standing in the gap."

Thaddeus smiled. "I'm beginning to think I was born to litigate."

"Well, you're way behind the rest of us then. Your admirers have known this for a long time."

"Now I'm blushing."

"Just get them for me, Thad. Knock their dicks in the dirt."

"You've got it. But you have to promise me one thing."

"I promise. What is it?"

"That you'll let my guys take care of Karli. You won't go looking for him."

"How could I do that? I have no idea where he is."

Thaddeus shook his head. "That doesn't mean jack. You know he's looking for you. You know how to make that confrontation happen. I'm just asking you not to. You've got a husband and two little kids. We want to see mommy get home to them safe and sound."

"Well, I do promise, since you put it that way. Okay, deal."

"Thank you."

54

After filing the Christine lawsuit on Monday, Thaddeus went home early. He was tired; they had worked all weekend putting the lawsuit together and he hadn't slept that well, knowing that Karli was lurking somewhere nearby. He pulled the Tesla into the garage and waited while the door shut behind him. Meanwhile, Sarai opened the door that connected the garage to the house and stuck her head out.

"Mama says you in trouble, Dad."

He came to the front of his car. "I'm in trouble? What did I do wrong?"

"Mommy says you probably didn't go to bed all weekend. She said she's going to stick you in bed whether you want to or not."

"Well, I better behave myself, then. Now come here and give your dad a big hug."

Sarai held the door open and reached for Thaddeus as he came up the steps leading into the house. He bent down to her and she wrapped her chubby arms around his neck.

He stood up, holding her with his forearm under her butt, and walked inside like a monkey carrying its young.

"Hello?" he called. "Anybody home?"

Sarai gripped his face in one hand and squeezed his cheeks.

"I'm home. Miss Margot is here."

Miss Margot was Sarai's nanny. She hailed from Mexico City and was working on a Ph.D. in finance. Days were spent caring for Sarai and writing her dissertation while Sarai attended first grade. It was a win-win for everyone and Katy had nothing but the highest regard for Miss Margot. As did Thaddeus.

Miss Margot came into the kitchen, winding up an Elmo doll as she entered. "Here, Thaddeus let Elmo sing you a lullaby. We heard you didn't sleep all weekend."

Thaddeus shrugged. "Where's that coming from? I crashed on Christine's couch Friday and Saturday night and got good sleep. Well, not that good. But not bad. Who's been saying things about me around here?" he said, and bent low to place Sarai on the floor. He grabbed her from behind and swung her around. "You the one who's been telling tales about daddy? It was you, wasn't it?"

Sarai squealed and begged for more.

Another ten seconds of swinging and Miss Margot said, "She's going to throw up Cheerios on you if you keep that up, Thad."

He stopped suddenly. "Whoa, then. We don't wanna go there."

Sarai snatched the Elmo doll and ran for the family room.

"Let me get changed. Then you can update me on my daughter's life."

Miss Margot smiled. "You're a busy man. She misses you."

"It's mutual. Hey, where's Turquoise?"

"She gets home from school around four. You're a couple hours early for her."

"All right. Be down in a few."

He climbed the stairs to their bedroom, which was actually three rooms, divided into three areas: bathroom/walk-in closet, sleeping area, and sitting area. Off came the suit pants, white shirt, tie, suit coat, what he called "goofy shoes" (loafers with tassels) and Glock 19 in shoulder holster with two clips. He carefully placed the gun inside his gun safe and spun the combination lock. On came the 501's, black T-shirt with pocket, Teva sandals and red hoodie. He went into the bathroom and looked into the mirror. He peered into his blue eyes and brushed a hand back through his longish brown hair. The round eyeglasses reminded him that someone had once called him "owlish." But at the same party someone else had called him, "Mr. Magoo-ish." So there it was, he thought, take your pick. I am what I am, as the spinach man says.

Back downstairs and into the family room. He flopped on the second of two couches, this one in the much-hated floral cover, though he would never tell Katy that. There was a who-could-tell-how-old bowl of popcorn on the octagonal coffee table, so he began munching. Soon, Sarai crawled up out of the beanbag she had occupied and came to the couch and motioned him to move over.

"Lie down, Daddy, so I can too."

He moved back against the cushions and Sarai climbed up and lay down beside her dad. He closed his eyes and smelled her hair. Anything, Lord. I would do anything for this one, he thought. I am a lucky man to have this family and these people in my life. So lucky. Thank you, God. Lately he had begun praying sometimes. He didn't know why or to whom, but it seemed like he owed something or someone for all his blessings and he wanted the universe to know he was grateful. He inhaled his child's hair again, eyes closed, and his breathing shallowed. He slept.

While he was under, Sarai—the restless one—lifted his arm from around her and crawled off across the floor.

"Miss Margot, I need a sandwich."

Miss Margot had been reading a paperback on macroeconomics by Hubbard. She was testing to see how his theories compared to those discussed by Krugman in his book on the same topic. She looked across the top of the book at Sarai.

"Did you say something?"

"PBJ. I'm *star*ved."

"Coming up. But it's three. You only get a half, so we don't ruin your dinner."

"Ruin it! Ruin it!" the six-year-old cried and began running wildly around the room.

On the second pass around, Sarai stopped at Thaddeus' head and reached out a tiny hand. With forefinger and thumb she opened his left eyelid.

"What?" he mumbled.

"You in there?" said the daughter.

He playfully swatted her hand away. "Let daddy sleep, Sarai. Please now."

"Let's go out and make a snowman.

"Later. Bring daddy his blanket and cover him up, okay?"

"You never play."

"I always play. How about Thursday when we made the snowman and decorated him with your watercolors? Wasn't that play?"

"Daddy, that wasn't Thursday. That was last Monday. Mommy says you're never here even when you're here."

"Who did Mommy say that to?"

"Henry Landers. Her grandpa. On the phone. I heard her."

"You're probably mistaken. Mommy knows I only have eyes for her."

A voice suddenly interrupted from behind, in the doorway. It was Katy, home from the community center for the homeless.

"Mommy knows what?" she said to Thaddeus. She moved swiftly over to him and tickled the bottom of his top foot.

He kicked out. "Don't, please. You know I hate that."

"I know you do. That's why I do it. Hey, stranger, long time no see."

"Sorry about that. I got busy again."

"All weekend. Where, at the condo?"

"Yeah, I've got Christine holed up there."

"I know. Christine called and told me where you were."

"I called too."

"I know. I got your voice mail."

"Then we got busy."

She pushed his legs up to his chest and sat at the end of his couch.

"You got so busy you couldn't try me back?"

"Why, did you need me?"

Sarai and Miss Margot were off making PBJ's. So Katy said, in a stage-whisper, "I don't know that I need you so much as I need your arrows."

"Damn, girl," he said, "don't I have you with child yet? Papoose, you goose?"

"Nice try last time. But no blue."

Blue, as in the pregnancy test strip turning blue to indicate conception.

"I'm blue. But I can certainly service you again, m'love. Wanta try right now? I'm about ready for a go at it."

"Tonight, chief. When all the little kids are in bed and the fire's burned down in the fireplace. Then we'll get naked and bump bellies."

"Oh, God, I hate when you say that! Say something nicer."

"How about 'have intercourse'?"

"Now you sound like a damn doctor."

She slipped her hand up and under his hoodie. "That's because I am a doctor. And doctors sometimes say doctor things."

"Intercourse? Nobody says intercourse."

"Of course they do," said Miss Margot, suddenly appearing with Sarai in tow. "I can name two economists who talk all the time about economic intercourse and freighted discourse. I've got the books to prove it."

"Hello, MM," said Katy. "How's it going round here today?"

"Oh...you know. Same old same old."

"Good to hear. Well, I'm going to run up and change. Thaddeus, you make me some coffee and bring it up, please."

"Sumatra or French Roast?"

"Sumatra. I might need to drive. Gotta keep my wits about me."

"Sumatra it is. Give me five minutes."

"That'll be about right. Sarai, what you eating, girl?"

"PBJ."

"Great. But you're going to eat vegetables tonight. I promise you that. So don't fill up."

"I hate vegetables. Except for popcorn."

"Not that again."

55

"**S**o what you're telling me is we forget about resisting this case in court?" asked Piotor Irunyaev. He was seated behind his gilt-edged desk in the Kremlin, weighing a letter opener on one finger, seeking the center of gravity, the balance point, much as he was seeking the middle ground on the lawsuit filed by Thaddeus Murfee. With him were two senior cabinet member advisors, both schooled in American law and one of whom was admitted to practice in New York, Illinois, and California. His name was Dzhokan Ansazi and he was educated at Boston University and Harvard Law School.

Ansazi was the type of lawyer who was ready and willing—and able, especially able—to fight and win just about any case in any court in any jurisdiction. He was known among his cabinet staff as Mad Dog and his official title was Registrar of Laws. Which meant he was the senior legal representative of the Russian Federation on all matters legal. His role and title were equivalent to the U.S. Solicitor General.

"We should not resist this case in court, Mr. President. Here's why."

Ansazi indicated his assistant should dim the lights and he began with a frame-by-frame review of the .wmv video file taken of Christine Susmann during her so-called assault on the Russian President.

"Now, Mr. President, especially look here—" said Ansazi, stopping the frame by frame with a small remote unit—"and again here, frame 788. See the woman's left eye? See the protrusion above the supraorbital ridge there?"

"Yes, I can see that," said Irunyaev. "What of it?"

"Well, Mr. President, if we can see it without magnification, just sitting here in your office, imagine how patently obvious this will be when the plaintiff's attorneys blow it up and review it frame-by-frame in court. The finder-of-fact is going to be enraged, because these injuries to the American woman pre-date the alleged attack she made against you."

"Speak plainly, man. Damn it all!"

"Plainly speaking, she had been beaten before the attack. You can review multiple injuries to her face and hands if you continue with this review. Which I am more than happy to do for you."

"So we don't resist because that would allow this Thaddeus Murfee to get his hands on our video?"

"Precisely that. He will have his experts review it if we turn it over to him. Which we would be forced to do if you make an appearance in the American courts. As it stands now, they cannot access our .wmv file, our original file. We should stand on that."

"And that's your considered opinion?"

"It is, Mr. President."

"All right, we'll do as you say. With one reservation. What can we expect in measure of an award for damages?"

Ansazi leaned back in his chair. He pulled a Cuban cigar from a pocket and began unwrapping its cellophane cover. He stopped and looked up.

"Amount? In cases such as this, U.S. District Court judges are awarding around fifteen to twenty million dollars. Somewhere in that neighborhood."

"Can you guarantee that?" asked the president with a small smile, as he clearly was relieved the payout would be such a minor sum.

"All but guarantee. I'm going to go on the record and project twenty million USD."

"We can work with that. Definitely."

"So we stand silent and don't answer the complaint? Is that your final instruction to my office?"

"You'll receive that memo from me before six o'clock today. It will say as much."

Ansazi stood, the unlighted cigar clenched in his left hand. With his right hand, he shook the president's offered hand. The deal was thus made.

It wasn't until they were in the anteroom and leaving the president's suite of offices that Ansazi looked down at the cigar he had been clutching. Halved—it had been snapped in half by the left hand.

He wondered: where did that come from, the absent-minded force necessary to crush a cigar in my hand? Am I that fearful about this case? Am I?

He retreated to his own suite of offices and told his staff to divert all calls.

He was deep into personal injury awards handed down by American District Court judges in the past ten years. Surely there would be one with an equivalency to the Christine Susmann lawsuit.

Six hours later he relaxed. It looked like he had been

spot on. Damage awards ranged from five million to twenty-five million.

At 5:55 he received the president's signed memo authorizing him to leave unanswered the complaint this Thaddeus Murfee had filed.

With a light heart, he headed home for dinner. It had been an instructive day and he had given his president excellent advice.

He was almost sure of it.

56

After Russian troops invaded Eastern Ukraine, the U.S. decided to hit them back. So they froze the assets of two Russian banks worth $637 million. Three billionaire friends of Piotor Irunyaev controlled the banks, the *Wall Street Journal* reported.

So Thaddeus made some calls to the lawyers for the government. He learned that Bank Rossiya in New York held about $572 million in U.S. accounts and about $145 million of that belonged to President Piotor Irunyaev himself. The money reportedly came from the president's skim from profits made on Gazprom petroleum exports. Other exporters whose funds were frozen were Neft, Lukoil, Srgutneftegaz and Rosneft. Another bank holding Irunyaev funds was SMP bank, majority-owned by Malich and Oligci Rottenzic, two brothers with close ties to the Russian president. At SMP the Russian president was said to own $75 million of the $235 million on deposit there.

Now he had his targets. So he hit the Russian president

with a TRO—temporary restraining order, and the court took control of the Irunyaev funds, almost $625 million.

"This is like shooting ducks on a pond," Thaddeus told Christine. "And we're just getting started."

He filed a motion for accelerated discovery and fast track calendaring of the case for trial. The Russian president had been served with process. Summit DocWorx in Moscow had personally served the president's secretary with the summons and complaint and TRO. The TRO was made permanent ten days after service when the president failed to file a response.

Almost incredibly, the Russian president failed to file an answer to the complaint.

Which meant he was subject to a default judgment being taken against him.

Which Thaddeus did, early in March. He took Christine into court, the judge called the court into session, and Thaddeus put Christine on the witness stand. As she testified, Angelina was in the front row, taking notes and readying the story she was going to file.

Christine testified about the hijacking, about being taken prisoner and interrogated at the airport. She then went into the detail she remembered from the country encampment where she had been Tasered and beaten and had fingers amputated.

Christine recounted the torture in the prison at Matrosskaya Tishina and what happened after she was moved to isolation in Special Isolation Unit No. 4. Water boarding, at least 150 times. She knew because she counted. A story had made the rounds after the U.S. invasion of Iraq how one of its key leaders had been water boarded 150 times. Christine had been part of the MP group charged with guarding the leader. She had known of the water boarding and torture by electric shock. She had heard the numbers, the times he had been almost drowned. So, she had decided to keep track of her own abuse.

As she testified about what the Russian guards and GRU officers had done to her, the Honorable Edward M. Mackie of the U.S. District Court for the Northern District of Illinois grew increasingly incensed. During one break in the testimony, he called Thaddeus forward and they whispered off the record.

"Mr. Murfee, what I'm hearing here today defies belief. How did the CIA not help your client? I mean, how could they refuse? They had to know what was going on."

Thaddeus nodded and half-smiled. "My point, exactly, Your Honor. It would seem that Christine was totally abandoned by her country when the plane touched down in Russia. It's almost inconceivable."

"Well, how much will you be seeking in damages?"

"All of it. All of Irunyaev's money in the U.S."

Judge Mackie nodded solemnly. "My guess is, you're going to get that award. Times three, for treble damages under RICO. So move it along. I've heard quite enough."

When the hearing resumed, Thaddeus asked four more quick questions and then rested his case.

Closing statement followed. He laid it all out and, as he spoke, the judge looked preoccupied. He was writing on a yellow pad and seemed all but oblivious to what Thaddeus was saying. Finally, Thaddeus ended by submitting the case to the court for its decision.

"Mr. Murfee," the judge responded, "let me read to you the gist of the order and findings the court will be filing in writing later today. One, that the President of the Russian Federation, one Piotor Irunyaev, in concert with many others, engaged in acts that rose to the level of criminal behavior under our RICO statutes. Second, the acts of the President directly and/or indirectly cause great bodily and emotional and mental harm to Christine Susmann, a United States citizen lawfully in Russia. Third, that, while many of the actions occurred inside Russia, many of the acts also occurred in the United States, including two attacks wherein the Russian president's agents were armed with automatic weapons and staged attacks aimed at the murder of Christine Susmann. These attacks were avoided only because of the defenses set up for Christine Susmann by Thaddeus Murfee, her attorney and employer. Fourth, that the acts of the Russian president directly caused severe bodily harm and emotional and mental harm to the plaintiff, Christine Susmann. Fifth, as a result of his acts, president of Russia is found guilty of one-hundred-fifty-seven counts of violation of the RICO act. Sixth, that damages are awarded to Christine Susmann in the amount of $150 million dollars, which equates to one million dollars for each time she was water boarded at the direction of the Russian president. Seventh, that Christine Susmann is entitled to treble those damages under the RICO statute and her damages are thereby increased to the sum of $450 million. Judgment is hereby entered in favor of Christine Susmann and against President Piotor Irunyaev of the Russian Federation in the amount of $450 million plus costs. Counsel, what are your costs?"

"We will provide a detailed list, Your Honor," Thaddeus said.

"Remember the cost of the jet fuel to bring her home. I don't want you to miss a dime of it, Mr. Murfee."

"We will list every penny, Your Honor."

"Is there anything further here today?"

"No, sir."

"Very well, the Court stands in recess."

Everyone stood, the judge filed out, and Christine turned to Thaddeus.

"Did I actually hear what I just heard?"

Thaddeus smiled ear to ear. "You sure as hell did."

"My kids just got their college paid for."

"And you can buy Sonny his own dump truck."

"And now I can pay my hysterectomy bill. We didn't have insurance for that."

"But we gave the hospital a lien and so they waited."

"Thank you for doing all that, Thaddeus."

Thaddeus was busily stuffing files and books in his brief-case on wheels.

"Hey, you deserve every penny."

"What happens now?"

"Now I execute your judgment on the president's bank funds and the banks cut you a check for $450 million."

Christine dropped into her chair. She dropped her head to her hands and turned her face sideways.

"I can't talk right now," she said. "Go on without me."

"Not a chance. We still have Karli Guryshenko to deal with."

He sat beside her and stared straight ahead.

"Come on, Karli," he said. "Come to Thaddeus."

"Better yet, come to Christine. I'm ready for you."

Outside in the hall, four XFBI agents patiently waited. Two would accompany Christine to the condo; two would accompany Thaddeus back to the office.

In the meantime, several U.S. banks holding Russian funds began cutting checks.

They were holding $450 million that now belonged to Christine Susmann.

She would want it without delay.

57

L ess than forty-eight hours after judgment was entered in the case of *Christine Susmann v. Piotor Irunyaev, et al.*, Thaddeus received a call from XFBI. He was sitting in his office, reading and re-reading the court's order when the light blinked on his phone.

"Thaddeus Murfee here"

"Thad, George Leyvas. Our network has intercepted a passenger jet manifest that includes the name of your boy."

"Slow down, please. Tell me again."

"Your boy, Karli Guryshenko, is listed among the passengers flying on a chartered Aeroflot jet of the Russian Federation. The flight is nonstop, Chicago to Moscow."

"Leaving when?"

"Tomorrow. 11:55 a.m."

"Out of O'Hare."

"Out of O'Hare. General Aviation hanger nine."

"Excellent work. Thanks, George."

"Go get 'em, Tiger."

"Will do."

Thaddeus hung up and dialed Christine on his cell phone. He brought her up to speed on the latest news about Karli.

She was angry, of course.

"He thinks he can just run off? Back to Russia without consequences? I guess not!"

"Well, you now know as much as I do. Frankly, I think we should call the police."

"Please, no police."

"No, I think we get the police involved."

"Thad, how many kids do I have?"

"Two. You have two children."

"How many did Sonny and I plan on having?"

"You always said four."

"Do you think I can have them now?"

"Not since the hysterectomy, no."

He thought long and hard. He looked at the window and the soft rain cutting patterns down the glass.

Finally, he said, "No police."

"Thank you," she said, and hung up.

58

O'Hare International Airport has often been designated the busiest airport in the world. O'Hare is located about twenty minutes from downtown Chicago and the Loop by El Train. O'Hare belongs to the City of Chicago and is administered in all respects by the CDA—Chicago Department of Aviation.

It's a busy place. In January 2015 the airport logged flights in and out of 66,567. That's over thirty-one days. Which figures out to be about two flights coming or going every minute of every day for thirty-one days.

Traffic problems in and around the airport are huge. Eighteen-wheelers have special cargo lanes and loading/unloading zones. Drivers are specially licensed and all trucks, cargo and even the smallest packages are X-rayed. Some are even searched. Metal detectors and dogs interpret the contents of every item riding the conveyor belts loading the planes.

Eight runways are kept open 365 days out of the year, ranging in length from 7500 feet to over 13,000 feet.

Hilton Chicago O'Hare is the only hotel located directly inside O'Hare International Airport. It is connected to three terminals by underground walkways and is directly across from departing international flights from Terminal 2.

So it only made sense for Christine to insist on a terminal-side room on the tenth floor when she checked in the night Thaddeus received departure information on Karli Guryshenko. She wanted to arouse no suspicion, so she arrived with two large suitcases and one electric guitar case that said FENDER along the topside.

"Do you play that thing?" asked the clerk behind the counter, indicating the guitar case.

"You know what, I do," said Christine. "But I only have three fingers on my pick hand, so I've had to really work at flat-picking."

"Wow, I bet," said the clerk.

The young woman handed Christine a brochure about the hotel and a small white envelope with the keycard.

"Just the one key, correct?"

"Correct," said Christine. "I'm traveling alone tonight."

"Well, welcome to the O'Hare Hilton. Please enjoy your stay. Ronald will help with your bags."

Ronald led her to the elevator, opened the doors, and ushered her inside. He followed with the luggage cart and pressed the 10 button.

"What kind of stuff do you play?" he asked.

"Mostly cover songs. I try to play a lot of Mark Knopfler's stuff. *Sultans of Swing* is a real challenge for this hand," she said, holding up the hand with three fingers.

"Wow, I'll bet. Is there someplace I can come hear you?"

"We're not playing tonight. Sorry."

He ushered her off at the tenth floor and walked

halfway down the hall. He inserted her keycard and allowed her to enter the room first.

"This is it. Luxury suite. Excellent view of hotel, Checkout is noon tomorrow."

"I'll be leaving at 11:56," she smiled.

"Oh, down to the minute, are we?"

"Indeed. I insist on punctuality for my band."

"Are they here too?"

"Arriving tomorrow. I'm a day early. We'll be leaving by bus. One big happy family."

"Anything else I can get you?" asked Ronald.

It was time to make the mandatory swap: a five-dollar bill for his manufactured niceness. They made the trade and Ronald left the room.

Christine slipped two latex gloves from her coat pocket and worked them onto her hands and fingers. Two of the fingers on the right glove were collapsed. But ignored. She was too far along in her rehab to allow such things to affect her. They were gone, the fingers, and that was that. All the therapy in the world, all the tears in the world weren't going to bring them back or grow new ones. It was time to suck it up and move along, nothing new here.

Christine stuffed the suitcases into the closet, unopened. Suitcase one was filled with newspaper and some old magazines, none of it traceable.

Then she laid the guitar case on the queen bed nearest the window. She clicked the four locks and their hasps popped open. She lifted the lid.

Except it wasn't a Fender Strat guitar. Nor was it a Fender Telecaster.

Fitted perfectly in its own custom foam rubber bed was a rifle, an M24 Sniper Weapons System (SWS) made by Remington. It was the military and police version of the

Remington 700 rifle. M24 was the model name assigned by the U.S. Army after adoption as their standard sniper rifle in 1988. The M24 was called a "weapons system" because it consisted not only of a rifle, but also a detachable telescopic sight and other accessories. It was chambered for the 7.62x51 mm NATO "short-action" cartridge, the configuration preferred by Christine. It was also the configuration on which she had qualified as "Expert" while serving in the U.S. Army in Afghanistan.

She lovingly lifted the rifle and ran her gloved hand along its stock. She then sat on the bed beside the case and assembled her weapon. She extended the stock and spread the bipod on the front barrel. She loaded it and worked the bolt action. Now it was chambered with a round ready to fire. Placing the weapon on the nylon bedspread, she went to the drawn curtains and pulled them open.

At her feet was a direct view of the exact gate where Karli Guryshenko would exit the terminal, walk about thirty paces, and then climb the stairway to his chartered Aeroflot jet.

She turned back to the guitar case and lifted the glass cutting system.

TEN O'CLOCK THE next morning and XFBI agents Jenner and Morrison were finishing off their coffees as they waited in the loading zone at the Palmer House, where their quarry was registered. At 10:10 he appeared beneath the sidewalk canopy and stood to the side as the valet motioned the next cab to pull forward.

A dozen photographs were taken with Jenner's Android phone.

"Perfect. Topcoat with fur around the collar and down the lapels. Perfect."

The photographs were emailed to c.susmann@murfee-hightower.pro, along with this notation, "Check out the fur collar. Place your shot three inches above."

No one said XFBI was on the side of law and order.

XFBI was on the side of whomsoever paid them. And today's activities were funded by a source known only to them as Timber Cutting, Hauling, and Boating, Minnetonka, Minnesota. That's all the accountants needed to know, that and the fact all payments were in cash, which was a common method of payment in the world of black ops.

The two men pulled their Dodge out into moving traffic. As they passed the cab carrying Guryshenko, both men looked to the left, just another precaution. He wouldn't have known them anyway. XFBI rotated agents in and out on a daily basis, sometimes even an hourly basis. There were 275 agents located in Cook County and they were all booked up for the next thirty days around the world.

———

SHE WOULD LATER DESCRIBE it as a droplet flare. Also as a red flare. She would be talking about the split-second after the NATO round entered the target's skull and punched out the opposing cranial vault.

Getting hit with that round was tantamount to getting hit with a sledgehammer. The single round knocked Guryshenko over the side of the stairway he was climbing to enter the waiting aircraft for the trip back to Russia. The woman leaning out the door of the aircraft to welcome him aboard, ducked back inside and pulled the door closed.

The pilots could be seen sliding down behind the glass of the aircraft's cockpit, but there was no reason for it.

Christine was already out of the room and trotting for the stairwells. She was still wearing the latex gloves she had worn since entering the room the day before. No prints, no latents, no DNA left behind, nothing. Cleaning chemicals had been carried into the room in suitcase number two. They were designed to remove all traces of DNA, even destroying the DNA left behind in the traps and drains of the bathroom. A glass-cutter and a used-but-one-time M24 weapons system occupied the slate top of the dining table shoved up against the terminal-side window.

"I'm an American patriot," she whispered to herself as she hustled down the stairs.

"I am an American patriot."

59

T ony Folachnaya waived the fee. Christine wanted to pay him the full fifty thousand dollars, but Tony refused.

Oleg Valadnikov was the wiry Russian from the Urals, the man who had been trained as a guard while serving in the Russian army. He hated Americans. He had even raped one while she was a prisoner in his prison.

When the new guard named Jacques cut his throat and left him to bleed out on the basketball court where the non-dangerous penitents played round ball, Oleg never saw it coming. He sat there, waving wildly about, in his own widening pool of blood.

"Christine says she will see you in hell," said the new guard, wiping the razor blade on Oleg's shoulder. His accent was French, which brought a look of puzzlement to the dying man's face.

"I-I-I-I—"

"Yez, you. She will see you in hell."

The new guard then left the prison. No one asked any

questions as he passed by their stations and doors. No one looked at him or even dared to look at him.

Out front of the prison a black Mercedes was waiting, its diesel engine chugging in the cold.

The new guard climbed in and dropped the razor inside the console.

"Drive," he told the man behind the wheel. "American Embassy."

"Yes, Mr. Lemoneux."

60

"Thaddeus," said Katy the following Saturday. "Come in here, please."

He rolled over in bed. Propping himself on one arm, he squinted in the bright morning light.

"What is it?"

"Come *here*, I said, please."

He rolled upright and swung his legs over the side. A pair of black briefs lay on the floor and he stood and stepped into them. He walked to the bathroom door.

"What's up?"

She held up the rectangular piece of plastic. An inch long opening along its spine was blue.

"Boy or girl?" he said.

"Boy."

"I can see it now, Murfee, Hightower, and Murfee."

"No, no law, no medicine, not for this one."

"What then?"

"I haven't decided. School teacher, maybe."

"Why not lawyer?"

"If I'm reading my newspapers correctly, Thaddeus Murfee is way more than just a lawyer. There's an article in today's paper."

"You've been downstairs and got the paper already?"

"Made pancakes for Turquoise. She's off to play tennis."

"And you read the paper?"

"Go read the article. You'll see."

He took her in his arms and kissed her firmly on the mouth.

"Congratulations, wife."

"Thank you. Now. Go. Newspaper."

61

What Makes a Bestseller Sell?
by Angelina Sosa

H*e was a man who would abide no lowering of his principles.*
  He had traded vows with her. He loved her and would love, honor, and obey her all of his life. Until death parted them.

 The first night in Moscow was spent in the presence of two beautiful women. (Forgive us if we call ourselves beautiful. Just know that others have.)

 The younger one smiled and brushed up against him in the room. She fixed him a cup of coffee and set it before him on the desk where he was working with his laptop. He refused to look into her eyes, though she invited him to look there.

 The next day his friend was arrested and taken away. Which left the younger woman with the man. Alone in the hotel suite that they occupied for the next fourteen days. Sometimes there would be robes and showers, sometimes there would be sleeping clothes and partial nudity, sometimes there would be moments together, at dinner, where their eyes met.

At those times, his eyes didn't look away from her.

But neither did his eyes look inside of her, as she would have preferred.

They only looked at.

Always at, never in.

At last she became frustrated and came to his office. There was a meeting there, including the older woman who had been arrested by the Russian authorities. She was now back in the States and becoming active in her own defense. The meeting finally ended and a plan was made.

The older woman left first. The younger woman dawdled.

Alone for the moment, the younger woman turned to him and came right out with it.

"Why wouldn't you take me? You could have, you know?"

He smiled broadly. His entire face beamed.

"It's not that you're not beautiful and attractive, believe me, you most certainly are."

"We knew each other once in law school, you know?"

"Yes, I have known that."

"And you wanted me then, I could tell."

"Yes, I did."

"So am I less attractive to you now?"

His grin faded away. "Not at all. You're even more attractive to me now."

"Then why did you avoid me? Why didn't you take me?"

He had sat down at his desk and clasped his hands behind his head. He looked thoughtfully at the ceiling. Then he said, "It's the book you're writing, you know."

"What difference would a dumb book make?"

"Dumb? A New York Times best seller dumb? I don't think so."

"You know what? I'm going to tell the story of you. The story of

the man whose head couldn't be turned. Not even by his own Bathsheba."

"People won't give a damn about a book like that."

"My readers will. They'll give a damn about the man who won't cheat."

"You write that book, Angelina. We'll just have to see."

And with that, he shrugged into his shoulder holster and gun and put on his coat.

"Now you go catch up with Christine. We've got a little task ahead of us."

"Us?"

"You're going to her condo. I'll see you over there."

In the next thirty minutes, two Russian agents lay dead in a lobby, killed by this same man. The police came, no charges were ever filed, defense-of-others was accepted as a reasonable basis for the shooting.

That's the last your intrepid reporter ever saw of this man.

Is there enough story here to make this a best seller? A story about a man so devoted to his wife and family that he wouldn't cheat, even when he was ten thousand miles away and nobody would ever have known?

Only time will tell.

THE END

Next in the Thaddeus Murfee series

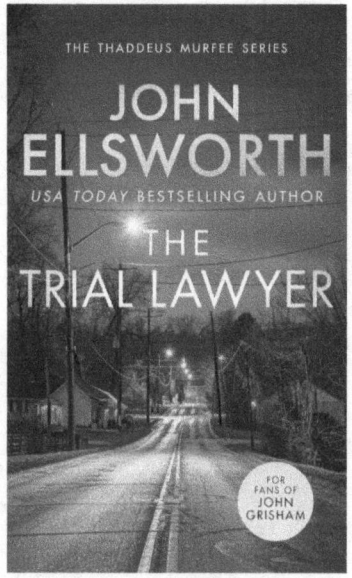

vinci-books.com/trial

**Betrayed, wounded and facing a dire case.
Thaddeus Murfee's life is about to change forever.**

Turn the page for a free preview.

The Trial Lawyer - Preview

CHAPTER 1

Killen Erwin wanted Mary Roberta to come home to him and the kids. He wanted her to stop drinking and dancing with other men as she did several nights a week. Most of all, he wanted her to stop picking them up and bedding them. He begged, he bribed; he appealed to the mother in her: "Celena and Parkus miss their mom. They cry themselves to sleep!"

But nothing worked.

So he followed her to the Copperhead Tavern and got himself good and drunk while he watched her dancing and rubbing up against Dave Daniels. A slow song played. Killen tried to cut in. Dave laughed at him, and Mary Roberta turned her face away, burying her beauty in the man's shoulder. She refused to look at her husband, refused to acknowledge him and wouldn't give him even one dance.

Killen poured down the booze. There was a fire down below, and it refused to die.

As he watched his wife dance a slow dance, he saw the man take a step to the side and the woman step into his groin with her own. It was intentional, and it was sexual and they hung there together, joined through their clothing, missing a full step of the dance. Killen broke a Cutty Sark bottle on the bar and threatened the old-timers who were perched along the bar like magpies on a wire. They scattered and broke for the door.

Then he screamed, the sound of a cougar with its foot in a trap, "Mary Roberta! I'm coming for you, baby!" And he began making his way across the floor. He held the broken bottle out in front of him like a lance, away from his body, slashing at the air, scattering the dance crowd left and right.

Mitt Henry, the massive bartender, pulled his baseball bat from behind the bar. It was a thirty-two inch Louisville Slugger spotted with blood.

It was Killen's luck that he had an ally in the crowd of drinkers that night, a young, quiet man named Johnny Albertson. Johnny liked Killen and knew what he was going through. Johnny ran to him and slapped away the bottle. The green glass hit the cement dance floor and shattered, shards spinning out and out. Johnny shook his head at Mitt, who was stalking Killen with his baseball bat like a pinch-hitter intent on ending a tie game. "He's knee-walking," Johnny said and positioned himself between Killen and Mitt. Mitt pounded the sweet spot of the bat into the palm of his hand.

"You've got ten seconds," Mitt told Johnny.

Johnny bear-hugged Killen and began pulling him away.

"Johnny?" Killen said. "You saved her!"

Johnny dragged Killen outside. In the parking lot, he demanded the keys to Killen's pickup. Killen refused.

So Johnny climbed in the passenger seat, resolute, arms crossed on his chest. "Then I'm coming too," he said. He would make sure Killen got home safely.

Then the driver's side door opened and, as Killen was climbing in, Johnny heard a woman's voice tell Killen, to "Move your ass over, sit down and don't throw up."

"Mary Roberta?" said Johnny. "What are you doing?"

"If dumbass kills himself I lose my best babysitter!" She spat. "I'm taking him home. Then I'm coming back."

Five minutes of bouncing along and Killen was passed out, chin to chest, bobbing and swaying with the road.

"You think that string of slobber makes you irresistible," Mary Roberta said to her comatose husband. "But I'm onto your tricks," she laughed. She rapped Killen's head with her knuckles. He didn't move except to swing and sway with the road.

Five minutes later they were coursing through the pitch black Illinois countryside, images of tall corn swaying in the soft summer breeze, dry leaves clashing together above a screaming chorus of riverine bugs and night fliers so in love and lust they soundtracked the landscape. Mary Roberta, chain-smoking, intent on the road, but every so often turning her head to answer or query Johnny on some fine point of furniture refinishing, his day job at his mother's antique shop.

The pickup's headlights swept a quarter mile ahead and illuminated the Algonquin Levee Bridge. Mary Roberta's eyes were turned to Johnny and then swept to the front as Johnny's mouth fell open, and he soundlessly pointed at the road ahead and she turned to see what he had seen. Johnny

337

heard the driver curse. "Son of a—" she cried as their lane ended.

Upon impact, the bridge girder sheared away the truck's right side and Johnny went airborne in the night sky over the edge of the bridge. The spinning crew cab door tattooed him. He plunged to the sandy river bed where once there had flowed water but now there were dredge marks from the scoop line that had reclaimed that good earth. Shoes were found twenty yards beyond; one contained a foot. The catastrophic crash caused a farmer two miles north to sit up in bed.

Killen survived. His Ford truck spun 360's along the asphalt, blocking all lanes where it came to rest. Traffic snarled and backed up. Someone dialed 911.

A state trooper named Bill Janes, who lived on a farm less than two miles back the way the Ford had traveled, took the call. He dressed and fired up his squad and ran Code 3 out to the scene. The driver was ID'd as Killen Erwin. Sergeant Janes observed Erwin, smelled his breath, and spoke briefly. He needed no first aid. Erwin found himself handcuffed in the rear of the squad.

(*The driver was sitting in the center of his Ford's front seat, now sitting on the asphalt, cursing because the truck wouldn't go. He still possessed the steering wheel* said the police report.)

The trooper placed flares and reflectors. Traffic was stopped in both directions. Now he could look the scene over while help came on.

Sergeant Janes pulled out his Canon and began snapping. He gave particular attention to the northwest lane, which was under repair. The vehicle had shredded the blinking sawhorses and sent the orange cones flying. The paint markings on the roadway remained as at the time of the accident.

Erwin cursed from the back seat. He vomited down his Rolling Stones T-shirt.

(*Words were slurred and the eyes bloodshot and there was a strong odor of alcoholic beverage* said the police report.)

The officer backed up fifty yards, lights flashing. He snapped the approach to the bridge. He pulled forward. He snapped the roadway paint indicating a lane drop. The paint job puzzled the veteran highway cop. He made a note to check the traffic engineering rules adopted by Illinois.

EMTs came and scattered into the dry river bed, looking for the shorn half of the Ford. Among the debris, they found Johnny. Stethoscopes returned only silence. A stretcher was packed in and the body loaded.

The Ford was removed. Wreckers tugged and hoisted as the frame, the engine, glass and debris were winched and swept away. Then an EMT dually removed the body from the scene and headed to the morgue.

After the Ford had been taken away, Sergeant Janes spoke to the two vehicles waiting to cross from the south. These would be the vehicles that were following Killen's truck when it struck the bridge. In the first car, a yellow Mitsubishi, sat a seventy-year-old woman named Anita Brushkart. She told Janes that she had witnessed a figure fleeing the scene of the accident. Was it a man or a woman? She said she could only guess because the figure was wearing blue jeans and a shapeless top, but she would have to suppose that was a woman.

"Where did the fleeing woman go?" asked the officer.

"Why, she run off the bridge and jumped in a pickup that stopped ahead of the one that crashed. It was already across. It was red and had lights on the roof that was pointed back at us. Blinded us but I could clearly see the gal run up to the truck and then she was gone. Ain't nothin more to add."

Anita Brushkart lived in Summer Hill, and she had been going to the hospital in Orbit because she was dizzy, and her chest felt tight. Later that morning, Sergeant Janes filled out some of his police report. But he left out the part about the fleeing woman. The witness was sick and probably hallucinating, so he purposely omitted her comment. She had agreed to ride into Orbit with Sergeant Janes as he was going to the hospital anyway. Nothing further had been said about the phantom woman driver.

Sergeant Janes rushed Erwin and Brushkart into Orbit. She was admitted to the hospital for tests. Erwin refused to submit to a blood draw, so Sergeant Janes read the mandatory consent form and Erwin fell to his side on the examining table, asleep.

(*Subject passed out and physician revived with smelling salts and requested consent for blood draw. Consent to blood draw was refused* said the police report.)

So Sergeant Janes ordered the blood be drawn: the sergeant's legal right and obligation.

The needle bit into the vein. Erwin struggled awake. His free arm beat the air. "I want to see my lawyer."

"Mr. Erwin, it's Sergeant Bill Janes. You *are* a lawyer."

"I'm a lawyer? Well."

"You are the District Attorney. We have cases together."

The ER physician capped a purple tube of blood. "He is? How's that gonna work?"

"It will be politics as usual," said the sergeant.

Sergeant Janes drove the District Attorney back to the Orbit Jail. He was single-celled because the District Attorney couldn't be commingled with the general jail population—consisting of two drunks and a domestic violence enthusiast.

By noon the next day the DA was regaining sobriety. He demanded to make his phone call.

"Hello, Thaddeus?" he said into the pay phone in the jail hallway. "It's Killen Erwin. I've been arrested."

CHAPTER 2

He turned off the ignition switch.

Here he was back in Orbit, south of Chicago on a slant to the Mississippi River. The stately Hickam County Courthouse filled his windshield like a wedding cake.

A woman walking by on the courthouse sidewalk recognized him through the windshield. She was well-fed and round and looked to Thaddeus like a woman who served pork chops every week. She waved and smiled. He waved back and smiled at her. He was a clear-eyed, hard-driving attorney with almost eight years of experience in the trial game and he felt every minute of it deep in his bones where he carried the pain of the people he represented. Their agony always became his own; he was just that kind of lawyer. Thaddeus was tall—he had played college basketball —and wore his brown hair down to his collar in back and short on the sides. Sunglasses were Oakley amber with interchangeable lenses for mountain biking and skiing. A day's growth—maybe two—wasn't unusual. But wife Katy hated it and made him shave before entertaining his advances.

The clerk had faxed him the police report. Thaddeus read it while he listened to Pearl Jam and kept time with his fingers drumming against the leather seat.

He drew a deep breath and looked up again.

A silver dome capped the courthouse. Each ninety on the compass offered stairs and double doors. An acre of green August grass, sprinklers tossing long combs of water, enough dandelions to rank second on the agenda of the County Board, and very busy mom-and-pops all around the square—a postcard of a town. On the north side was a state bank; on the south a federal bank. According to their digital signs, both were paying less than two percent on savings. They also blinked out hog prices, time and temperature and a welcome back to the seniors of 2015-16.

At least fifty pickups sat nosed-in all around while their owners did their weekly shopping, for it was late Friday afternoon, and everything would be open until nine.

At the moment he shut off his engine, both the federal and state bank had it at 4:10 p.m. Just enough time to accompany his best friend to court.

Killen Erwin had called when Thaddeus was chewing his first bite of lunch pita stuffed with hummus and walnuts —wife Katy's idea—no mayo. Nine hundred feet above Chicago in his office at Federal Tower, Thaddeus accepted the collect call.

"I'm in jail, man. I need you."

"Slow down, Kill. Have you been charged with a crime?"

"Last night, man, I was driving—"

"Don't say it on the phone."

"I've already said too damn much."

"Just stop there. You've been charged with a crime?"

"Yes. I go to court today. Four forty-five.'

"What crime?"

"Negligent homicide."

"Okay. Don't speak about the facts. Is it in Hickam County?"

"Yes."

"That's where you're going to court?"

"Yes."

It just so happened it was Thaddeus' birthday. He would miss the surprise birthday party. But he had no choice. His wife was his best friend in the world. But Killen was his second best. He had referred Thaddeus' first hundred clients to him; Thaddeus felt he owed him his law practice.

"Who's the judge?"

"Richard Mason Wren."

"Bird Nest? What's he doing in Hickam County? Judge Veinne recused herself?"

"Sure she recused herself. We're bridge buddies."

"Okay, sit tight, I'm on my way."

"Sitting tight is easy. No bail. Johnny Albertson was in my truck. I didn't know it. He died."

"I say this to everyone, Kill. I'll say it to you: Don't talk to anyone about the case. Got me?"

"Hell, I already have. I've talked to everyone."

"Why?"

"Waggle tongue. It comes in a Stoli vodka bottle."

"Okay, that's enough."

Drinking and driving. Hard cases to beat under the best of circumstances. But a dead body in the aftermath? Damn near impossible. Thaddeus had tried hundreds of fender-benders, rear-enders, and DWIs—he was an expert on vehicle cases—and none was so hard to beat as a drunk-driving case. Why? Because the cops loved those cases. The evidence was chemistry and physics—easy to prove in court using the right experts, plus the state provided the experts free to the prosecution. The HGN test, the heel-to-toe test, touch your nose test, alphabet test—hard to pass even stone cold sober; impossible if you were knee-walking drunk.

So that's what it sounded like. Drunk-driving and a negligent homicide. Thaddeus wouldn't have wished that on his worst enemy.

Much less his best friend.

"Cancel me out," he told Janet on the intercom. "I'm going to Orbit. Call Katy, tell her I'm sorry about the surprise party but it's about Killen and I had no choice. JT will pick her up from the shelter."

Three bottles of Aquafina went with him when he pulled out. Two hours south of Chicago, a mad dash inside a rest area. Another two hours and he was on the Orbit town square recovering from road hypnosis.

An internal debate was underway as his eyes roamed over the wedding cake courthouse. Did he go inside and defend the guy or did he just throw up his hands and leave? The case was crap to begin with, and any trial lawyer would tell you that crap cases don't get better with time. But he was Thaddeus' best friend, and he had killed a guy. Which didn't reduce him in the young lawyer's sight because he'd seen all the sins. None of them offended him, and he forgave them all because he wasn't put there to judge. He was put there to defend.

It was the only way he ever found it possible to do such dirty work.

———

The Mustang's A/C popped as it cooled.

He looked both ways across the square.

Now both banks agreed it was 4:20 p.m. In a fit of what

could only be price-fixing, they both blinked they would pay 1.04% on savings.

He resisted going inside. He would give it another ten.

His mental image of Killen was of a professional District Attorney, a guy maybe mid-thirties, five-six, weighing in at 125, dressed resplendently in expensive suits with pocket squares, tie tacks, and a heavy gold Rolex on his wrist, something with serious diamonds. He was effusive when he talked, explosive almost. High, high energy level, forever challenging everyone about the facts of any case in court when he was prosecuting. He thought himself always right. He protected his cops and to hell with those who did evil. He made sure he returned evil tenfold with long jury trials and refusals to plea bargain, preferring prison terms to probation.

Now there he was in jail, with it all falling down around him.

Thaddeus considered what he would tell the judge about Killen when he made an argument for bail. He knew Killen was an ex-jock. When he was sixteen, he started racing thoroughbreds at county fairs. Wearing silks sewn for men, he swam in the garments and people often laughed.

But he loved racing. He loved being a jockey.

The horses got bigger and faster. Some of them got clumsier.

He told the story of the conclusion of turf and thoroughbreds.

Churchill Downs. Betty's Erotic Handicap hauling ass with Killen up top charging the final turn when she stepped in a gopher hole. Of course there was no gopher, and there was no hole. Betty just made that up. So she had an excuse for going down like she'd been head shot. The Daily Racing Form said Killen was a human comet, head-over-

heels into the turf. Betty the horse? Twice a mother since her retirement to Tennessee.

When he hit the dirt, the hoof of the lead horse caught his eye and pitted his eyeball from its socket, leaving him without a left eye. Worse, he heard the bones in his neck pop as he skidded on his chin.

After he broke his neck, he never swung a leg over another nag. And that was lucky because *Betty's Erotic Handicap* cratered the next Sunday and popped the jock's head like an egg. It was a jockey tradition, roses for the funeral, so Killen wired one dozen. Jocks attending their dead colleague's funeral said he had finally made the winners' circle.

When news of the dead jock first reached him, Killen grimaced from his hospital bed. He questioned whether he had in fact been all that lucky. Spinal fusion—enough pins, wires, and metal to supply an Erector Set. Followed by three months facedown. The guys in the white coats said the next stop was diapers if he torqued his neck just once more.

How to pass three months facedown? Killen read everything the nurses brought him. One, working on her master's degree, forgot it was her day to bring books and so she left behind her college catalog. Curious, Killen cracked it and tried on a hundred possible careers, archeology to zoology. Two weeks later he found himself enrolled in law school. A titanium rod in his C-Spine corrected his posture like a West Point plebe.

He graduated law school and purchased *Money's* "100 Best Places to Live." Into a bowl twelve of the hundred best places were dumped. Shutting his eyes and plunging his hand into the choices, he surfaced clutching Orbit, Illinois.

Thaddeus was waiting in his Mustang for 4:30, watching Mr. Hatch drag the sprinkler around. What a great job, he was thinking. Mowing, watering, painting, snow plowing, changing neons. No clients, no stinking jails, no bad cops, no temperamental judges and other mental losers in black robes. He had almost forgotten it was his thirtieth birthday. Then his watch beeped, and it was time to go inside.

Goodbye Mr. Hatch, goodbye grass rainbow.

Up the stairs he trotted, each step seeming higher than the last. A few heads turned in the Circuit Clerk's office as he passed. A few smiles of recognition, then he was entering the second-floor courtroom.

It was packed; the arrest of the District Attorney on murder charges was a guaranteed draw.

The Hickam County Democrat was represented by no less than the publisher along with the local reporter. The police reporter from the *Quincy Herald-Whig* was in the crowd, and an anxious team of TV journalists were poised as they waited for the judge to rule on their motion to allow TV cameras inside.

Killen Erwin was already at counsel table.

From the back, as Thaddeus came up the aisle, the jock looked like a large boy. His shoulders were hunched, and Thaddeus knew that was because he was handcuffed.

Just behind him sat Mitt Gaffney, the rotund deputy who had walked Killen over from the jail. He wasn't smiling like his usual jocular, double-dipping self. He was all frowns.

They'd all been there a thousand times, but this time was different. Thaddeus realized it was the light that was different: in every surface, every wood and linoleum and wall he could see stark reality. Something had gone bad in Orbit. Really bad.

Killen turned when he heard Thaddeus step through the gate.

"Thaddeus. Thank God."

"Hey, Kill. How's tricks?"

"I was afraid you wouldn't come."

The young lawyer laid his hand on the DA's shoulder. "That, little brother, would never happen. You need me; I'm here."

"How can I ever pay you back, man?"

"Give me a surprise birthday party."

"What?"

"Nothing. So where's Bird Nest?"

"Judge Wren? He's back in chambers conferring with the special prosecutor the Twelfth sent down."

The Twelfth Judicial Circuit had rallied from the shock of Killen's arrest enough to locate an experienced prosecutor and send her to court that afternoon.

"Sounds like a blow job to me."

"You never know," Killen said at Thaddeus' weak attempt at humor.

They were alone at the table, so Thaddeus went for some particulars.

"You told me Johnny Albertson died last night?"

"Johnny Albertson."

"He was a passenger?"

"Yeah. We hadn't been drinking together. He saw me leaving and asked for a ride."

"And you said what?"

"I told him no. I said it wasn't smart, that I'd had too much to drink."

"So how was he in your truck?"

"The truth is, I don't even remember pulling away. I was in a blackout."

"Down at the Copperhead?"

"Yep. Three day weekend to kick off Pork Week."

Hickam County proudly touted itself as "Pork Capital of the World," a dubious honor in most circles, but one to which its citizens clung like fat on lean. There was the annual *Miss Pork County* contest and a thousand dollar gift certificate from the Orbit Chamber of Commerce.

"How'd it happen?

"Hit a bridge."

"Where?"

"Algonquin Levee Bridge. Smacked it head-on. Shit, did I just say that? Oh my God!"

"This was last night?"

"It was. I'm still drunk. Head's on fire, seeing spots."

"Okay, take a deep breath and count to ten."

At that moment, the courtroom's double doors flew open.

"Oh shit," muttered Killen.

"Who?"

"Johnny's brothers, Markey, and Mikey. They're here to hang me."

Thaddeus shot a look back over his shoulder. They were identical, the two young men. Sandy hair, unkempt and silvering as their natural blonde gave it up for the nagging gray of middle age; eyes rheumy and lackluster; arms and shoulders powerful enough to wrestle tag team—they were just the sort of survivors it would take all the guile and cunning Killen could muster if he were to avoid them and stay alive.

The twins took over the front row and turned on the harangue. Thaddeus knew they were the type who would watch their sons play football and curse the coach anytime the boys fell short. Fair-minded they were not.

"Who's the loser with the killer?" Asked one twin in his loud, sideline voice.

"Thaddeus Murfee. He used to live here. I remember his picture from the paper. He sued the state and made off with a hundred million of taxpayers' money. Total asshole." It was the almost-identical voice of the identical twin.

"Hey, Murfee," the first twin said. "What are you driving? We wanna be sure we don't run you off the road after court."

Thaddeus shook his head, trying hard not to provoke them.

Just then the Honorable Richard Mason Wren of the Twelfth Circuit entered the courtroom from offstage left. He looked very elegant in his black robe. Silver hair combed back on the sides and top and clipped to perfection around his ears, he looked like a soap opera businessman, the guy who owned the company. He happened to be the Chief Judge of the Twelfth, and he was a no-nonsense jurist who'd never been overturned on appeal. A phenomenal record, to say the least. Steely eyes with the ability to pierce a defendant—or hapless defense attorney—like a bug under the pin. The local bar called him Bird Nest in their futile effort to downsize a man larger-than-life.

"All right," said Bird Nest, "we're back on the record."

"I don't hear no record!" said one of the twins in a rancorous drawl. While Hickam County was all-Yankee, it was far enough south in the state that many citizens spoke in a southern patois. It was strange to hear "Y'all" in the north, but it happened.

Bird Nest ignored the remark and the few sniggers it elicited from the crowd.

"Counsel, identify yourselves for the record, please."

The special prosecutor went first. "Eleanor Rammelskamp," said the stout middle-aged woman with thick neck and eyeglasses hung from a gold chain. She reminded Thaddeus more of a member of the local garden club than the seasoned prosecutor he knew she was. She was nobody's fool, and she would be throwing the proverbial book at Killen Erwin, for he had let down the elite: the prosecutors. "I represent the people of the State of Illinois."

Now Thaddeus stood. "Thaddeus Murfee for the defendant Killen Erwin. We are prepared to enter our plea of not guilty, Your Honor."

Before His Honor could respond one of the twins erupted with, "Not guilty my ass! Killed my brother, the son of a bitch did!"

Whereupon Judge Wren's eyes narrowed, and he moved his gaze to the twins.

"Gentlemen—yes, you two, no need to look around. That will be quite enough with the outbursts in my courtroom. If I need to hear from you, I will tell you. Otherwise please shut the hell up!"

His words settled the courtroom. The participants knew his reign was a *fait accompli*, and he wasn't going to allow anything to detract from his station. Much less a set of hillbillies from a lesser county than his own.

"Sorry, Judge," said the verbal twin. "We thought this was like wrestling."

"Well, it's not. So silence, please, gentlemen."

"You got it judge," said the same idiot voice, and Thaddeus turned just in time to see him make the zipper motion across his mouth, turn the key and toss it. Judge Wren nodded and got back to his script.

"Counsel, has your client received a copy of the charging document?"

"He has, Your Honor. He showed me a copy of the information he'd been given as soon as I walked in."

"And he's aware of the charges against him?"

"He is, Your Honor."

"Mr. Erwin, please step to the podium with your attorney."

They stepped to the podium. Killen stood on Thaddeus' right, and the young lawyer would have sworn he saw him wobble.

The judge saw it too.

"Are you all right, Mr. Erwin?"

"Yessir. Just upset."

"Damn well oughta be," drawled verbal. "Killed my baby brother!"

Judge Wren snapped his gavel hard against its base plate. "Enough! Sir, one more outburst and you will be held in contempt and removed from my courtroom. No more!"

That time there was no reply. The judge and defense counsel then went through the standard question-and-answer dialogue interspersed with the occasional standard response of the defendant himself. It was rote for all of them.

"Now, the question of conditions of release. Madam District Attorney, you may be heard first."

Ms. Rammelskamp was quick to her feet.

"The defendant is a resident of the county, owns property here, and has well-known contacts with the area. All of that is true, and defense counsel will hammer on these facts. But the truth remains, Judge, this is a murder case. The court must set bail enough to guarantee the defendant's return to court. We're asking bail of one million and his passport."

"Counsel?" said the judge to Thaddeus.

"Your Honor, it's true there are a great many connections between Mr. Erwin and this county. He owns real estate here, owns livestock here, has a wife and two children here, and even holds elected office here. More important, perhaps, is the fact he has no prior convictions—much less indictments—for anything. He's an example of decency and good citizenship to all of us. I say this keeping in mind he hasn't been convicted of anything. The information the state has filed against him is allegations only. There's no proof of any wrongdoing, not yet at least. So the court is asked to release him OR—on his own recognizance. No bail bond necessary, Your Honor. Thank you."

"What the fuck!" cried a twin in his twangy drawl. "Fuck that no wrongdoing kind of bullshit talk. He killed our fucking brother!"

Without a word Judge Wren nodded at big old Gaffney, the luckless deputy who was the sole law enforcement officer in attendance. Gaffney pushed up to his feet from the bailiff's chair and made a beeline for the twins. Thaddeus turned to watch the fracas.

Gaffney grabbed the closer one by the arm and the twin immediately twisted free of his grasp. "Back off, fat boy," said the twin. "I'm gonna have to hurt you, son." The twin danced away and taunted the deputy now with some distance between them.

Gaffney then reached for the arm of the second twin—now the closer one—only to have his hammy fist pounded away by the much faster fist of twin two. A startled look passed over Gaffney's face. He'd never been physically overwhelmed in the courtroom. Not in twenty years. He reflexively felt for his firearm, but all guns were checked downstairs in the clerk's office before law enforcement was allowed upstairs in the courtroom. Gaffney was outnumbered, and the force he faced was overwhelming. He turned and looked at the judge.

Judge Wren was momentarily dumbstruck. In Quincy, where he regularly held court, he would be joined in the courtroom by a dozen or more police officers, deputy sheriffs, and state police on any given day. But now he found himself in this backwater without recourse to force. What to do?

Which was when Thaddeus climbed to his feet.

"Your Honor," he said, "can I be of any help? As an officer of the court, I too want to see justice done here in an orderly manner. These outbursts are contemptuous, and I would join Deputy Gaffney in his effort to remove the offenders." Thaddeus was way outside his weight class. It was all an act.

Judge Wren's expression changed to relief.

"Thank you, counsel," said the jurist. "I think Mr. Gaffney can show them the door, and I think they'll leave now without any further outbursts. Gentlemen? Am I right?"

The twin with the fast fist waved off the judge.

"We're just leaving," he declared.

The two left the courtroom, sputtering and cursing as they departed.

So Thaddeus sat back down, but he knew he had made his spurs with the judge. It was the exact moment to renew the defendant's motion for release OR. This meant Killen might leave the courtroom without posting a dollar.

"Again, Judge, we ask OR release," Thaddeus said.

"That is certainly appropriate, given the circumstances of the case," said the judge. "It is so ordered. Preliminary hearing on Monday at ten a.m. Anything further?"

They shook their heads. They had nothing further.

Court fell into recess, and Killen and Thaddeus stood up. Handshakes and thanks followed.

"Thanks, Thad," Killen whispered. "Now what?"

"Now I start interviewing witnesses. My weekend is spoken for."

"Too bad. I could use your help shoveling shit."

"I could do that for an hour."

"Well, come by the barn in the morning."

"I'll be there. Put the pot on."

"Done."

"And say hello to Mary Roberta. Tell her I'm on it."

"She doesn't give a damn. I go to jail, and everything falls into place for her."

"Sure. I've heard." Mary Roberta's lifestyle was common knowledge and even though Thaddeus had been away he'd heard things through the grapevine.

"How can I thank you enough?"

"Don't worry about it. Just keep inviting me out to shovel shit and we're good."

He left the courtroom after the judge had, to everyone's surprise, granted bail. He escaped out the back, down the judge's private entrance, avoiding the milling press. It was a violent death, and it had attracted a loud, insistent crowd of journalists bent on a sound byte.

As he drove off to the motel, he looked around the square. Same buildings—though some with different names above the stores. But everything pretty much just like he had left it five years ago.

It was good to be home.

Two miles west of town, Thaddeus parked and checked into the motel Killen owned. He carried his laptop, brief-case, and suitcase inside. He made the two cups of coffee in the mini-pot. In the bathroom, he ran water and lifted it to his face. Then he called Katy.

The disappointment was evident in her voice when she heard he wasn't coming home yet. He would miss the birthday celebration they both knew she had planned in secret. She sounded resigned.

Another client had stepped to the head of the line.

vinci-books.com/trial

About the Author

For thirty years John defended criminal clients across the United States. He defended cases ranging from shoplifting to First Degree Murder to RICO to Tax Evasion, and has gone to jury trial on hundreds. His first book, *The Defendants*, was published in January, 2014. John is presently at work on his 31st thriller.

Reception to John's books have been phenomenal; more than 4,000,000 have been downloaded in 6 years! Every one of them are Amazon best-sellers. He is an Amazon All-Star every month and is a *U.S.A Today* bestseller.

John Ellsworth lives in the Arizona region with three dogs that ignore him but worship his wife, and bark day and night until another home must be abandoned in yet another move.